WILLOWS vs. WOLVERINES

WILLOWS vs. WOLVERINES

Alison Cherry

Aladdin
New York   London   Toronto   Sydney   New Delhi

ALADDIN

An imprint of Simon & Schuster Children's Publishing Division

1230 Avenue of the Americas, New York, New York 10020

First Aladdin hardcover edition April 2017

Text copyright © 2017 by Alison Cherry

Jacket illustration copyright © 2017 by Angela Li

All rights reserved, including the right of reproduction in whole or in part in any form.

ALADDIN and related logo are registered trademarks of Simon & Schuster, Inc.

For information about special discounts for bulk purchases, please contact Simon & Schuster Special Sales at 1-866-506-1949 or business@simonandschuster.com.

The Simon & Schuster Speakers Bureau can bring authors to your live event. For more information or to book an event contact the Simon & Schuster Speakers Bureau at 1-866-248-3049 or visit our website at www.simonspeakers.com.

Jacket designed by Jessica Handelman

Interior designed by Mike Rosamilia

The text of this book was set in Bembo Std.

Manufactured in the United States of America 0317 FFG

2 4 6 8 10 9 7 5 3 1

This book has been cataloged with the Library of Congress.

ISBN 978-1-4814-6354-6 (hc)

ISBN 978-1-4814-6356-0 (eBook)

To my cabinmates of choice:
the ladies of the Bearsville retreat house

CHAPTER 1

Mackenzie and I are on an ugly orange bus filled with strangers, and all of them are singing off-key.

"Foxtail, Foxtail, burning bright, you're my heart's one true delight!" shrieks a chorus of piercing voices, and I slump farther down in my ripped vinyl seat, hoping some of the sound waves will fly over my head and miss my ears. I don't understand how anyone could be so excited about Camp Foxtail. Then again, the rest of these kids probably don't know what they've been missing at Camp Sweetwater, where Mackenzie and I have spent summers since we were eight. And where we *would* be headed right now, if there were any justice in the world.

"No singing until we're on camp grounds!" shouts the driver. He's got about twelve pieces of gum in his mouth, so the words sound garbled, but his exasperation comes through loud and clear. I can tell he'd rather be doing pretty much anything other than chauffeuring a bunch of kids to middle-of-nowhere Michigan—going to the dentist, shoveling snow, getting all his leg hair waxed off.

I know how he feels. This is the last place I want to be too.

Mackenzie rubs her eyes under her purple-framed glasses. "I can't believe we're missing Midnight Snack at Camp Sweetwater," she grumbles.

"I *know*," I say. "I've been dreaming about it all year." After the Welcome Campfire there was always this enormous late-night snack buffet in the mess hall—sundae ingredients, popcorn, cookies, you name it. Mackenzie couldn't eat most of it because of her dairy allergy, so we invented these special dessert sandwiches made of toaster waffles, peanut butter, bananas, Marshmallow Fluff, and chocolate syrup: the ChocoNanaFlufferNutter Delight. We've tried to replicate them at home a million times, but they never taste the same. Mackenzie once read about this Chinese restaurant that put drugs in its disgusting food so people got addicted and kept coming back, and we have a theory Camp Sweetwater might do the same thing with their peanut butter. We even pooled our allowances and bought a drug-testing kit so we could investigate our hypothesis this summer. I wasn't exactly looking forward to peeing in a cup in the spider-filled cabin bathroom, but I was totally prepared to do it for science.

Of course, that was all for nothing now that my parents and Mackenzie's had some stupid falling out with Delilah, their friend who runs Camp Sweetwater. Why do adults have to be so dramatic about their friendships? Don't they realize camp is way more important than whatever they're fighting about?

"I bet Camp Foxtail won't even *have* peanut butter," I say.

"They'll probably feed us eggplant casserole and chicken feet and those disgusting Jell-O molds with canned fruit that my great-aunt Doreen makes," Mackenzie says.

"They'll probably make us eat dog food." All this talk of food reminds me of the package of Red Vines in my backpack, so I dig it out. Mackenzie takes a whole handful. There's not much that can improve this situation, but candy makes everything at least a *little* better.

"I bet the lake will be full of seaweed and trash and leeches," she says with her mouth full. "I bet we won't even be able to swim."

"I bet they won't have *beds*. We'll have to sleep on the floor."

"Or on the lawn."

"Or in the *woods*."

"Or in a *pit of snakes*."

"And what kind of name is Camp *Foxtail*, anyway?" I ask. "It's like they were too cheap to name it after an actual animal, so they named it after a piece of fuzz hanging from an animal's butt."

Mackenzie finally cracks a smile. "Camp Fuzzbutt," she says, which makes us both start giggling. At least she's with me on this horrible orange bus. There's no way I could make it through an entire month of this horror show without her.

The ride takes four hours. By the time we finally turn onto the dirt road marked with a huge wooden sign in the shape of a fox, I'm restless and cranky and thirsty from all the sugar I've eaten. The second we bump past the sign, everyone starts scream-singing *"Foxtail, Foxtail, burning bright"* again, and this time the driver lets them get all the way through it. There are only about three other people on the bus who don't seem to know the words, and despite the fact that I don't want to be here, I feel left out.

I know I should feel lucky that I get to go to camp at all—none of my aunts and uncles went, and they won't let my cousins go either, even though they've been begging for years. The rest of my family thinks my parents are totally nuts for letting me go away for an entire month, but my mom has all these amazing memories of spending her summers at Camp Pine Needle in Minnesota, and she wants me to have similar experiences. Then again, if that's the case, she should really send me to a camp where I'll actually have *fun*. I wish more than anything that Mackenzie and I were riding through the familiar arch that marks the boundary of Camp Sweetwater right now, belting out the Sweetwater Anthem Delilah taught us when we were little kids.

The bus winds through the woods, and I brace myself for what I'm going to see when it pulls out the other side. I know how much photos on websites can lie. But the woods open up onto a wide green lawn, and then the bus lurches to a stop in front of an old-timey-looking wooden building. There's a sign that says FRIENDSHIP SOCIAL LODGE above the front door, which is super cheesy, but the lodge itself actually looks pretty nice.

I turn to Mackenzie. "Hey, do you think—" I start to say, but she's staring out the window in the other direction.

"Whoa," she says quietly.

My eyes bug out when I see what she's looking at. I knew Camp Foxtail was bigger than our old camp, but I didn't realize it was *this* much bigger—there are easily *two hundred* kids on the lawn. I knew practically everyone at Camp Sweetwater, but here I don't recognize a single face.

At school, I'm never the most popular or the best at anything—Dani Alvarez and Nick Riccardi get the highest grades, Sasha Hollingsworth always beats me on swim team, and Lily Greer-Whipple is the teacher's pet. I'm not even the class clown—Gavin Yeh's jokes are *so* dumb, but the whole sixth grade still thinks he's the funniest. But at Sweetwater I was always the pranking queen. Dozens of girls always swarmed me the second I got off the bus, eager to hug me and take selfies with me and hear about the hijinks Mackenzie and I had planned for the summer ahead. Camp was the only place where I was cool and interesting and fun without having to try.

Now I'm going to have to start all over again at the very bottom of the social ladder, and just thinking about it is so exhausting that I want to cry. Nobody at this camp even cares that I'm here. It might be *forever* before I have a solid group of friends. For all I know, it might not happen at all.

I'm about to complain about all of it to Mackenzie, but before I can say anything, she reaches out her pinkie finger. It's our secret signal for "I need moral support," and I realize how terrified she must be right now. The first day of Camp Sweetwater was always hard for her even though Delilah was there, so I can only imagine how she feels surrounded by strangers in this brand-new place. I shouldn't be thinking about making new friends when the best friend I already have needs my help.

I link my finger through hers and hold on tight. "It's gonna be okay," I say. "We can get through anything as long as we're together, right? Even leeches. Even *eggplant casserole.*"

Mackenzie shrugs and says, "I guess," instead of smiling like I'd hoped, but when the girls in front of us get up and push toward the bus doors, she lets go of me and stands up too, so I guess maybe I helped a little. I stay right behind her as we climb off the bus so she knows I have her back.

A counselor in a bright orange T-shirt that says I'M FOXY across the chest is standing at the bottom of the steps with a clipboard. "Name?" he asks.

"Izzy Cervantes."

He traces his pen down the page until he finds my name, and I see that I'm listed as Isobel, which I hate. The counselor makes a neat check mark on the paper and smiles at me. "Have a great summer, Isobel," he says, and then his eyes skate right past me and onto the next boy. If this were Camp Sweetwater, Delilah would be rushing over right now to welcome Mackenzie and me and sneak us some of the sour candies she always carries in her pockets. It's so weird and sad to be just another couple of names on a list.

We must be the last group to arrive, because I'm not done gathering my duffel and my sleeping bag before the counselors start blowing whistles and herding everyone into one big group in the center of the enormous oval-shaped field. There's a flagpole at one end and soccer goals at the other, and the cabins are spaced evenly around the edge. Camp Sweetwater only had twelve cabins, but here I count twenty. Mackenzie sits down all the way at the edge of the group, and I join her, though I always prefer to be closer to the center. I look around and guess which of the other girls might be in our cabin, and when I spot a couple of friendly-looking ones our age, I try to make eye contact. But they're busy talking and showing each other pictures before their counselors make them put their phones away, and none of them notice I exist. I tell myself it's not an omen for how the rest of the summer will go.

Another counselor in a FOXY shirt gets up in front of the group. "Who is stronger than an ox?" she shouts.

I barely have time to shoot Mackenzie a look like *What?* before everyone on the lawn shouts back, *"I am! I am! I'm a fox!"* They're all holding up three fingers next to each temple, which I guess is supposed to represent fox ears.

"Who here thinks outside the box?"

"I do! I do! I'm a fox!"

"Who's as steady as the rocks?"

"I am! I am! I'm a fox!"

"Who's more graceful than the hawks?"

"I am! I am! I'm a fox!"

"Dumbest chant *ever*," Mackenzie grumbles. "How is a fox stronger than an *ox*?" I know she's thinking about the cheer she made up last year that became part of the standard Camp Sweetwater repertoire; it's so sad to think of our friends singing it around their Welcome Campfire without us. But even though the fox call-and-response is way stupider than our old cheer, part of me wants to join in, just to be part of the group.

I'm about to make fox ears with my fingers like everyone else, but the chant is already over, and the counselor shouts, "Welcome back, campers! Who's ready to have an *amaaaaazing* summer?"

Everyone screams, and I feel stupid sitting there in silence, so I clap. Mackenzie keeps her hands folded in her lap.

"Let's get started, then! First, I'd like to welcome all our brand-new Foxes! Raise your hand if this is your first summer at Camp Foxtail!"

A bunch of hands go up, but almost all of them belong to little kids, and for a second I'm not sure what to do. I don't really want to call attention to the fact that I'm an outsider, in the same category as a bunch of eight-year-olds. But at the same time, I *do* want everyone to notice I'm here. So I put my hand in the air and smile to let the other campers know I'm friendly. Mackenzie glances at me, then looks at the ground and raises her hand to shoulder height.

"How about a big round of applause to make them feel welcome?" the counselor shouts, and everyone claps. "Perfect! We're so glad to have you all with us, and we know you'll love Camp Foxtail as much as we do! And now . . . are you ready for some *cabin assignments*?"

Everyone screams again, and the counselor starts calling out names, starting with the littlest kids. The wide-eyed third graders follow their counselors to their cabins, lugging their too-heavy bags behind them. One tiny girl sitting near us starts crying when her name is called, and an older boy who has the same dark hair and eyes wraps an arm around her shoulders. "Don't be scared," he says. "You're going to love Cottonwood Lodge. That's the one I told you about with the purple door, remember? Maybe later today you can help your counselor teach your cabin all the Camp Foxtail songs you know. That would be cool, right?" The little girl nods and wipes her eyes, and when her counselor beckons her over, she puts on a brave face and goes.

It's stupid, but for a second I wish I had a big brother to hug me and tell me everything's going to be fine. I'm twelve years old, and I should be able to take care of myself. But no matter how brave you are, it's nice to have someone to show you the ropes when you're in a new place. When you're the oldest kid in the family, you always have to figure everything out for yourself.

At least Mackenzie and I have each other. I nudge her with my shoulder. "You want the bottom bunk again?"

"Yeah," she says, and she gives me a tiny smile. I start looking forward to tonight after lights-out, when we can whisper together until we fall asleep. One of the best things about camp is that it's like having a four-week-long sleepover party with your best friend.

The kids who are getting called now look about our age, so we start listening for our names. The boys' cabins are all named after woodland animals—Badger, Chipmunk, Raccoon, Owl—and the girls' cabins are named after trees—Cottonwood, Birch, Poplar, Cedar. Mackenzie's name is the third one called for Maple Lodge, and I grab my backpack and get ready to stand up too. *I'm a Maple,* I tell myself, and I try to feel some pride in that—cabin loyalty is a big deal. I wonder what our cabin cheers will be like. I can't think of anything that rhymes with "maple" besides "staple."

But then the counselor finishes reading off the names of the Maples, and I realize I haven't heard mine. I probably wasn't paying enough attention. "She called me, right?" I whisper to Mackenzie, but then I see that my best friend's eyes are wide and scared. She shakes her head.

"But how is that possible? They can't put us in different cabins. They must've made a mistake, right?" Mackenzie's only six weeks younger than me, and we've never been in different cabins before. We've never been apart for *anything* at camp; Delilah always made sure we were in the same activities and on the same team for capture the flag and the Sweetwater Olympics. We were together so much that everyone referred to us as IzzyAndMackenzie, one word.

A short counselor with a black ponytail raises a hand above her head and shouts, "Follow me, Maples!" and girls start making their way over to her. But Mackenzie's still standing next to me, staring wildly around like she's forgotten how to walk. I'm upset, but she's clearly full-on panicked. If she had known we'd be separated, I doubt she would've agreed to come to Camp Foxtail at all.

"You should go over there," I whisper, and I try to keep my voice as calm and brave as possible. "It's okay. We'll still see each other all the time, right?"

"I guess," she says, but she doesn't sound convinced. We both know how much time everyone spends with their own cabins.

I link my pinkie with hers and give it a squeeze. "Go," I whisper. "I'm sure they're all really nice. I'll see you at dinner, okay? And in the meantime I'll talk to someone about getting you switched into my cabin." No matter how miserable Mackenzie is, she never makes a fuss, so fixing this will be up to me. Not that I mind helping her, obviously.

Mackenzie nods. She takes a deep breath, and then she turns and walks away, head down, her purple-sneakered feet dragging in the dirt. I try to keep a reassuring smile on my face in case she looks back at me.

But once she's out of sight and I'm left alone with a bunch of strangers, I suddenly don't feel very brave anymore either.

CHAPTER 2

A few minutes later I'm the first one called for my cabin, Willow Lodge. My counselor is really pretty; she's got long, wavy strawberry blond hair, almost the same color as my mom's, and she has freckles everywhere, including on her elbows and knees. She's not that tall, but she looks strong, and I imagine she could probably rescue a drowning swimmer or break up a fight with no problem. It's reassuring.

"Hey!" she says when I make my way over to her. "My first camper of the summer!" She says it in this way that makes me feel special and singled out, like I got called first because I'm the best and not because my last name is early in the alphabet. She holds up her hand for a high five, and I put down my stuff so I can slap her palm. It's not as good as the giant hugs I always got from the counselors at Camp Sweetwater, but her smile is warm and friendly, and it makes me like her right away.

"Nice," she says. "I like a girl with a strong high five. And I love your yellow sleeping bag—that's my favorite color. I'm Valerie, by the way. What's your name? I don't recognize you from last year."

She seems almost as sunny and bright as Delilah; it makes sense that yellow would be her favorite color. Even the sound of her name is happy. "I'm Izzy Cervantes," I say. "I'm new."

"It's great to meet you. I think you're going to love it here at Camp Foxtail."

"I hope so," I say, and she laughs like I've said something really funny.

I'm about to ask her if there's any way Mackenzie can transfer into our cabin, but then I notice three more girls heading toward us, arranged in a triangle shape with one in front and the other two slightly behind her. My stomach does a little flip; the meanest girls in my school walk down the hall that way, always on the lookout for something to mock. I try to scope them out without making eye contact.

"Hey, welcome back!" Valerie says when she sees them, like they're not intimidating at all. She gives each of them a hug, and the high five she offered me suddenly doesn't feel so special. "How are you, ladies? Did you meet our new camper? This is Izzy Cervantes."

The leader of the triangle turns and inspects me, and the tiny rhinestone studs on the earpieces of her glasses flash and gleam in the sun. Then she reaches out to shake my hand like we're at a business meeting, which is totally weird, but I try to look like I'm not surprised at all. For someone so short and delicate-looking, she has a surprisingly strong grip, and I remember something my dad once said about how a strong handshake is the sign of a strong leader.

"I'm Rupali," she says. "Everyone calls me Roo."

"I've never heard that name before," I say. "It's really pretty."

"Thanks. It's Indian." Roo flips her shiny black hair over her shoulder and gestures to the girls behind her. "That's Lexi, and that's Ava."

Ava looks me over, head to toe and back again, and then she yawns, which isn't exactly a huge vote of confidence. Her hair and clothes are flawless, and so is her dark skin—she seems like the kind of person who has never had a pimple in her life. But Lexi shoots me a big smile, revealing a mouth full of braces. She's wearing a T-shirt with a cartoon fox on it and a Camp Foxtail baseball cap, her blond ponytail pulled through the opening in the back.

"Hey," she says. "Nice to meet you! Your last name is Cervantes? That's my cousin's girlfriend's last name. She's from Mexico. Is that where your family's from too? Maybe you're related!"

I laugh. "Probably not, it's a really common name. But yeah, my dad's parents are from there."

A few steps away, Valerie's chatting with another girl wearing a ruffly pink outfit. The girl's voice has this chirpy student-council tone to it, almost exactly like this girl in my class at school who spends recess color-coding her notes. She comes over and gives us a smile that looks practiced, like she rehearsed it in the mirror. "Hey, guys!"

Roo turns her back to me, and I feel like I've been dismissed. "Hey, Summer. How's it going?"

"Great! It's going to be an *amazing* month. Don't you think, Hannah?" It's only then that I realize there's another girl behind her, sticking so close to Summer it's like she's trying to hide in her shadow. She's twisting a piece of blond hair around her finger so tightly the tip is turning white. She gives a tiny nod, then lets out a wet sniffle, and I realize she's crying.

"Are you okay?" I ask.

"She'll be fine," Roo says. "She's just a little home-sick. Right, Hannah?" She reaches out and roughly pats Hannah twice on the shoulder, and Hannah flinches, then hiccups and nods. She's holding her breath in an effort to stop crying, but I can't tell if it's because Roo has made her feel better or scared her into silence. Lexi slips an arm around her shoulders, and she starts breathing again.

A lanky redhead has joined the group, and Ava goes over to hug her. "Where's Juliet?" I hear her ask.

"She's not coming this year. Her family moved to Minneapolis."

"Oh *nooooo*," Lexi says. "I was counting on her to do the karaoke competition with us!"

The rest of the Willows have gathered around Valerie now, and she gestures for us to follow her toward the flagpole end of the field. A short Asian girl falls into step beside me. "Hey," she says. "You're new, right?"

I'm starting to feel like I should get that printed on a T-shirt or something: I'M IZZY, AND I'M NEW! But she actually seems interested in talking to me, so I introduce myself, and she tells me her name is Mei. "You're going to love Camp Foxtail," she says. "It's the best. I've been coming here since I was eight. Did you meet everyone?"

"Not everyone." I point out the girls whose names I don't know—the redhead, and two girls with matching sneakers and tons of beaded bracelets up their wrists. I can tell they're best friends by the way they lean toward each other even when they're talking to other people.

"The one with the red hair is Petra," Mei says. "She's a supertalented horseback rider—she wins competitions and stuff. And those two are BaileyAndHope." The way she says it like it's one word makes me miss Mackenzie so much it hurts.

"What's up with that girl?" I tip my head toward Hannah, who's still sniffling as she drags her pink wheeled suitcase across the grass.

"Oh, she's fine. She always spends all of camp saying she's homesick and wants to leave, but then she comes back every year anyway."

"Why doesn't she stay home if she doesn't like camp?"

Mei shrugs. "No idea. She's sweet when she's not crying, though."

Up ahead, Summer says something to Petra, who lets out a loud, bubbly laugh. "So, the rest of you guys know each other already?" I ask.

"Yeah. Pretty much all of us have been coming here since third grade. Not BaileyAndHope, I think they came when we were ten. Are you going into eighth grade?"

"Seventh," I say.

"Huh, weird. Most of the seventh-graders are in Maple. I wonder why they put you with us? I guess it's because Juliet's not here."

Mei doesn't say it meanly or anything, but now I feel more out of place than I already did. I bet everyone here would rather have Juliet than me. "My best friend's in Maple," I say. "Do they ever let people switch cabins? Not that I don't want to be with you guys. But if I went to the camp director's office and explained the situation, do you think maybe they'd move her into Willow?"

Mei shakes her head. "People try that every year, but it never works."

Man, getting this fixed would be so easy if we were at Camp Sweetwater. "Are you sure?" I ask. "Should I talk to Valerie, maybe?"

"You can try, but trust me, Val's going to say no. There's only room for ten people per cabin, so you'd have to kick someone out, and that wouldn't be fair."

I guess that makes sense, but I'm not looking forward to telling Mackenzie. She's going to be devastated. I cross my fingers that she'll make some new friends right away and decide Maple isn't so bad.

Willow Lodge is a weathered brown cabin with peeling green paint on the screen door. Mei holds it open for me, and I squeeze through the doorway with all my stuff. The cabin smells musty, but aside from a few cobwebs high up in the exposed beams of the ceiling, it looks surprisingly clean. Five sets of bunk beds and one single bed are pushed up against the walls, which are made of wooden planks that don't quite match the wide floorboards. There's a bathroom in the back, and next to it is a little screened-in porch that looks out onto a dirt trail through the woods.

We've been inside all of ten seconds before an argument breaks out in front of the bunk beds on the left side of the cabin, near the biggest window. "But you said *I* could bunk with you this year!" Lexi whines.

"I said *maybe*." Roo sounds very patient, like this isn't the first time they've had this discussion. "I sleep better when I bunk with Ava. She doesn't snore."

"I don't snore!"

"No offense, Lexi, but you kind of do," Summer says.

"I *don't*! And even if I did, you'd still be able to hear me four feet away."

"Bunk with Petra," Roo says as Ava starts unloading her clothes into the dresser. "She wouldn't wake up if you punched her in the face."

"It's true," Petra says like it's a point of pride. "My little brother tried it once."

"*Fine.* Whatever." Lexi drags her bag across the floor.

BaileyAndHope are whispering to each other as they spread out their stuff on the bunks at the back of the room, and a stab of panic shoots through me as I realize almost everyone has paired off. I've never had to think about who my bunkmate would be before, and now I'm in danger of getting stuck with sniffly Hannah.

"Hey," I say to Mei. "Do you want to bunk with me?"

"Sure," she says, to my relief. "Do you want the top or the bottom? Either one's fine with me."

"I'll take the top, if that's okay," I say. "Thanks." I wonder who Mackenzie's bunking with. I hope she found someone who let her have the bottom. She's afraid of falling from the top—she flails her arms and legs around so much in her sleep that my mom calls her the Octopus—but I'm sure she was too embarrassed to tell that to a total stranger. I should probably go over to her cabin later and make sure she's not going to get hurt.

"Hey, guys, gather around for a second!" Val shouts, and everyone goes quiet and moves toward her. "First of all, welcome to Willow Lodge! Almost all of you took sailing with me last year, but I'm so excited to be your counselor this time around and get to know you better. Does everyone have a bunkmate? Who's with Hannah?"

"Hannah, come bunk with me," Summer calls. I try to find an edge of annoyance in her voice, but she sounds totally willing to share with the resident weeper. I wonder if she's genuinely okay with it or if she's just trying to get credit for being nice.

"Great," Val says. She looks around and smiles at each of us. "This is such an awesome group, you guys. I definitely got the very best cabin in the camp."

I'm sure every other counselor is saying the same exact thing to their own cabins right now, but Val sounds so genuine that it makes me feel like this really *is* the best cabin. A little blossom of Willow pride opens in my chest, followed immediately by a twinge of discomfort that I'm being unfaithful to Camp Sweetwater.

"And we're also the *luckiest* cabin," Val continues, "because we have Camp Foxtail's very own official photographer!"

Everyone cheers, and Roo takes a big, showy bow. "She has a super fancy camera," Mei whispers to me. "She takes really amazing pictures all summer, and the camp director puts them all in this big slide show on the last day. Being in her cabin is basically like being a celebrity. But don't get on her bad side. Last year there was a picture in the slideshow of Sophia Waldron from Poplar with her finger up her nose."

"Thanks," I whisper back, and then I shoot Roo a big smile. It sounds like she could make or break my reputation here.

"So, first order of business," Val says. "The Willow cheer. Most of you have heard it a million times during your last few summers at camp, so you've probably picked it up. Do it with me if you remember it, and everyone else follow along the best you can. Ready?"

Everyone but me raises their hands into the air and starts to chant.

"Willows, willows, sweep the ground, with a gentle rustling sound!
Prettiest of all the trees, tendrils dancing in the breeze!
We hide mysteries in our boughs, secret loves and private vows!
Don't believe us? Think we're nuts? We will kick your leafy butts!"

There are hand motions that go with the cheer, and at first I try to follow along. But I'm always a beat behind, and it makes me feel stupider than if I were standing still. After a minute I stop trying.

The rest of the girls clap and whoop when they're finished, and Val beams at us. "Excellent. You've got half an hour to get settled now, and then we're going to head down to the lake for your swim test. Dinner is at six, and then we'll have our opening night treasure hunt! But it's not all fun and games; I also need you guys to start thinking about something very important."

She gestures for us to come closer, and we all lean in. Her freckled face has gone deadly serious, and I wonder if she's going to give us a lecture about water safety or bullying or something. But then she says the very last thing I expect to hear.

"We need to start planning our first prank on the Wolverines."

Everyone starts talking at once, and my heart leaps. If the skill I was known for at Camp Sweetwater is *very important* here, I shouldn't have a hard time fitting in at Camp Foxtail at all. As soon as the Willows see how good I am at this, they'll accept me as one of them—probably as one of their leaders—and camp can go back to being the way it's always been.

But I don't have time to ask any questions before Val raises her hand for silence. "The Willows' prank war with the Wolverines is a sacred and time-honored tradition," she says, like it's the beginning of a fairy tale. "Way back in 1990, before any of us were born, a pair of twins named

Scarlett and Daniel Paddington came to Camp Foxtail. They had spent their whole lives pranking each other— they were probably doing it in the womb—and they were both masters at it. Daniel lived in Wolverine that summer, and Scarlett was a Willow, and they got their whole cabins involved in their rivalry and pulled the most spectacular pranks the world had ever seen."

"One of the pranks involved a blimp, right?" says Lexi.

"And Scarlett released five hundred toads inside the Wolverines' cabin," Summer adds.

"Where would you get five hundred toads?" asks Mei.

"The lake," Lexi says. "Duh."

"The old pranks aren't important," Val says. "What's important is that even though the Paddington twins are too old to be Foxes now, the rivalry continues to this very day. I'm sorry to say that the Wolverines bested the Willows last year. But now that *you* ladies are here, they don't have a chance, do they?"

Everyone cheers, and I do too. I know 1990 isn't exactly historical, but I still get tingles up my spine when I think about participating in something so much bigger than myself. If this is the focus of our cabin, the summer's going to be *way* better than I expected.

"I can definitely come up with some ideas," I say. "My

best friend Mackenzie and I did all kinds of great pranks at our old camp. There was this one with a ceiling fan and raw hamburger meat and—"

Lexi starts talking right over me. "I was thinking we could steal all the boys' underwear and run it up the flagpole," she says. "It would be *so* hilarious."

"Or we could hide an alarm clock somewhere in their cabin and set it for three in the morning, and everyone will go crazy looking for it," says Roo.

Those are the oldest, most boring pranks in the world—I don't believe these girls think they'll be good enough to win a sacred, time-honored prank war. "That's exactly the sort of stuff they'll expect, though, right?" I say. "We need to do something really creative. But don't worry, I have a ton of experience with this. Last year at my old camp—"

Roo cuts me off. "No offense, Izzy, but this isn't your old camp, and you don't know how anything works around here."

"I know, but pranks are kind of the same everywhere, right? Maybe we could—"

"I'm sure we can find a way for you to participate, even though you're new," says Lexi. "Is there anything you're especially good at? Like climbing flagpoles or spying or picking locks or anything?"

And just like that, my excitement rolls over and plays dead. I'm probably better at pranking than all these girls put together, and they're writing me off before they see what I can do.

I realize that if I really want them to respect me and accept me as one of them—and I *do*, I so do—I'm going to have to distinguish myself by doing something really incredible. Should I go rogue and pull an amazing prank on the Wolverines all by myself? Should I prank the girls in my own cabin to prove how sneaky and creative I am?

Or . . . maybe it's a lot simpler than that. Maybe all I need to do is make the Willows believe I'm already one of them, that I have roots at Camp Foxtail, too.

I think about that boy I saw comforting his little sister earlier, and the spark of an idea ignites in my brain. Before I have time to consider whether it's stupid or not, I square my shoulders and look Lexi right in the eyes.

"I can do better than that," I say. "My older brother used to be a Wolverine. He was the most amazing prank-ster since the Paddington twins, and he taught me everything he knows."

CHAPTER 3

The change is instantaneous. A second ago I was just the anonymous new girl. But now the Willows look intrigued, like I might have value to them. At Camp Sweetwater someone would've called me out immediately and said, "What are you talking about? Your brother is *four*." But nobody knows me here. And that means I can be whoever I want.

Val is looking at me like I've handed her a puppy wearing a diamond collar. *"Seriously?"* she says. "Oh man, Izzy, that's *such* fantastic news." She sounds so sincerely happy that I almost feel bad for misleading her. But it's so great to have someone look at me like I belong here that it's easy to push those guilty feelings aside. Once I show Val and the Willows what an amazing addition I am to this group, it won't matter that I started out by telling a harmless white lie. They'll probably never have to know.

"Wow," Mei says. "We're *so* lucky you're in our cabin. You would've been totally wasted in Maple."

Lexi scoots closer to me. "This is seriously the greatest! Don't you think, Roo?"

"Yeah, definitely," Roo says, but her expression doesn't match her words. It's like she suddenly sees me as a threat, now that I've proven myself to be more interesting than she expected.

I remember what Mei said about being on Roo's bad side, and I backpedal a little. "I'm sure you guys have some great ideas too," I say. It's not like I have to be in charge right away. I'm willing to work up to it.

"What's your big brother's name?" Lexi asks. "My brother's sixteen. Ben Silverman. Do you think maybe they knew each other?"

"My brother's name is Tomás," I say, which is actually true. "He's much older, though; he turned twenty in May. I don't think he would've known your brother. His last summer here was, um . . ." I quickly do the math—this camp only goes up to age fourteen, and I need to make sure my fictional big brother wouldn't have overlapped with any of the girls. ". . . six years ago, I think."

Lexi looks disappointed. "Aw, too bad."

"I think I might remember a Tomás Cervantes," Val says, and although there's no way she possibly could, part of me thrills that she thinks there's a connection between us. "He's only a little younger than me. There was this one time all the Willows woke up with these huge dead fish in their beds. Was that him?"

"Yeah! He tested that one on my parents. You should've heard my mom scream. She woke up the whole neighborhood."

"Where did he get the fish?" Ava asks. It's the first time she's spoken to me, and it feels like a small victory.

"I don't know, I was pretty little back then. But I can ask him if you want."

"How come you went to a different camp if your brother liked it here so much?" asks Roo.

I decide to stick as close to the truth as possible. "My parents' friend started a camp, and they wanted me to go there," I say. "I always wanted to come here, though. I finally convinced them this year."

"And we're so glad you did," Val says. She slings an arm around my shoulders, like I'm as much a part of the group as Roo or Lexi, and it makes me warm and happy all the way through. "All right, everyone, put your stuff away and get your bathing suits on. We'll have plenty of time to toss ideas around later. You'll tell us some of your brilliant plans during Cabin Chat tonight, right, Izzy?"

Cabin Chat *tonight*? I had no idea I was going to have to come up with something that quickly. It usually takes Mackenzie and me days to work out all the details of a prank. And if I'm honest, *she's* usually the one who thinks of all the best ideas, not me. We've always been a perfect team because we have such different skills—she's great at coming up with concepts and working out how all the little details fit together, and I'm better at stuff like making props, sneaking into places I'm not supposed to be, and lying with a straight face. But none of those skills are going to help me if I can't make a plan on my own.

Why did I think I could do this without my best friend?

"Izzy?" Val asks. "Everything okay?"

I give her my calmest, most confident smile and pray she can't tell that my stomach is doing a series of backflips. "Of course," I say. "The Wolverines won't know which way is up by the time I'm done with them."

The swim test is easier than the one at Camp Sweetwater; all we have to do is swim out to a buoy and back and tread water for five minutes. The lake is beautiful, shimmery and blue, and there's not a leech or a piece of trash in sight. I scan the pier for Mackenzie so I can tell her everything that's happened, but the Maples are running behind, and they don't arrive until all ten Willows are done swimming. (Everyone passes except Hannah, who immediately starts crying again, even when Summer reminds her that she doesn't *like* water sports.) I lag behind as the Willows head off across the lawn, hoping I can at least stick around long enough to cheer my best friend on—no matter how prepared she is, Mackenzie gets nervous taking tests. But when Val calls, "Izzy, come on!" I realize I'm not totally sure how to get back to the cabin on my own, so I scurry after her. I'll see Mackenzie at dinner.

When I get to the mess hall an hour later, my long braid still dripping down my back, Val leads us straight to the Willow table all the way on the left side of the room. It's marked by a plaque in the shape of a weeping willow tree. I glance at the tables next to us, hoping to spot a maple leaf, but we're surrounded by the Magnolias, the Porcupines, and the Owls. I finally find the Maple table two whole rows away. When Mackenzie spots me, she returns my wave and tries to smile, but it doesn't reach her eyes.

"Do we always have to eat with our cabins?" I ask Mei

34

as she climbs onto the bench next to me. It's heavy and old, rubbed shiny and smooth by decades of camper butts.

Roo shoots me a hard look from across the table. "Why, you don't want to sit with us?"

"No, I do. It's just . . . my best friend's over there in Maple, and I want to make sure she's settling in okay. She's really shy, and I'm the only one she knows here." I leave out the part about desperately needing her help to think up a prank.

Val sits down at the end of the table. "We do always sit with our cabins, Izzy. But that's thoughtful of you, and you can check on your friend after we're done eating, okay?"

"Okay," I say. Roo doesn't say anything else, but she raises the huge camera that's hanging around her neck and snaps my picture while I'm scratching my nose.

"Candid shot," she says, and I vow to win her over no matter what it takes. If I'm going to be somebody at this camp, I need her as an ally.

The mess hall is huge, with hardwood floors and exposed beams in the ceiling, and shouts and laughter echo everywhere as the room fills up. There's a series of thirty or so framed all-camp photos on the walls, one for each year, and I hope nobody asks me to point out Tomás in one of the older ones. Over the fireplace in the corner is a mangy taxidermy moose head, its antlers draped with Mardi Gras beads, tinsel, and a few random Christmas ornaments. Everything smells like dust and tater tots.

"The kitchen staff will serve us tonight," Val tells us, "but starting tomorrow, you guys will switch off being waiters. I'll pass out the schedule later. Your responsibilities are to set the table, fetch the food from the serving window, return the serving dishes after the meal, and wipe down our space. Most of you know the drill, and you'll pick it up fast, Izzy."

I wish people would stop reminding everyone that I'm new. "I know how it works," I say. "We had waiters at my old camp."

Val smiles. "Great. Thanks for making my job easy."

A group of boys our age enters the dining hall and marches directly toward us, and Val sits up straighter. "You guys," she says quietly. "That's them."

"Who?" I ask, but it immediately becomes obvious when they start shouting, *"Wol-ver-ine! Wol-ver-ine! The fiercest furry mammal that you ever have seen!"* They're all wearing those sticky HELLO, MY NAME IS name tags, but most of them are blank. As they do a complete loop around our table, I catch a few that are filled out:

GROUCHO, BEANS, CHOMPERS. A redheaded boy with a sticker that says TWIZZLER makes his hands into claws and hisses right in my face, and I hiss back, which makes Mei laugh. When the Willows start shouting our cabin cheer to drown out the boys, I try to join in, but I only remember about a quarter of the words.

The Wolverines head back to their table, and their counselor comes up beside Val and bumps her with his hip so hard she almost slides off the bench. He's tall and lanky, and his hair is all messed up, like he rolled out of bed two minutes ago. There's a hole in the shoulder of his FOXY T-shirt, though everyone else's looks brand-new.

"I hope you're ready for us, *Fail*-erie," he says with a smirk. "Get it? 'Cause you guys are going to *fail*?"

Val rolls her eyes. "Dude, that's not remotely clever. And was that little charade supposed to scare us? Because you're the ones who should be nervous. My Willows are going to wipe the floor with you. Right, girls?"

We all cheer, and the guy raises one eyebrow. "Oh, is that so?"

"It is, actually," Val says. "We've got a secret weapon this year." She looks right at me and winks, and I stop feeling even the tiniest bit sorry that I lied.

"A secret weapon?" the guy repeats in a super-high-pitched snotty voice that sounds nothing like Val. "And what might that be?"

"If I told you, it wouldn't be a secret, would it?"

"Whatever," says the guy. "Watch your backs. We're gonna make you Willows *weep*."

All the Wolverines start pumping their fists and chanting, "Weep! Weep! Weep!" Their counselor walks backward toward them while doing that cheesy thing where he points two fingers at his eyes, then back at us. He's been over here all of thirty seconds, and I'm already incredibly annoyed by him; he reminds me a lot of Mateo Mendoza, this loud, irritating guy in my class at school. But Val seems pretty good-natured about the whole thing. Actually, she kind of seems like she's trying not to laugh.

"That's Stuart," she says when he's gone. "Otherwise known as Public Enemy Number One."

Mei leans closer to me. "I heard Stuart stole all of Val's bathing suits last year, dipped them in water, and froze them, and in the morning—"

"We do not speak of that incident," Val says, mock-stern, and Mei giggles. "We concentrate on *taking him down*."

A guy from the kitchen comes over and puts two huge pizzas and a bowl of salad on our table, and the conversa-

tion stops as everyone scrambles for the kind they want.
I manage to grab a slice of pepperoni—clearly the best
topping—and then I make a point of sliding the tray
directly across the table to Roo. But she wrinkles her
nose and says, "I'm a vegetarian," like I should somehow
know that already.

"Oh, okay," I say. I take a bite of my own pizza, and she
snaps another photo of me as a bunch of sauce drips down
my chin. Perfect.

I try as hard as I can to be part of the conversation
during dinner, but I'm totally lost most of the time. The
first night of camp is always about telling stories from
past summers, and every sentence begins with "Remember that time . . ." and "Wasn't it hilarious when . . ." At
first Mei tries to fill me in on some of the Willows' inside
jokes, but there are way too many of them, and she can't
keep up. I glance over at Mackenzie and see that she's not
talking to anyone either. She's picking all the cheese off a
slice of pizza, looking completely miserable, and I wonder
why she doesn't have the special meal she's supposed to
get because of her dairy allergy.

I stand up and go around the table to Val. "I'm done
eating," I say. "Is it okay if I check on Mackenzie now?"

Roo and Ava look up at me like I have a thing or two

to learn about Willow loyalty, but Val says, "Yeah, that's fine. We're going to head out in ten minutes, so be back by then."

I narrowly avoid being hit by a flying piece of cucumber on my way to the Maple table, but Mackenzie's face brightens when she sees me. "Hey!" she says. "Are you allowed to come eat over here?"

"No, but my counselor said I could visit for a little while. How're you holding up?"

"Um." Mackenzie side-eyes the girls next to her. They don't seem to be paying any attention to us, but she clearly doesn't want to say anything personal in front of them.

"I have to go to the bathroom," I say. "Do you want to come with me?"

"Yeah," she says, obviously eager to get out of here.

Neither of us says anything until we're inside the bathroom at the back of the mess hall. But the second we've checked under the stalls to make sure we're alone, Mackenzie's words pour out in a rush, like she's been saving them up for hours. "This place is the *worst*. I hate not knowing where anything is or which people are nice or how anything *works*. And the nurse's office lost the form that says I have a dairy allergy, so there's nothing for me to eat besides pizza crust. I'm *starving*."

"I'm so sorry," I say. "You can still eat the salad, right?"

"Well, yeah, I guess. But it's *salad*."

"Good point. Don't worry about it, okay? I'll talk to the nurse's office for you in the morning and make sure it gets fixed."

"Eleanor already did, I think. That's my counselor. Did you ask if we could switch into the same cabin?"

"I did, but it's not allowed," I say. "I'm really sorry. I think we might be stuck where we are."

"Of course." Mackenzie slumps against the wall next to the paper towel dispenser. "Ugh, why did we bother coming to camp at all if we couldn't go to Sweetwater? I wish we'd just stayed home. Don't you?"

Now that the prank war is on the table, I actually feel like this summer has potential, even if Mackenzie's not in my cabin. But I can't really say that to her, so I try to distract her instead. "Have you met anyone cool?" I ask. "Who are you bunking with?"

"This girl Lauren. She's okay, I guess, but she doesn't really talk to me. Nobody does. Are people ignoring you, too?"

"Not really," I say. "But only because I did something kind of bad."

I tell Mackenzie about the rivalry with the Wolverines

and my fictional prank-master older brother, and by the time I'm done, her eyes are huge. "You told them Tomás is *twenty?*"

"I know, it's ridiculous, right? Good thing nobody knows that he stuffed pinto beans up both his nostrils last week."

"Man, why can't *my* cabin have a prank war?" Mackenzie says. "This is so unfair."

"Maybe you could start one. Like, pick a boys' cabin and attack? Maybe you'd be legendary, like the Paddington twins."

"The Maples don't seem like they'd be into that kind of thing. All they talk about is converting our cabin into a spa. They want to have a 'hair-braiding clinic' for Cabin Group tomorrow, whatever that means." Mackenzie runs her fingers through her own light brown hair, which is way too short for braids. "Plus, it's not like they'd listen to *me* if I suggested doing something different."

"I would seriously give anything to have you in my cabin right now," I say. "All the Willows expect me to come up with something perfect by tonight, and Val's calling me her secret weapon, and I've got *nothing.* I'm going to look so stupid."

I feel a little bad that I'm complaining about the thing

Mackenzie wants most, but she doesn't look annoyed at all. Actually, she's starting to look kind of hopeful. "I'll help you think of something, if you want," she says. "I could help you plan pranks all summer. We'd have to keep it a secret, but it would make this place *so* much more fun." Then her eyes light up. "Wait! What if you did the spaghetti prank?"

I can't believe I didn't think of it myself. The spaghetti prank is *killer*. We thought of it at a sleepover way back in April, and we were so excited to test it out that we sneaked downstairs and cooked a bunch of pasta at one in the morning. We laughed so loudly at the result that we woke up my mom, and we had to shove all the pasta under my bed so she wouldn't see it. In the morning, we totally forgot about it, and it stayed there an entire week before I found it again, covered in mold.

"That prank would be *perfect*," I say. "Is it really okay if I use it for this, though? I wouldn't be able to give you any credit. I'd have to say the idea came from Tomás."

Mackenzie shrugs. "Pranking for credit is for amateurs. The fun part is seeing how everyone reacts when you pull off something really great, right?"

"Yeah," I say. I know that's how I'm supposed to feel. But secretly, I love when everyone knows it's me.

"Besides," Mackenzie says, "you won't get any credit either if you say it was all your brother's idea. It'll be like we're secret agents."

Actually, I wasn't planning to give Fictional Tomás *all* the credit for my ideas, but Mackenzie doesn't need to know that. It's not like it'll affect her if I move up the ranks in my own cabin. This still seems like a way better deal for me than it is for her, but if she's satisfied, I'm not going to try to talk her out of it. With my best friend behind me, I'll have an endless supply of hilarious pranks. I could go from total unknown to leader of Willow Lodge in no time, and then camp will finally feel *right* again.

"Great," I say. I extend my pinkie to her. "Let's do this. Partners in crime?"

Mackenzie links her pinkie with mine. "Partners in crime," she says. "We're going to do way better than any college dude ever could, even if he *were* real."

CHAPTER 1

I wasn't the star of the treasure hunts at Camp Sweetwater, exactly. Whatever cabin Emma Foster was in always won; she ran like a gazelle and always managed to figure out the clues faster than I could read them. But I was pretty good too, and my cabin was usually in the top three, at least. Even if I wasn't the absolute best, I was close.

Here at Camp Foxtail, I'm so far from the best it's like I'm not on the same *planet*.

I haven't gotten slower; when the Willows run from one place to another, I'm always near the front of the pack. But I'm completely useless at figuring out the clues. How am I supposed to know the infirmary is "home of the biscuits" because Nurse Patchett is from England and doesn't know the right word for cookies? How could I possibly guess that "Doobie doobie doo" means we're supposed to go to Camp Director Dana's office? (Doobie is her nickname because her last name is Duberman, apparently.) I know I shouldn't feel dumb for not knowing my way around—the whole point of an opening night treasure hunt is to learn about the camp if you haven't been here before. But I hate not being able to contribute when even people like weepy Hannah know exactly what's going on.

We come in fourth out of twenty, but I can't enjoy it because I'm too stressed about being dead weight. I wish we could fast-forward to later tonight, when I've already told the other girls my plan for the prank and proven I'm an asset to this cabin.

Everyone's still pretty riled up by the time we get back to Willow Lodge. Petra, BaileyAndHope, and Mei start squealing over some guy named Caden from Owl Lodge, who got really cute since last year. Summer and Hannah giggle together in the corner, and Roo, Lexi, and Ava curl up on Ava's bed and scroll through Roo's photos from earlier today. They keep laughing hysterically and imitating people's unflattering facial expressions, and I wonder if Roo's showing them the one of me sloppily eating pizza.

Nobody talks to me as I change into my oversize Snoopy T-shirt and blue plaid boxers, and I know

Mackenzie's probably feeling equally alone as she puts on her seahorse pajamas. Her cabin's only a short walk down the field, but she feels impossibly far away. I didn't get to say good night to her after the treasure hunt, and I wonder whether she's scared to sleep in a new place without me.

To make me feel less lonely, I climb up onto my bunk with a roll of tape and start putting up the photos I brought from home: Mackenzie and me in front of the Camp Sweetwater sign, me holding my little cousin Julio, my grandma and me curled up together on the couch, watching her favorite telenovela. I'm about to put up one of my whole family from my birthday last year, but then I realize I can't; if the other girls see it, they'll wonder why there's a little brother in the picture and no big brother. So I take one last look at the photo and fix all the details in my mind—the laugh lines around my dad's eyes, my mom's wild strawberry blond hair, my siblings' gap-toothed smiles. And then I tuck it away in my sock drawer, right next to the St. Christopher medal and the picture of the Virgin of Guadalupe that my grandma insisted I bring for protection. I figure it'll be extra safe there.

"All right, ladies," Val calls. "Settle down. Everyone

brush your teeth. We're starting Cabin Chat in five minutes, and I don't want to smell any stinky breath."

It's pretty chaotic trying to share two sinks with nine other people, but we manage, and pretty soon we're all in our sleeping bags. Roo, Lexi, and Ava have matching purple ones with silver stars, and Summer's is bright pink with ruffles around the edges, like her outfit today. (Her bathing suit and nightgown are pink with ruffles, too, and I wonder if she owns any clothes in other colors.) Hannah refuses to get into her bed until Summer checks for toads and giant dead fish; apparently our discussion earlier made quite an impression on her.

"There's no way the Wolverines have pranked us already," Summer says. "It's much too early." But she does a pretty thorough check anyway, and I catch her feeling around the bottom of her own sleeping bag after she's done with Hannah's.

Val switches off the overhead lights, and like the first night of camp every year, I'm surprised by how ridiculously dark it gets. There's a streetlight right outside the window of the bedroom I share with my sister, Carolina, and it's so bright that we've never needed a night-light. I'm not afraid of the dark or anything, but I still tuck my flashlight into my sleeping bag, and it makes me feel safer. I kind of wish I had my stuffed owl from home, but I push that thought away. I've never been homesick at camp before, and I'm not going to start now.

"Guys, this was an awesome first day," Val says, and the sound of her voice makes me feel calmer. "I think we're going to have such a fun four weeks together. For our first Cabin Chat, I thought we could each say a goal we have for this summer. Maybe you want to try an activity you've never done before, or improve a skill, or make friends with someone new, or overcome a fear. Anything, really."

"Ugh, can't we say something more fun?" Roo says, and I wonder if she'd be brave enough to challenge Val like this if the lights were on. "Like, which actor would play us in the movie of our life?"

"Taylor Swift!" Lexi immediately says.

"Taylor Swift isn't really an actor," says Ava.

"Yes she is! She's been in a bunch of movies."

"She's, like, twice your age," says Roo. "Can you imagine Taylor Swift playing you at your bat mitzvah? It would be ridiculous."

Lexi giggles. "It would be *amazing*, is what it would be."

"I thought we were going to talk about the prank war," says Petra.

"Let's say our goals, and then we can talk about that,

I promise," Val says. "I'll go first. My goal for the next four weeks is to learn about each and every one of you extraordinary young women and to help make this the most fantastic summer of your lives."

"OMG, soooo cheesy," Petra says, and a few people giggle.

I feel bad for Val—I think what she said was nice. It is cheesy, but I still really want her to learn about me. For a second I think she might reprimand Petra and tell her not to cut other people down, but instead she says, "That's me: Cheeseball McCheddar!" She sounds totally cheerful about it, and everyone laughs. I make a secret goal to be more like her—cool and in control and totally unconcerned with what everyone else thinks.

"Who wants to go next?" Val asks.

"I'll go," Roo says. "My goal is to be a Color Wars captain this year."

Lexi sighs in a frustrated way. "Roo, I told you yesterday at dance class that *I* want to be a Color Wars captain!"

"I'm not saying that can't be *your* goal. I'm just saying it's mine." I don't even know what Color Wars is, but if captains are involved, it's probably something like Sweetwater Olympics.

"There are only twelve captains all together, and

probably half will be boys," Lexi says. "So we're probably not both going to be able to do it, like, statistically. Why do *you* want to be a captain? You don't care about Color Wars."

"I'd probably care about it more if I were a captain," says Roo.

"No offense, you guys, but *I'd* be the best Color Wars captain," says Summer. "I have excellent leadership skills. I'm student council vice president, and I'm the captain of my debate team, and I volunteer at my church, and—"

"God, Summer, this isn't a campaign speech," says Roo. "And who cares about any of that stuff? It only matters if you're a good leader *at camp.*"

I wonder if maybe I could be one of the captains; if everything goes as planned with the prank war, everyone will see what an amazing leader I can be. But I don't say anything about it out loud. It's way too early, and I don't want Roo and Lexi and Summer to see me as competition.

"Okay, let's talk about some goals other than Color Wars," Val says. "Things we can achieve by ourselves. Ava? Do you have a goal?"

"I want to stay up on water skis all the way around the lake," Ava says. "I almost did it last year, but then Chloe Sapperstein started puking over the side of the boat, and I got distracted because it was bright green from the Jell-O she had at lunch." All the girls squeal and gag, and suddenly it seems like everyone's on the same side again.

Petra says her goal is to convince the woman who runs the stables to let her go on an early-morning solo ride. She wants to gallop a horse named George Harrison through a particular field as the sun is coming up so she can be like the heroine of a book she loves. BaileyAndHope talk about some soccer technique they want to improve, but it's so technical and specific that I don't understand most of the words. In a tiny voice, Hannah tells us that she wants to have more fun at camp this year than she did last year, which is kind of general, but I guess it makes sense for her. Mei says her goal is to get to the top of the hardest climbing wall in less than five minutes, her personal best from last year.

And then it's my turn. "My goal is to kick the Wolverines' butts in the prank war," I say. "And I know exactly how to do it."

"I still think the underwear thing would be really funny," Lexi says. "We could—"

Roo cuts her off. "Lex, let her talk. Her brother has way more experience than us, and we need something really professional." She's giving me an opening to impress her, and I am so ready to take it.

I'm a little nervous at first as I explain the logistics of the spaghetti prank—one "Tomás and I came up with together"—but as I talk, I start to calm down and enjoy it. After being ignored at dinner and during the treasure hunt, having everyone's rapt attention is pretty much the best. This is what camp has always been like. It's what camp is *supposed* to be like.

When I'm done talking, nobody says anything at first, and for a minute I wonder if I misread the situation— maybe the Willows think the prank is stupid, and they're trying to find a polite way to tell me. But then Roo says, "Wow, that's actually much better than what I was going to say. And it's *way* better than Lexi's underwear thing. Your brother is really funny."

"*So* funny," echoes Lexi. She doesn't seem offended that Roo insulted her.

"If you guys think of anything that would make it better, let me know," I say, but I'm sure nobody will. This prank is perfect the way it is.

"Izzy Cervantes," Val says slowly, giving weight to every syllable of my name, like each one is incredibly important. "I've been the Willows' counselor for three years now, and that is the most hilarious prank idea I've ever heard. The Wolverines are going to *flip out*."

"They totally are," says Summer, and Mei whispers, "Nice going."

There's a high, manic giggle from the corner of the cabin, and it takes me a minute to realize it's Hannah. "I can't wait to see their faces," she says, and then everyone cracks up, because she actually sounds kind of evil.

"What do we think, ladies?" Val asks when the noise dies down. "Does Izzy's prank get the Willow stamp of approval?"

There's a chorus of enthusiastic yeses, and since no one can see me in the dark, I let a goofy smile break over my face and do a fist-pump. This afternoon, these girls thought I was completely useless. And now, thanks to my pranking genius (and a few harmless lies, and Mackenzie's help), I'm already in charge of something.

It has only taken me eight hours to go from dead weight to rock star.

Dear Mom, Dad, Lina, Tomás, and Abuela,

I got to camp okay. Mackenzie and I are in different cabins, which is TOTALLY UNFAIR, but everyone says the cabin assignments are final and we can't switch. UGH. My counselor's name is Valerie, and she's really cool, and some of the girls seem pretty nice. We had our swim test and I passed, obviously. I'm bunking with this girl Mei, and I got the top bunk. Lina and Tomás, if you send me drawings, I'll hang them right over my bed so I can see them first thing when I wake up.

Mom and Dad, I know this is weird, but you know that noise-activated dancing Santa toy Tomás hates? Can you send it to me as quick as you can? We need it for a project, and it's kind of urgent. Maybe you could overnight it?

Abuela, you know how I asked you to sneak candy into my care packages? (Sorry, Mom, don't get mad.) Anyway, don't bother. The camp director opens everyone's packages in the office and takes the food before it gets to us. She says having food in the cabins attracts mice, which is ridiculous, because there's NO WAY we'd let it sit around long enough for any mice to get it. I think she's eating it all herself.

Love,
Izzy

CHAPTER 5

I wake up in the morning to the sound of a bugle fanfare. For a second I think there's an actual guy with a bugle outside—what is this, the army? But then the fanfare finishes and starts over from the beginning, and I realize it's the alarm on Val's phone.

"Up and at 'em, ladies," she calls in her croaky early-morning voice. "Flag raising is in fifteen minutes." She rolls out of her bunk and stumbles toward the bathroom, her T-shirt all askew and her hair sticking up in a million different directions.

Fifteen minutes later, we're out in the early-morning sunshine, making our way toward the group of campers around the flagpole. As Mei and I walk together across the dew-sparkly grass and listen to Lexi and Roo argue about whether Lexi was snoring, I think, *Yeah, I could get used to this.* For some reason, sleeping somewhere makes that place feel more like yours. I hope Mackenzie's settling in a little bit too. I spot her across the circle, and she looks pretty tired, but at least she returns my smile and wave.

All two hundred of us gather in a giant circle and watch as Stuart (a.k.a. Public Enemy Number One) raises the flag. When he's finished, he bows with a huge flourish, like he's done something superimpressive, and I roll my eyes. I almost feel bad for the Wolverines, who have to deal with him all the time. But only *almost*, because you're not supposed to feel sympathy for the enemy.

There's no wind today, so the flag hangs limply as everyone puts their hands over their hearts and recites the camp pledge: *"Today, I dedicate myself to fun, friendship, and my fellow Foxes. I pledge to learn all I can, be the best I can be, and serve my camp, my country, and my world."* It sounds like kind of a lot to accomplish, but I try to remember the words anyway so I can recite them tomorrow.

When we're done, Camp Director Dana steps into the middle of the circle, and everyone starts pumping their fists and chanting, "Doo-bie! Doo-bie!" She raises her hands for silence, and when everyone finally quiets down, she says, "Good morning, Foxes! Welcome back. I hope you're all ready to make this summer the best one yet!"

Everyone goes crazy, and she has to pause again before she can continue. Making announcements at camp always takes way longer than it does anywhere else.

"I don't want to keep you from your food, but since this is the first day, I thought we'd talk through the schedule quickly. After breakfast you'll head to your first two activities—your counselors have your schedules, and they'll pass them out when you're done eating. Activity three is after lunch, followed by Cabin Group and Free Time. After-dinner activities are different every day, and the counselors and I have planned some seriously awesome things for you this year. You ready to get started?" Everyone cheers. "Perfect! No other big announcements today. Let's go get some grub!"

Breakfast is cinnamon French toast sticks, which we eat with our fingers (except for Summer, who calls us animals and cuts hers up with a knife and fork). I look over at Mackenzie's table and spot her slumped at the end of the bench again, picking at her French toast and not talking to anyone. Part of me wants to ask Val if I can go over and cheer her up again. But I know Roo's watching me closely, and I don't want to undo all the progress I made with the Willows last night by showing them someone else is my top priority. I stay put and eat my breakfast.

When Val finally pulls out a folder full of schedules near the end of the meal, everyone starts talking at once and making grabby-hands. Mackenzie and I filled out our activity preference forms almost identically, so hopefully we'll finally get to spend some time together.

"Look these over, and come talk to me if you have any concerns," Val says as she passes them out. "Please don't ask to change your schedule unless you have a medical issue with an activity you've been assigned. If you've been placed in Horseback Riding and you're allergic to horses, that's a medical issue. If you're not in Arts and Crafts in the same time slot as your friend, that's not a medical issue."

I take a look at the paper Val hands me.

CERVANTES, ISOBEL:

Week 1:

9:15: Ropes Course

10:30: Boating and Canoeing

1:00: Arts and Crafts

Week 2:

9:15: Archery

10:30: Horseback Riding

1:00: Sailing

Week 3:

9:15: Nature

10:30: Soccer

1:00: Fishing

Week 4:

9:15: Rock Climbing

10:30: Water Skiing

1:00: Ultimate Frisbee

It looks pretty good overall. I'm not thrilled about the fishing part, but it could be worse. At least I didn't get any of the other activities I listed as my lowest priorities, like tennis or softball.

Across the table, Lexi's trying to convince Val that she's medically unable to go on nature walks because she might see a snake and have a heart attack. I get up and try to find Mackenzie so we can compare schedules, but everyone is moving around now, and there are so many people between us that I can't see her. I still haven't found her by the time Val herds us out the door.

I'm superexcited to have Ropes Course first thing, even though it means I definitely won't be with Mackenzie, who's scared of heights. Mei gives me directions, but I don't really need them—I took special note of where the course was last night during the treasure hunt. The counselor in charge has shaggy hair and those weird plastic plugs that stretch out your earlobes and make them look like tunnels, and I try not to stare at them.

"Hey," he says. "I'm Aaron."

I introduce myself, and he gestures to the ropes course above us. "You ever done this before?"

"Not this particular one, but it looks a lot like the one at my old camp."

Aaron nods. "Sweet."

The other kids trickle in, including two boys I vaguely recognize. One of them is short and skinny, and he's wearing a shirt that says THE MILITANT UNICORNS across the front. I think his nametag last night said BEANS. The other one is the redhead who hissed in my face at dinner, the one whose tag said TWIZZLER, but he doesn't pay any attention to me, so he probably doesn't remember.

Aaron looks around and counts us. "Is that everyone? I think it is. Hello, little monkeys! Welcome to the ropes course. I'm Aaron, your handsome and clever leader. And this is Carl, our counselor-in-training." He gestures to a lanky blond guy who looks a few years older than me. He's got about seven hairs on his chin, and he's let them grow really long; I bet he thinks they make him look manly or something. "Today we'll teach you how to put on your harnesses, tie some knots, and safely communicate with us when we're belaying you from the ground. That means anchoring the rope you're attached to so you can't fall if you slip when you're high in the air. I know you're anxious to get up there, but safety is our first priority. What's our first priority?"

"Safety," we parrot back.

"What good little monkeys. All right, everyone grab a harness out of that box, and let's get started."

It takes me about thirty seconds to clip myself into a harness, so I help some of the younger kids, which makes me feel grown-up and knowledgeable. The next forty minutes are pretty boring, since I already know how to lock a carabiner, tie a figure-eight knot, and communicate with the person belaying me. But I dutifully shout out the commands over and over until everybody has them down.

There are still twenty minutes left when Aaron's satisfied that everyone knows the rules, so he asks if any of the more experienced climbers want to go up in the air for a little bit. I raise my hand faster and higher than anyone, and he picks me right away. There are two side-by-side vine walks on this ropes course, each with a single thin cable you're supposed to walk like a tightrope and a bunch of knotted ropes of different lengths hanging down from above, which you grab for support. Aaron picks the redheaded Wolverine to go up and race me, and I clip Aaron's line to the front of my harness while Twizzler does the same with Carl's.

"On belay?" I ask Aaron.

"Belay on," he says, which means he's ready.

"Climbing," I say, and my heart starts pitter-pattering with excitement. I scale the rope ladder that leads up to one of the wooden platforms as fast as I can, and I hear one of the younger kids below me go, *"Whoa."* I smile to myself as I step onto the platform fifteen feet in the air. I didn't really need to climb so fast, but it's possible I wanted to show off a little.

"Permission to transfer?" I call down, and Aaron calls back, "Permission granted." I clip my harness to one of the safety ropes that slides along the track at the top of the vine walk, then unclip the belay rope and send it down. I love being up here in the trees all alone, and I lean against the platform railing and listen to the wind rustle through the trees as I wait for Twizzler to join me.

He takes his sweet time going up the ladder, but he seems totally comfortable on it, and he's not winded or sweaty at all by the time he gets to the platform. "You're that girl from Willow," he says as he clips into the safety ropes on the other vine walk.

"Yeah," I say. "And you're that guy from Wolverine."

"Yup." He gives me what's probably supposed to be an evil smile, but combined with his face full of freckles and the way his ears stick out, he just looks kind of goofy. "You guys are going *down*," he says.

I shrug. "We'll see about that. What's with the Twizzler thing, anyway? That's not actually your name, is it?"

He snorts. "No. It's Josh. Stuart gave everyone nick-names last night."

It makes sense—Josh is tall and skinny and red, like a Twizzler. "Why did he call your friend Beans?" I ask. "Does he really like beans or something?"

"No, it's beans like coffee beans. He was whining about how only counselors can get coffee in the mess hall. We got off easy, honestly. Nick showed up wearing a Hungry Hungry Hippos T-shirt, so now he's Hippo. And Sebastian was trying to get some of the guys to do that Bloody Mary thing in the bathroom mirror with him last night, so now for the next four weeks, he's—"

"Bloody Mary," I finish, and Josh nods.

"Is this a ropes course or a tea party?" Aaron calls up. "Less chatting, more racing!"

65

Josh and I move toward the edges of our platforms and get ready. "I hope you know you don't have a chance of winning," I tell him. "I was second fastest in my entire camp last year."

"I hope you're prepared to feel like an idiot, because I was the *first* fastest here last year," Josh says.

"Ready . . . ," Aaron shouts from the ground, "set . . . go!"

I face away from Josh so he can't distract me, grab the first knotted rope, and scootch out onto the cable. The first few seconds without anything solid under my feet are always scarier than I expect, and a rush of nervous adrenaline sweeps through me as the cable bows and sways. I take deep breaths and remind myself I'm safe, that I can't possibly fall. I bend my knees and try to keep my feet shoulder-width apart for maximum stability as I shuffle to the left and pass the ropes over my head from hand to hand. A gust of wind pushes at me from behind, and I almost tip over when one of my feet slips off the cable, but I'm able to pull myself back upright. I'm a little more than halfway across now.

"Go, Twizzler!" shouts Beans from the ground, and Josh whoops in response. It sounds like he's close by, but I can't tell if he's behind me or ahead. I wish I'd faced toward him instead, so I could track his progress.

About three quarters of the way across, I hear a yelp and a swear from behind me. I peek over my shoulder to see what's happening, and out of the corner of my eye I spot Josh dangling from his safety rope and one of the handholds. He's lost his footing entirely. "Hook the cable with your toe and give yourself a swing," calls Aaron from the ground, and I smile to myself as Josh mutters, "I *know*, jeez."

I want to shout something witty at him, but I can't think of anything good, and I don't want to lose my focus now. So I turn back around and concentrate on inching closer to the end platform. It would be pretty embarrassing if I stopped to laugh at him and fell myself.

Only ten feet to go . . . then five . . . and then I'm there.

I pull myself up onto the solid wooden platform, pump my fists in victory, and shout, "Done!" Josh has managed to right himself, but he's still about twenty feet behind me.

"Izzy wins with a time of three minutes and thirty-six seconds," Carl calls from the ground.

There's a peal of laughter, followed by Beans's voice. "Oh man, Twizzler, you got your butt kicked by a *girl*."

Josh's freckled cheeks are flaming pink, and he looks at

me with slitted eyes. He looks a lot more evil now than he did before, but I'm not worried. I shoot him my best angelic smile.

"Yup," I say. "And you better get used to it."

CHAPTER 6

I cross my fingers that Mackenzie will be in my second activity—we've never gone this long at camp without having a conversation, and she's probably freaking out by now. But the only people I know in Boating and Canoeing are Roo and Ava. I figure I'll be able to bond with them a little more now that they've heard my fantastic prank idea, and at first things seem to be going well; they're polite to me as we clip on our orange life jackets, and Roo helps me push my banana boat into the water. But once we're out on the lake, they paddle in the opposite direction, and it feels weird and stalkerish to follow them. I guess I shouldn't expect things to change overnight. I spend the next hour hanging out with two girls from Aspen and trying to flip each other's boats, which is pretty fun, but not nearly as fun as it would've been with

Mackenzie. Last year we tried to set a Sweetwater record for how many times we could flip our boats in a row, but we gave up after twenty-seven because we were too dizzy.

I finally spot her when I get to lunch, and I run up and hug her before she can get to the Maple table. My bathing suit is soaking through my T-shirt, and she squeals and pushes me away. "Gross, you're all wet," she says, but I can tell she's happy to see me.

"I can't believe we weren't together all morning," I say. "What do you have after lunch?"

"Arts and Crafts."

"Me too!"

Mackenzie gives me a huge, relieved smile. "Thank god. I've been dying to talk to you, 'cause I've got another really good idea for *you know what*. I thought maybe you could—"

A hand lands on my back, and I look up to see Val. "Hey, Iz, how was your morning?"

I love that she's already shortened my nickname to another nickname; I'm pretty sure that means she likes me. I smile up at her. "Good. It was fun."

"Excellent. You ready for some grilled cheese? It's my favorite thing the kitchen makes. They use, like, *triple* cheese. It oozes right out the sides."

"Sounds great. I'm starving." But then I notice the way Mackenzie's face has fallen. "Oh no, did you get your dairy-free thing worked out with the nurse? I can talk to someone if—"

"No, it's fine," she says. "I'm sure they'll give me peanut butter or something."

"We can talk about *the thing* right after lunch, all right? Meet me by the door and we'll walk over to Arts and Crafts together."

"Yeah, okay." Mackenzie gives me a little smile before she heads over to her table, but it looks kind of sad. I guess I'd be pretty upset too if I had to eat boring peanut butter while everyone else had triple grilled cheese.

I claim a seat next to Val at the table and tell her all about how I kicked some Wolverine butt on the ropes course this morning. When I repeat my snappy comebacks for her, she breaks into this huge belly laugh where she throws her head back and opens her mouth so wide I can practically see her tonsils. I wish my laugh sounded like that instead of the stupid giggle that always sneaks its way out of me. I wonder if I'd look dumb throwing my head back that way; I'll have to give it a test run in front of the mirror later.

The sandwiches are as delicious as Val promised, and she

spends the whole meal telling us stories about mortifying things that happened to her when she was a camper, like the time her wraparound skirt got caught in the cabin door and all of Porcupine Lodge got a good look at her rainbow-striped underwear. Unlike last night, we're all laughing together, and I totally feel like part of the conversation. It's amazing how much things can change in one day.

I'm feeling pretty great by the time Mackenzie and I head to Arts and Crafts. She asks to see my schedule, and we hold our papers up side by side as we walk across the field. Next week we have archery together first thing in the morning, and week three we have nature together. The fourth week our schedules don't overlap at all. "It's not a lot, but at least we have something together almost every day," I say. Hopefully by week four, she'll finally be comfortable enough here that she won't mind not seeing me during activities.

Mackenzie sighs. "I just wish it could be like at Camp Sweetwater, when we had *all* our activities together. Everything was better there. Don't you think?"

"Yeah," I say. But honestly, there are already some things I like better here. If someone told me I could transfer to Sweetwater tomorrow, I'm not positive I'd want to go, since it would mean giving up the prank war. And Val.

And the possibility of beating Twizzler Josh on the ropes course again tomorrow.

The Arts and Crafts lodge has one long table in the center, and Hannah's already sitting on one of the benches when we arrive. I know I should probably be a good Willow and sit with her, but she actually looks pretty happy for once, and Mackenzie and I need to talk privately about prank stuff. When I smile at Hannah and then sit down at the other end, she doesn't seem to mind. The back wall of the room is covered in rickety-looking wooden shelves crammed with construction paper and clay and markers and glue and paint. There are several industrial-size containers of glitter balanced precariously on top. I'm kind of afraid to touch anything for fear it'll all come crashing down.

When everyone has arrived, the counselor in charge gives us each a big lump of grayish clay and tells us to make whatever we want. Then she perches on a stool in the corner and opens one of those magazines with a cover story about how to get the perfect bikini body. I don't get the point of those articles. Any body is a bikini body if you put a bikini on it.

Mackenzie and I start rolling our clay into long snakes so we can make coil pots, and while we do, she fills me in on her brilliant new prank idea. It's classic Mackenzie—hilarious, subtle, and a little scary—and I'm reminded again how lucky I am to have her on my side. She finds a piece of paper and a marker on the supply shelf, and we abandon our clay for a while and make a supply list. Some of the stuff we can probably get right here in Arts and Crafts, but I might have to get my parents to send me something from home again. I hope they don't mind going to the post office over and over.

We're so absorbed that it seems like barely any time has passed when the counselor looks up from her magazine and calls, "Five more minutes!"

I look down at my sad half-finished pot. "Will we have time to work on these tomorrow?"

The counselor snaps her gum. "I guess," she says. "Whatever."

When I glance over at Hannah, I'm surprised to see that she's made an impressively realistic skull out of her clay. "Whoa," I say. "That's really good."

She smiles shyly. "Thanks. I'm going to paint it glossy black with neon green teeth and maybe a little bit of blood coming out of the left eye socket and the mouth." I think about her evil laugh last night during cabin group; seems like there's more to Hannah than I thought.

"Ooh, blood coming out of the eye sockets. *Nice*. I'm going to do that too." A boy at the end of the table holds up his project, a creepy doll with a long, pointy nose and snakes for hair.

Mackenzie wrinkles her nose. "What *is* that?"

"It's the Sea Witch, obviously."

"What's a sea witch?" I ask. "Like Ursula in *The Little Mermaid*?"

The boy's eyes widen. "How do you not know about the Sea Witch? *Everyone* knows about the Sea Witch!"

"She's new," Hannah says.

"Ohhhh," he says. "Okay. So, a long time ago, there was this beautiful blond counselor—"

"And every night, after it got dark, she'd go down to the lake to swim all by herself," a girl with two long braids cuts in.

The boy shoves her. "Shut up, Ally! I want to tell it!"

"We can both tell it!"

"I'm the one who made the Sea Witch. I get to tell it."

This seems like it might go on for a while, so I say, "What happened to the counselor?"

"One night," the boy says, "a camper from her cabin went down to the lake after dark because she'd left her backpack—"

"It was her towel," interrupts Ally.

"It doesn't *matter*! She went down to the lake to get it, and she saw someone swimming. But the swimmer didn't look like a pretty blond counselor anymore, because she'd changed into her true form—*the Sea Witch*."

"She had black sunken eyes and a craggy nose covered in warts, and her hair was made out of *snakes*, all coiling around and hissing," says Ally.

"But the counselor was still wearing the clothes she'd had on earlier, so the girl recognized her and figured out what had happened."

"Why was she swimming in her clothes?" I ask.

"And why is she the *Sea* Witch?" Mackenzie adds. "Shouldn't she be the Lake Witch?"

The boy rolls his eyes. "I don't know, that's how the story goes! The point is, the camper tried to run back to her cabin to tell everyone what she'd seen. But the Sea Witch couldn't let her secret get out, so she grabbed the girl with her long, pointy, witchy nails, and she dragged her into the lake and *drowned her*."

"They found her body the next day, floating in the water with a snake coiled around her neck," says Ally. She wraps one of her own braids around her neck for emphasis and sticks her tongue out.

"And of course the pretty blond counselor pretended to be super upset, so nobody suspected it was her. The rest of the summer was normal, and the counselor didn't come back the next year. But in the middle of the summer, *another* camper was found drowned with a snake around *his* neck!"

"And that's because the Sea Witch was *still there in a different body*. She can take any form she wants. And that's why you never know where she is. She could be anyone. She could be *me*!"

"So don't go down to the lake at night unless you want a snake around your neck," finishes the boy. He shoves his Sea Witch doll in Ally's face and makes a growling sound, and she screams and laughs.

"I hate that story," Hannah says. "It's so creepy."

Ally rolls her eyes. "Says the girl who made a *skull*."

"Skulls aren't creepy. Everyone has a skull."

The boy turns back to us. "So anyway, the night before Color Wars every year, we have this huge campfire at the fire pit near the dock, and Doobie tells that story. And then one of the counselors comes out of the water dressed as the Sea Witch and pretends to kidnap a camper, and that person is the first Color Wars captain."

The greatest thing about being best friends with

someone for almost your whole life is that you can look at each other and know exactly what the other one is thinking. And now, when I turn and meet Mackenzie's eyes, I know we're having the same exact idea.

Sounds like the perfect opportunity for a prank.

CHAPTER 7

The rest of the first week goes by quickly. Josh challenges me to a race on the vine walk each morning, and I leave him in the dust every time. Mackenzie and I spend Arts and Crafts and Free Time planning pranks for "Tomás" to suggest, and sometimes it almost feels like we're back at Camp Sweetwater. It's not that I don't like plotting with her, but part of me wishes my best friend were more interested in exploring our new surroundings. We could be going on trail rides or walks in the woods or canoeing excursions during Free Time, and I'd like to try them all. But Mackenzie still seems really uncomfortable at Camp Foxtail, and she's obviously happiest when we're sprawled under a tree with her notebook. I tell myself those activities can wait until she's ready, but the thing is, she doesn't seem to be making any progress. I rarely even see her *talk* to anyone but me; every time I glance over at the Maple table during meals, she's silently picking at her dairy-free food. I get that she's shy and everything, but I feel like she could be making a little more of an effort to fit in, like I am.

As the days pass, the Willows become increasingly paranoid about the Wolverines pranking us, and soon all of us are checking our sleeping bags every night and shielding our eyes before we open our drawers, in case something horrible pops out. Hannah refuses to go into the bathroom stalls or the shower unless Summer checks them for her first. But nothing happens, and nothing happens, and nothing happens. In a lot of ways it's actually worse than a prank, since it allows our imaginations to run wild, and I wonder if the boys are holding out on purpose so we'll freak ourselves out. Then again, they're probably thinking the same thing about us.

And then on Thursday the care package from my parents finally, *finally* comes. Lexi has mail call that day, and she arrives at dinner with my package, her eyes wild with excitement. We all rush back to our cabin before the all-camp activity—a massive game of capture the flag—and the Willows gather round and watch as I tear the box open. I pull out a pen shaped like a fish, new stationary, a stuffed hedgehog, a travel Boggle set. And then I finally get to the important thing: a six-inch-tall plastic Santa toy. I hold it up with great ceremony.

A crinkle appears between Roo's eyebrows. "Wait, that's *it*?"

"Just watch." I flip the switch on the bottom of the toy, stand it up on the edge of my dresser, and clap a couple times right in front of Santa's face. He comes to life immediately, raising and lowering his arms and twitching his hips from side to side, and a recording of my dad singing *"Feliz Navidad"* really off-key comes out of the speaker on the bottom.

"Santa shouldn't wiggle his butt like that," Petra says. "It's just *wrong*."

"It's noise-activated," I explain. "You can record any message you want. My dad did that one, but we can record over it."

"So we can make it say, 'Wolverines are the scum of the earth' or something?" asks Lexi. She has a huge smile on her face, but then she glances sideways at Roo, like she's looking for permission to be excited.

"Yup. We can make it say whatever we want." I look at Roo too, and after considering for a minute, she nods.

"Yeah, you're right. I think this'll probably work."

"It's perfect, Izzy." Val gives me a sideways hug. "Right now spaghetti night is scheduled for Saturday, but if you guys are ready, I'll talk to my friend Danny in the kitchen and see if we can move it to tomorrow." It sounds like she's talking to all of us, but she's looking straight at me, like I'm the leader, and I love it.

"Yup," I say. "We're ready." I get a shiver all the way up my spine. Our very first prank in an age-old prank war, and it's all because of me and Mackenzie.

The next day can't go by fast enough. I'm so excited I can barely eat during lunch, and I spill blue paint all over my shirt in Arts and Crafts. Mackenzie's no better, and the two of us keep bursting into hyper giggles as we glaze our clay pots. Surprisingly, Hannah's much better at keeping it together, though there's a secretive, gleeful smile on her face the entire time she's painting her skull. I spot Josh walking across the field as I head back to Willow Lodge for Cabin Group, and I wonder if I should've let him win our race on the ropes course this morning. I almost feel bad kicking his butt twice in one day.

Almost.

When it's finally time for Waiter Call, Roo and I walk over to the mess hall together. She's not exactly the friendliest accomplice, but it's good that she's here with me for the first prank. It's important to have her as an ally, and I wouldn't want her to resent me because she feels left out.

The two of us try to act normal as we set the table, but we keep a close eye on the serving window, and the moment the kitchen staff starts laying out the heavy serving platters of spaghetti, we race over and grab two. The Wolverine waiters don't seem to be paying us any attention, but Roo still shields me from them while I slip the plastic Santa out of my backpack and switch it on. And then, working very quietly so I don't activate it, I lift up a big pile of spaghetti with the serving tongs and nestle Santa into the pasta underneath. I arrange the noodles over him, then stack a couple of meatballs on top of the pile so it looks natural.

"Can you tell it's under there?" I whisper, and Roo shakes her head and smiles.

I pick up the serving platter, approach the Wolverine table, and intercept one of their waiters as he starts heading toward the serving window. Fortunately, it's a boy I've never met before. I wonder if it's Bloody Mary.

"Hey," I say. "We accidentally took two. You can have this one if you want."

The boy's eyes narrow, and for a second I'm afraid he

recognizes me; Stuart probably told him never to accept anything from a Willow. "What cabin are you in?" he says.

My heart is pounding, but my voice comes out steady and calm when I say. "Cedar. Why?"

"No reason," he says, and he takes the dish. "Thanks."

People start arriving for dinner, and Val shoots me a questioning look as I set down a pitcher of water. I smile and nod to show her everything went fine. When Roo passes me the stack of trays I'll need for phase two of our plan, I glance over at the Maple table to make sure Mackenzie's watching. She makes her hands into the shape of a flying bird—it's our long-distance way of saying "The crow flies at midnight," which is code for "The prank is ready to go." I tuck my trays under my arm and make the bird sign back, and she smiles and holds up her pinkie for luck.

As soon as all the Wolverines are seated, Roo and I make our way toward opposite ends of the aisle that runs along their table, then walk toward each other at a brisk clip. The spaghetti platter's right across from Stuart, and when we're as close to it as we can get, we slam into each other and drop our stacks of trays on the floor with an enormous clatter. A bunch of people laugh and applaud sarcastically as we fake apologize and stoop to gather them up. I cross my fingers and hope the noise was enough to activate the toy.

Seconds later there's a gasp behind me, and one of the Wolverines shouts, "Omigod, it's *moving!*"

"What is?" says Stuart's voice.

"The spaghetti! You guys, *look at it!*"

"There's a *rat* in there!" someone shrieks.

And then there's total chaos. The Wolverines all try to back up as the spaghetti undulates like a wave, but they're trapped in by the benches. Beans gets his feet tangled up and falls off the bench backward, and I have to bite my lip so I don't laugh as he sprawls at my feet. Two of the Wolverine boys yell and grab on to each other as a couple of meatballs go rolling down the sides of the pile and plop onto the table. People at the surrounding tables leap up on their benches when they hear the word "rat," and a couple of girls from Magnolia scream and sprint for the door.

Stuart half stands as he watches the spaghetti wriggle, his forehead all scrunched up with concentration. Lightning-quick, he reaches out and snatches the serving tongs. And just as he raises them above the dish like a weapon, the noodles start to speak.

"Willows ruuuuule . . . ," says Val's ghostly voice as the spaghetti dances and writhes. "Wolverines droooool!"

"Did it just *talk*?" one of the boys gasps.

"There's no such thing as a talking rat, you doofus!"

"It said something! I heard it!"

"You guys! Shut up!"

The Wolverine table falls silent. *"Willows ruuuuuuuule!"* the spaghetti says again, louder this time. *"Wolverines drooooool!"*

All the tension goes out of Stuart's body, and he stands all the way up. "Oh, come *on*," he says.

He pulls the platter of wriggling spaghetti toward him, rummages around with the tongs until he finds the Santa toy, and holds it up as it flails around and sheds noodles and sauce all over the table.

"It's not a rat," he says. "It's a very stupid prank."

"Didn't think it was so stupid ten seconds ago, did you?" comes Val's voice from the Willow table. "We *totally* got you!" All the Willows start laughing and cheering, and everyone at the neighboring tables joins in. When Roo holds up her hand, I slap her palm hard. I hope a forceful high five is a sign of a strong leader.

"Ha-ha," Stuart says, totally deadpan. "Very funny."

Nearby I hear a soft clicking noise, and I turn to find Ava right behind me with Roo's camera around her neck, snapping away. "Did you get his face?" I ask her.

"Ohhhh yeah," she says. "It was perfect."

"Is that *Santa*?" asks Beans.

The toy shakes its hips. "Willows ruuuuule," it says.

"What a dumb prank," says one of the other boys, who has literally *just* stopped cowering under the table. "I wasn't scared at all."

"You keep telling yourself that," Roo says. "Come on, girls."

As we turn and walk back to the table, she slips one arm through Ava's and one arm through mine, and I time my steps to theirs. Mackenzie catches my eye from across the room and shoots me a smile and a thumbs-up. Even though her prank went perfectly, she looks a little sad, and I figure it's because she wishes she were over here, strutting across the mess hall with us. I mean, who *wouldn't* wish that?

"Willows ruuuule!" I shout over my shoulder, and when all my cabinmates and Val join in with "Wolverines droooool!" I feel like the coolest person in the world.

When we get back to the cabin after capture the flag that night, I squeeze onto Lexi's bunk between her and Roo and flip through the pictures Ava took of the spaghetti prank. She's right—the Wolverines' terrified faces are absolutely perfect. "We should write a letter to Tomás tomorrow during Cabin Group and tell him how well his prank went," Lexi says.

"Sure," I say. "I'll make sure he gets it."

"And we should ask him for more ideas," Roo says. "You were right, he's amazing at this. We should get started on something else right away and hit the Wolverines again while they're down."

"Don't worry, we're already working on a couple other options," I say. I hope they catch the "we." It's fine if they think the original idea came from someone else, but the execution was all me, and I think I deserve some credit.

"What does Tomás look like?" Lexi asks. "Is he cute? I bet he's *so* cute."

"Eew, I don't know," I say. "He's my brother!"

Lexi rolls her eyes. "Come on, you can tell if he's objectively cute."

"I guess he's good-looking," I say. "Black hair and brown eyes, like me. Kind of tall. His skin's a little darker than mine, and his teeth are really straight—he never needed braces or anything. And he's got a dimple in his left cheek."

"Can we see a picture?" Ava asks.

"I don't have one. I didn't bring any pictures of my family."

"What about on your phone?"

"We're not supposed to use our phones," Summer chimes in.

"I don't think so," I say. "I don't really take a lot of pictures."

"He must be on Facebook, though, right?" Lexi presses.

"Val, can we use *your* phone to look him up? Pretty please?"

"I wish we could, but there's no signal out here," Val says.

"We could go to the main office. There's wireless there, right?"

"It's okay," I say quickly. "I'll write to my parents tomorrow and ask them to send a photo."

"What's it like living with him?" Roo asks. "Did he prank you all the time before he went away to college?"

"Constantly. You have to watch your back when he's around. It's kind of a relief that he doesn't live at home anymore, honestly."

"What's the funniest thing he ever did?" Lexi asks.

Everyone looks at me, eyes wide with anticipation, my mind goes completely blank. "Oh man," I say. "I don't know. There are too many to choose from."

"Pick one! It doesn't have to be the absolute funniest."

"Um, okay." I frantically try to remember some of the pranks Mackenzie and I have done, but none of them seem good enough. "There was this one time he transferred everything in our living room onto the front lawn while we were sleeping, including my grandma's slippers and my math homework and my sister's Legos," I say. I'm pretty sure I stole that from a movie. I hope none of them have seen it.

"How did he carry all the furniture by himself?" Summer asks.

"No idea. I never figured out how he did half the things he came up with."

"Man, you're so lucky," Roo says. "My big sister would never do anything that cool."

"Mine either," says Petra.

"Yeah," I say. "He's pretty funny, when he's not dyeing your body wash different colors."

Loud, peppy music starts blasting through the cabin, and when I look up, I see that Val has set up an iPod dock on her dresser. "Post-prank celebratory dance party!" she yells. "Come on, everyone up! It's a Willow tradition!" She throws her hands over her head and shakes her hips, which makes her look kind of like the Santa toy, but much less creepy.

Lexi's the first to join her, spinning around and waving her arms as she mouths the words to the song, and

Val shouts, "Woooo, go Lexi!" Roo and Ava and Mei join in next, and then Petra gets up and starts doing this silly butt-wiggling dance. I expect Summer's dancing to be uptight and prissy, but she starts flailing her arms and legs in a surprisingly wild way. BaileyAndHope abandon their card game and jump in circles to the beat. Like always, they're sort of part of the group, but still a little separate, like they exist in a best-friend bubble that none of us can pop.

I don't have a great sense of rhythm—at the sixth-grade dance last winter Mackenzie and I spent the whole time at the snack table, competing to see who could eat more mini cupcakes. But I'm so happy tonight that it's hard to feel self-conscious, and I get up and join the circle. I undo my braid and try to copy the way Val is shaking her hair around, and she laughs when she sees what I'm doing, but it's the good kind of laugh that means *you and I are in on something together.* She whips her hair faster, and I whip mine faster, and then Roo and Lexi and Petra start doing it too, and for a second, everything feels perfect.

But then Val dances over to where Hannah's huddled on her bunk and tries to coax her into joining us. Now that we've pranked the Wolverines, it's like she's afraid to even step on the floor of our cabin in case there's a booby trap, but she finally gets up and lets Val spin her around until she giggles. It's a little annoying that *she's* getting so much special attention when all she's done is act shy and scared. I try to forget about it and enjoy dancing with the other girls, but without Val watching, the hair-shaking thing doesn't feel the same, so I stop.

When the song ends, Val turns the iPod off. "That's enough for tonight," she says. "Time to get ready for bed." I'm about to beg for one more song, but then she says, "Oh, Izzy, c'mere a second. I have something for you."

"You do?" I trot over to her, and she pulls an orange shirt out of her drawer and holds it out to me with great ceremony.

"You want to wear this tomorrow?" she asks.

When I unfold the shirt, I see that it's the one she was wearing our first day here, the one that says I'M FOXY. BaileyAndHope go "Oooooh" in unison.

I must look confused, because Val laughs and says, "Sorry, you fit in so well here that I keep forgetting you're new. It's a Foxtail tradition. When a camper does something really extraordinary for her cabin, she gets to wear her counselor's Foxy shirt the next day. It's an honor."

My whole body goes warm; Val thinks I did something *extraordinary* for the cabin. I remember how I felt last Sunday, when I trailed behind my group during the treasure hunt and got ready for bed all by myself while everyone else chattered around me. I didn't think I'd ever belong here. And now, six short days later, here I am, the very first one getting rewarded.

"You don't have to wear it if you don't want," Val says. "But you've earned it."

I hug the shirt to my chest and smile. "I definitely want to," I say. "Thanks."

Tomorrow, everyone in the *whole camp* is going to know who Val's favorite Willow is.

Dear Abuela,

How are you? Do you miss me? Are Lina and
Tomás driving you crazy? It's weird to go
through an entire day without stepping on
any action figures or hearing anyone throw a
tantrum because different foods are touching.
I DO NOT MISS IT AT ALL.

Things are going really well here. I've made
a bunch of new friends, and I get to do
the ropes course first thing every morning
this week. Don't worry, it's safe. The food
is pretty decent, but I miss your cooking
SO MUCH—I don't know how I'm going to
make it through an entire month without
a homemade tortilla. They served us this
"cake" on Friday that tasted like a dried-
up sponge, and all I could think about the
whole rest of the day was the cinnamon-
chocolate cake you made for my birthday.
And now I'm thinking about it again and
getting really hungry.

Can you do me a favor? I need you to print
out a picture from the Internet of the actor
who plays Juan Carlos on "Corazón de Hielo,
Alma de Fuego" and send it to me. Not one
where he's on the red carpet or anything, just
one where he's wearing jeans and looks like a
normal guy who might be related to us. Lina
can help you do a Google image search and
use the printer if you don't remember how.
Speaking of "Corazón de Hielo," I hope nothing
TOO horrible has happened since I've been
gone. (Hahahaha, of course horrible stuff has
happened—it's a telenovela.) Catch me up on
the plot in your next letter, okay? Did Luz and
Umberto die in the desert? Did that old woman
in jail turn out to be Rosalinda's long-lost
mother?

Thanks in advance for the picture! You're the
best! Te amo mucho!

Izzy

CHAPTER 8

*Mackenzie's not at breakfast on Saturday morn-*ing, and I don't see her at lunch or in Arts and Crafts, either. The minute Cabin Group ends and Free Time starts, I head over to Maple to check on her, and I catch her on her way out the door. "Hey, I was coming to find you," she says. Then a weird expression comes over her face as she notices my shirt. "Why are you wearing that?"

"It's Val's," I say. "She said it was a tradition that if you do something really extraordinary for your cabin, you get to wear it." The shirt is pretty big on me and drapes off my shoulders like I'm a wire hanger, but the impressed looks I've been getting all day have been totally worth it. Plus, the shirt smells like Val's sunblock and moisturizer and deodorant, and wearing it makes me feel really grown-up.

"Oh," Mackenzie says. "That's cool, I guess."

"Sorry we can't tell anyone the prank was your idea. You should get a turn to wear it too."

"It's okay. I don't really care."

She seems to want to change the subject, so I ask, "Where were you this morning?"

Mackenzie toys with the earpiece of her glasses. "The infirmary."

"Are you sick?"

"Not anymore. It was my own fault. Jayla's parents sent her brownies for her birthday, and Eleanor convinced the main office to let us keep them if we promised to eat them all right away. And I knew they weren't dairy-free, but I didn't feel like being the new girl with weird allergies anymore, and I really, *really* wanted one, so I ate one."

"Oh *no*," I say. "Did you puke?"

"Three times."

It's so unfair that I had such a perfect night and my best friend had such a horrible one. I wish I had been there to convince her not to eat that evil brownie. "Oh man, Mackenzie. I'm sorry. Do you feel better now?"

"Yeah. I don't want to talk about it anymore."

"Do you feel like swimming?"

"Not really. Can we go lie in the field and plan pranks?"

I actually have a ton of energy and would much rather

do something else, but I don't want to force her into anything. So I say, "Sure, sounds perfect," and Mackenzie finally smiles.

She grabs her notebook, and we head toward the Social Lodge and spread out under the tree we like best. After we spend some time rehashing how perfect the spaghetti prank was, Mackenzie starts looking a lot better. "Did you see Stuart's face when he first heard the voice?" She giggles. "I thought he was going to faint." She makes an exaggerated terrified expression and bugs out her eyes, which makes her look like a lizard.

I throw my head back and try to replicate Val's giant belly laugh, and Mackenzie looks at me weird. "Why are you laughing like that?"

"Like what?" I say. "That's how I always laugh."

"No, it's definitely not. You sound like the Wicked Witch of the West."

Huh, I guess that was a failure. I'll have to practice some more when I'm alone.

"*Anyway*," I say, "the Willows were asking *so* many questions about 'Tomás' last night, I had to make up all this stuff. And they wanted to see a picture of him—thank god there was no Internet. And Lexi wrote him a letter during Cabin Group today asking for more prank ideas. I guess I'm going to have to disguise my handwriting and write back."

"Want me to do it?" Mackenzie asks. "I can make my handwriting all spiky and messy."

"Really?" I say. "Yeah, that would be great! Thank you!"

"It's no big deal," Mackenzie says. "So, when should we do another prank? I thought maybe—"

"Hey, Izzy," comes a voice from behind me, and Mackenzie slams her notebook shut. I turn around and see Roo and Lexi and Ava.

"Hey," I say. "Have you guys met? This is my best friend, Mackenzie. She's in Maple. And this is Roo, Lexi, and Ava. They're my cabinmates."

They all say hi, but nobody seems very interested in Mackenzie, who immediately looks down and starts pulling up tufts of grass. It's no wonder she hasn't made any new friends here, if she acts like this whenever she meets new people.

"So, the camp-wide karaoke competition is on Monday," Roo says. "We're going to sing 'Chillin'' by the Squeegeez."

"Cool, okay," I say. I have no idea why they've made a special effort to come tell me this.

"Do you like that song?" asks Ava.

"I don't really know it," I say. I probably heard it at

my cousin Bianca's quinceañera—her little sister spent the whole night begging the DJ to play Squeegeez songs. All she ever talks about is who the singers are dating and which one got a haircut.

Lexi gives me a huge smile. "Well, you're going to have to learn it, because"—she pauses and holds up her hands like she's about to make a big reveal—"we want you to sing with us!"

I look at Mackenzie for some sort of explanation, but she looks as baffled as I am. "Well, yeah. Aren't all the Willows singing it?"

Roo rolls her eyes like she's frustrated by how slow I'm being. "Not everyone in the cabin participates. I mean, they do in the little-kid cabins. But once you're older and the point is to *win*, you have to be more exclusive."

"Oh," I say. "Who else is doing it?"

"Just us," Lexi says. "Ava will sing lead, and the rest of us will sing backup and dance. I'm choreographing! We won last year when we did 'Your Diamond Eyes' by Shazamazon with Juliet. It was the best!" She bounces on her toes.

"Um, it's really nice of you guys to ask me," I say. "But you should probably get someone who actually knows the song. Plus, I'm not that good at dancing."

Roo sighs. "Izzy, we're offering you an *opportunity*. If

you don't want it, that's fine. But I want to make sure you understand what you're turning down."

I blink at them for a second, and then it clicks. This isn't really about the karaoke competition—it's much bigger than that. Roo and Ava and Lexi were impressed by my prank, and they're offering me a place at the tip-top of the cabin social ladder. Including me in the karaoke competition is their version of letting me wear the FOXY shirt.

"Oh," I say. "I— *Oh*. Okay. I guess I'll be a backup singer, then. Thanks."

"Perfect!" Lexi squeals. "Yay. Come on, let's go over to the amphitheater and start rehearsing!"

"Wait, now?"

"Well, yeah. It's Free Time. And it's not like you're doing anything."

I glance over at Mackenzie. "Actually, we were kind of in the middle of—" I start, but then I realize I can't tell them what we were doing. They have no idea Mackenzie's been helping with the prank war, and they can't ever know. If I tell them I can't rehearse right now, that sitting under a tree is more important than representing the Willows in an important competition, they might decide I'm not loyal enough to our cabin. And *then* they probably won't let me be in charge again when it's time for our next prank. It's pretty clear that I only have power because they're letting me have it, and that means they could take it away again if I make one false move.

"Never mind," I say. "We can finish this tomorrow, right, Mackenzie?"

My best friend's eyes widen. I try to send her a telepathic message—*please, please, please let me off the hook without asking any questions*—and she must get it, because she says, "I guess so."

"Great! Do you want to come watch us rehearse?" I look up at Roo. "That's okay, right?"

She looks at me like I'm nuts. "Um, she's our *competition*."

"But I'm not singing with the Maples," Mackenzie says.

"So? You could still report back to the people who *are* singing. How do we know you won't steal our routine?"

The idea of Mackenzie stealing our choreography is completely ridiculous, but all three of the Willows look serious, and I don't want to start an argument. "Um," I say to her, "I guess you should . . ." I don't want to say *leave us alone* out loud, so I give her a sort of half shrug instead.

"Yeah, okay," Mackenzie says. "I'll go write some letters or something."

"Great! I'll see you later." I give her a big smile as I stand up and brush off the back of my shorts. There's no reason to feel guilty, really—one day of Free Time without me isn't going to hurt Mackenzie. She should probably go back to her cabin and rest, anyway, after how sick she was last night.

I follow Roo and Lexi and Ava to the amphitheater. I haven't been here yet except during the treasure hunt, and it's pretty cool in the daylight—there's a stage area at the bottom, and rows of semicircular stone seats slope up away from them, like the bleachers at a football stadium. Trees surround it on all sides, so it feels really peaceful. Roo pulls her forbidden phone out of her pocket and cues up the Squeegeez song so I can learn it, and we all huddle around to listen through the tinny speakers. The second the singing starts, Lexi says, "That's Sven. He's soooo cute."

Ava shushes her. "How is Izzy going to learn the words if you talk over it?"

"I'm starting it over," Roo says. She taps her screen, and the introduction plays again.

From what I can tell, the song is about a girl who's so hot that she literally raises the temperature of the summer. It's unbelievably stupid, and it's also super catchy. I'm pretty sure it's going to be stuck in my head for the rest of my life. I try to pay special attention to the backup part. Fortunately, there's a lot of oohing and aahing during the verses, so Ava's the only one who has to sing lyrics like, "Baby, let me be the ice machine that brings your temperature down." (Throughout the course of the song, the lead singer also requests permission to be the girl's ceiling fan, swimming pool, and Popsicle.)

After we've listened to it a few times and I've got the tune down, Lexi starts teaching us the dance steps. They're way more complicated than I expect; there's spinning and kicking and a little fake tap dance in the middle. I don't believe she expects us to do this while we're singing, but Roo doesn't seem to have any trouble picking it up. When I stumble on a turn and crash into Lexi for the fourth time, I wonder if she's going to kick me out, but instead she smiles and says, "It's okay, you'll learn."

I'm sweaty and bruised by the time Roo says, "All right, that's enough for today. I have a surprise for you guys." She retrieves her backpack from the stone steps and unzips it. I hope the surprise is cookies or something—I definitely deserve one after what I've been through for the past hour—but instead, she pulls out a wad of shimmery fabric. "Look what I brought!" she sings.

At first I can't tell what I'm looking at, but when Lexi

grabs it and shakes it out, I see that it's a stretchy dress with a silver top and a blue-and-silver sequin skirt. "OMG, they're *perfect!*" she says. "I can't believe Miss Amanda let you borrow them!"

"Who's Miss Amanda?" I ask.

"She's the head of the dance studio we all go to," Roo tells me. "She's incredibly strict about taking costumes out, but she trusts me."

"That's cool," I say. Now that I know they all take dance together at home, their gracefulness makes a lot more sense.

Lexi hugs the dress to her chest. "I love them sooooo much. Let's try them on!"

"What, now?" I say.

"Just over our clothes." Lexi starts pulling the dress on over her tank top and shorts.

I'm hoping Roo will say she only brought one dress with her, but she reaches back into her bag and pulls out three more. "This one should fit you," she says, tossing it to me. "You and Juliet are about the same size."

I try to keep a pleasant expression on my face as I put the dress on over my FOXY shirt. It fits okay, but it's so short it barely covers the tops of my thighs. I try to tug it down, but it's made of stretchy fabric, so it springs right back up. "Isn't this kind of . . . small?" I say. "It'll fly up whenever we spin."

"It's supposed to," Roo says. "I've got silver spankies for us to wear underneath. Like what cheerleaders wear under their skirts."

Lexi's using the front-facing camera on Roo's phone as a mirror, and she turns it toward me so I can see myself. "You look great," she says. "See?"

It's not like the dress covers any less of me than my bathing suit, and the whole camp sees me in that every day. But I'm pretty sure I look a lot more ridiculous in this than I do in my red Speedo. I've never really thought that much about my body before, but now all I can see is elbows and knees and angles. Then again, if this is the price I have to pay to be part of the group, I guess I can shimmy my hips for three minutes in this silly sparkly skirt.

I swallow hard. "Looks great. We're definitely going to win."

I guess that was the right thing to say, because Roo beams. Then she reaches for her fancy camera and loops the strap around her neck. "All right, girls, squish together," she says, and Lexi and Ava sling their arms around my shoulders and pose.

I'm not thrilled by the idea of the whole camp seeing a photo of me wearing a sequin dress over a too-big orange T-shirt. But even if I look stupid, this photo will remind everyone that the most popular Willows sought out my company during Free Time *and* that I got to wear Val's shirt. I tug the dress down as far as possible so that the big white letters peek out, and then I look right into the lens and smile as wide as I can.

CHAPTER 9

It's always weird waking up the first Sunday at camp and realizing I don't have to put on nice clothes and go to church. When I was little, we never really went except on holidays, but my grandma started taking Lina and me every week when she moved in three years ago, after my grandpa died. Mass is pretty boring most of the time, but I do like the music and the stained glass, and lighting a candle for my grandpa after the service is nice. Before we head out for flag raising this morning, I open up my sock drawer, touch my Virgin of Guadalupe picture, and say a little prayer for him inside my head. It's not quite the same, but it still makes me feel calm.

Our second round of activities starts today, and Mackenzie and I have Archery together first thing in the morning. I mean to walk over to the range with her after breakfast, but Roo and Lexi waylay me to talk about our karaoke performance. Mackenzie waits for me by the door, glancing anxiously at the clock every thirty seconds or so, until I finally gesture that she should go ahead without me. It's only after she leaves that I remember I promised to show her the way, since it's the same direction as the ropes course. I'm sure someone else will help her, but I still feel bad.

By the time Lexi's done telling me about how she thinks we should replace one turn with another kind of turn, I'm so late that I have to run. I get to the range and jog up to Mackenzie just as the counselor in charge is handing out bows. "Hey," I pant. "Sorry. Lexi wouldn't stop talking. Did you find this place okay?"

"Yeah, Lauren walked me over," she says. "She has Ropes Course."

"Who's Lauren?" I ask as the counselor hands me a yellow bow.

Mackenzie looks at me funny. "She's my bunkmate, remember?"

"Oh, right. Didn't you say she was ignoring you?"

"Not anymore. She's actually super nice, and she's really funny. She told this joke at dinner the other night that almost made me snort juice out my nose."

"What was the joke?" I ask.

She shrugs. "I can't tell it right. You had to be there, I think."

"Yeah, I get that. Val told a joke like that the other night that involved porcupines and balloons, and it was *so* funny at the time, but I can't really remember why now."

Mackenzie makes a noncommittal humming sound, and then the conversation ends because the counselor starts teaching us archery range commands. Then she calls us over to get arrows from a giant bin. As I'm picking some out, someone pokes the back of my shoulder, and when I turn around, there's Twizzler Josh. He must've been lurking behind me this whole time.

"Hello, nemesis," he says.

"Greetings, archrival. How was your breakfast this morning? Did it wriggle?"

He starts picking out arrows. "I've got to admit, I was impressed by your first attempt at a prank. Not bad for a bunch of girls."

I roll my eyes. "Oh, please. There was no 'attempt' about it. We have an *amazing* picture of your face when that spaghetti started moving." I demonstrate the expression, eyes bugged out and mouth open wide.

Josh shrugs, and against my will, I'm impressed by how

unruffled he seems. "It's nothing compared to how you're going to look when you see what we've got planned for you."

"I'll believe it when I see it. You Wolverines are all talk and no action. It's been an entire week, and you still haven't managed a single prank."

Josh backs slowly away from the arrow bin. "Juuuust you wait. It'll be worth it when it comes. And in the meantime, I'm gonna kick your butt at archery."

"Like you kicked my butt on the ropes course?"

"It'll be easier if I imagine your face as the bull's-eye." I watch as he walks over to the target at the end of the row and drops his arrows into the quiver. He does it with a little flourish, like he expects me to still be watching him. I turn away quickly so he doesn't get the satisfaction of knowing I actually was.

Mackenzie's not quite done getting her arrows, but I grab her arm anyway and tug her toward the target next to his. "Come on, let's go to that one."

"What? Why?" she says. "Who is that guy? Wait, do you *like* him?"

I make a face like I've licked a dead fish. "Eew, Josh? *No!* He's a *Wolverine.* We have to be close so we can spy on him. For pranking purposes."

"Sure. Right." Mackenzie looks like she doesn't believe me at all, but it's *true*. I don't want to be near him, I just feel like I should be for the sake of my cabin. Plus, I want to beat him at archery. And pranking. And *everything*.

"Archers to the shooting line!" calls the counselor, and I step forward so I can shoot at the same time as Josh. Since we're both right-handed, my back is to him, and I try to nock my arrow and draw my bow with perfect form, in case he's watching. When the counselor shouts, "Fire at will!" I let my arrow fly, willing it to plunge deep into the center of the target. Instead, it bounces off the edge and falls onto the grass. I'm annoyed to see that his arrow is sticking out of the red ring of his target, only a few inches from the bull's-eye.

"Whatever," I say. "I'm just warming up."

Josh gives me an innocent look. "I didn't say anything."

Unfortunately, he really is much better at archery than I am. Even with Mackenzie's gentle encouragement, I don't improve much, and only two of my six arrows hit the target at all. Josh hits his target with all six arrows, including two in the yellow bull's-eye area. When our counselor blows her whistle three times, which means we should stop shooting and collect our arrows, I trudge angrily toward my target.

"It's okay," Josh says. "Not everyone can be good at everything."

"Oh, shut up," I say, and then I turn my back to him so I can gather up my arrows in peace. I refuse to let him see how red my face has gotten.

Mackenzie shoots next, and she does better than me, but she's not as good as Josh either. Of course, I don't mind if *she* does well. When she's done collecting her arrows, she steps back and stands with me so the third girl in our line can shoot. "I swear I used to be better at this," I grumble.

Mackenzie shrugs. "We haven't done it in a whole year. We could come practice some more during Free Time, if you want."

I look down at the grass so I don't have to meet my best friend's eyes. "Oh, umm . . . I actually have to rehearse with Roo and Lexi and Ava during Free Time."

"Really? Again?"

"And probably tomorrow, too. I'm sorry. I didn't realize what a big deal this whole karaoke thing was. I mean, it's not a big deal, that's not what I mean. But I have to learn this whole dance routine, and it's actually pretty hard."

"Oh," Mackenzie says. "Okay. I guess I can hang out with Lauren again. We played cards yesterday."

"Yeah, that's a good idea." It's so great that Mackenzie has finally made another friend; now I don't have to feel guilty every time I have to do other stuff without her.

"Lauren says the karaoke competition is dumb," Mackenzie says. "She said she wouldn't want to participate even if someone begged her."

"It *is* dumb. 'Chillin'' is going to be stuck in my head for the rest of my life, and it's the stupidest song *ever*. Plus, we have to wear these awful sequin costumes that Roo borrowed from her ballet school. They're so short that we have to wear special silver booty shorts underneath."

"If you don't like it, why are you doing it? You can tell them you don't want to."

I lower my voice. "You know why I'm doing it. Those girls are in charge of everything in our cabin. If I want them to let me run the prank war, I have to make them like me."

"To let *us* run the prank war," Mackenzie corrects.

I glance over to Josh to make sure he didn't hear, but he doesn't seem to be paying any attention to us. "Right. Anyway, it's a give and take, you know? If I do what they want, they'll do what *I* want."

"Okay, whatever," Mackenzie says, but she doesn't sound like she thinks it's okay at all.

"Archers to the shooting line!" calls our counselor, and I give Mackenzie a quick smile before I turn back to the target, relieved that this conversation is over.

I've got Horseback Riding with Mei as my second activity of the day, but all we do is learn to lead the horses with a rope, then ride them around a small dirt track at a slow walk. My horse is named Spike, and he has no interest in following my instructions—he'd rather hang out with Mei's horse, Drusilla, who obviously doesn't share his feelings and keeps flicking him in the face with her tail. It's pretty funny, and Mei and I can't stop giggling. We don't blame the horses at all; we'd be bored too if all we ever got to do was walk in a circle.

So far today has been kind of a bust, but everything improves when I get to Sailing and discover that Val's the counselor in charge. She's wearing huge red-framed sunglasses and a red polka-dotted swimsuit with gym shorts over it, and her hair is in two braids. It's weird how braids are okay on little kids, and then they make you look babyish for a while, but then when you get older, they magically make you look cool again.

She smiles at me when I bounce up to the dock. "Hey, you! I'm so glad you're in my class!"

"Me too," I say. "Are there any other Willows on the list?"

She looks at her attendance sheet. "Nope. Just you and me."

I try to look disappointed, but I'm secretly glad that I get her to myself. I mean, there will be other people here too, obviously. But nobody who has the same connection to her that I do.

During the next hour Val teaches us the names of all the parts of the boat, how to tie some knots and do basic rigging, and how to fold and tie a sail. Then we all take turns practicing while she watches and gives us pointers. I remember a little bit from last year at Camp Sweetwater, but I want to impress Val so badly that I keep losing focus and mixing up which side of the boat is "port" and which is "starboard." By the time class is over, I'm feeling pretty stupid and frustrated. This karaoke thing is making me all spacey and throwing off my entire life.

Val comes over as I'm getting ready to leave. "Have fun?" she asks.

"Yeah," I say. "You're a great teacher. Sorry I didn't do that well. I'll be better tomorrow."

"You did fine, Iz," Val says. "Tomorrow we're going to split up into pairs and take the boats out." She leans in close and lowers her voice. "If there's anyone you really want to be with—or *not* be with—let me know."

That makes me feel a little better, and I smile up at her. "Thanks."

"Of course. I've got your back, lady." She grabs her towel and slings it around her neck. "Want to walk back to the cabin with me?"

The dock is pretty far from our cabin—at least eight or ten minutes of walking. I can't believe Val's offering me her undivided attention for that long. "Yeah, definitely," I say, and I suddenly feel 100 percent happy again. It's like the sun has come out from behind the clouds.

We head down the path through the woods, and I try to match my steps to hers so our flip-flops slap our heels at the same time. There are a million things I want to know about Val, and this is a perfect opportunity to ask all my questions, but now that I'm alone with her, I've completely forgotten how to start a conversation. Fortunately, she remembers how to act like a normal person, so she asks, "What other activities did you have this morning?"

I tell her about Archery and Horseback Riding, and my voice comes out all fast and breathless at first. But by the time I'm done talking about how my horse was obsessed with Mei's horse, I'm starting to sound like myself again. "What was your favorite activity when you were a camper?" I ask.

"I've always liked sailing best. I was on a competitive sailing team in high school, actually. We were pretty good."

"Whoa. Did you learn how when you were really little?"

"Yeah. My family has a boat. We used to live on it for a couple of weeks every summer. But we don't do that anymore, now that my sisters and I are grown-up. I miss it."

I can't imagine an entire family living on a boat; it would be so chaotic. I picture Tomás dropping his stuffed bunny overboard and throwing a tantrum.

"What's your boat called?" I ask.

"Stormy Weather." I wrinkle my nose, and she laughs. "What? You don't like it?"

"My grandma would say that's tempting fate," I say. "Couldn't you guys have called it *Clear Skies* or something?"

"'Stormy Weather' is an old jazz song my dad likes," she says, and she sings me a few lines. Her voice is beautiful, full and sweet, and the lullaby quality of the song makes me feel safe and happy, like when my mom used to sing me to sleep. I wonder if there's anything Val can't do.

"You're *really* good," I say when she stops. "You should go on one of those singing reality shows."

She laughs. "I don't think so. That's nice of you, though."

"I'm serious. My mom's always watching *The Voice*, and you're way better than most of the people on there."

"Speaking of singing . . ." Val bumps my shoulder. "You ready for the karaoke competition?"

"Ugh, no. Lexi's choreography is *so* hard. Hopefully I'll get it by tomorrow."

"It doesn't matter if you do it perfectly as long as you have fun," Val says. "I'm sure you guys are going to be great."

I don't really want to talk about the karaoke competition, so I say, "Hey, do you think it's weird that it's taking the Wolverines so long to prank us?"

Val shrugs. "They're probably not as proactive and clever as you girls."

"Do you think they're planning something huge? Or are they just terrible at this?"

"I'm not sure, honestly. It always takes Stuart and his boys awhile to get their act together, but it's not usually this long."

"I kind of wish they'd *do* something already," I say. "This is making me nervous."

"Yeah, I totally get that. The anticipation is always the worst part."

We come out of the woods, and I realize we haven't been heading toward the cabin. "Wait, why are we going this way?" I ask.

"I thought we'd make a detour before Cabin Group, if that's okay with you." We're right near the mess hall, and Val leads me around to the screen door that leads to the kitchen. It's propped open, and inside I hear running water and mariachi music. It reminds me of the radio station my aunt Lupe listens to while she cooks for family parties; she always sings along really loudly, even though she's completely tone deaf. Thinking about that makes me homesick all of a sudden.

Val knocks on the door frame and calls, "Hello?" then walks right in before anyone answers. I hesitate outside, but she gestures for me to follow her.

A guy peeling potatoes looks up and smiles at us. "Hey!" He wipes his hands on a dish towel and gives Val a hug. He's got shaggy brown hair under a worn blue baseball cap and a nice smile.

"This is my friend Danny," Val says. "Danny, this is Izzy.

We're on our way back from sailing, and it's *super* hot out, and we wondered if you had anything in the freezer that might cool us down." She fans herself with her hand like a damsel in distress and bats her eyelashes in this dramatic way, and I giggle.

Danny sighs. "I should've known. You never come by to see me unless you want Popsicles."

"Yes I do! I was here on Friday."

"And I gave you a Popsicle."

"Well, I didn't *ask* for one. You offered it to me. And if you wanted to give me another, I wouldn't say no. And one for Izzy, of course."

"Val, you know I'm not supposed to give food to campers between meals."

"Oh, whatever. She's not a camper right now. She's with me. You're not going to tell anyone, right, Izzy?"

"Definitely not," I say. I smile as I think about the sour candies Delilah used to sneak me at Camp Sweetwater. There must be something about me that makes adults want to give me forbidden sugar.

"Please, Danny?" Val begs. "Please, please, please? Pretty please? With a whole jar of cherries on top?"

"You're not going to stop until you get what you want, are you?"

She smiles. "Nope."

"Fine. What color?"

"Red," Val and I say at the same time, and then we grin at each other.

Danny comes back with two red Popsicles, and we thank him. "Gotta go," Val says. "It's time for Cabin Group. You're my favorite, Danny. I'll come back soon."

"Yeah, probably tomorrow, when you want more treats," he says, but he doesn't really seem annoyed. Val blows him a kiss before the screen door slams shut behind us.

"Do you *like* him?" I ask as we head down the path toward the cabin. Ordinarily I wouldn't be so forward, but I have a contraband Popsicle, and I'm feeling giddy and reckless. According to Val, I'm not a camper right now, which I guess makes me her friend.

Val laughs. "*Danny?* No. He's like my brother. Why, do *you* like him?"

I'm mortified and thrilled all at once that she would ask that, and even though I know she's teasing, I start laughing and can't stop. "I met him one second ago!"

"Do you like someone else?" She nudges me with her elbow. "Come on, you can tell me. Is it a Wolverine? Are you having a *secret romance*?"

An image of Josh springs into my mind for no reason, and I feel my face turning as red as my Popsicle. "No! Eew. I could never like a Wolverine. They're Public Enemy Number One, right?"

"Right," Val says. "You've learned well, young grasshopper."

We smile at each other with our Popsicle-dyed mouths, and then we walk back to the cabin together while the breeze rustles the trees above us and the sun kisses our shoulders. I close my eyes and turn my face up to it. I can't remember ever feeling happier in my entire life.

CHAPTER 10

I expect the Popsicles to be a one-time thing, but it turns out they're not. Val and I leave sailing together again the next day, and we walk straight to the kitchen like it's something we've always done. Now that I've had a little practice being alone with her, I'm less babbly and more comfortable asking her questions. She tells me that she's studying communications at college (though I don't know what that *is*, exactly). She tells me about her oldest sister, Analise, who got married and had twin boys as soon as she got out of college, and her middle sister, Sophia, who's in Ecuador building houses. She even tells me that she broke up with her last boyfriend, Liam, six and a half months ago and that she still misses him sometimes.

It's thrilling to be her confidante, and I love that she

trusts me enough to spill personal details the rest of the Willows don't know. In return, I tell her how much I'm going to miss my favorite teacher, who's moving to California, and that I'm worried my times might not get any faster in swim team this year. I try to stay away from the topic of my family in case she asks more questions about Tomás—it feels really wrong to lie to her when we're alone like this. Before we reach Willow Lodge for Cabin Group each day, we duck into the Social Lodge to toss our Popsicle sticks and rinse our bright red mouths so the other girls won't know we're getting treats without them.

Forget my fake brother. If I had an older sibling in real life, I'd want one exactly like Val.

I spend pretty much every spare second of Free Time practicing for the karaoke competition, and by the time Roo, Lexi, Ava, and I do a run-through for the rest of the Willows during Cabin Group on Monday afternoon, I finally get all the kicks and spins right. I'm still iffy on some of the words—it's hard to remember them while I'm concentrating on dancing—but it helps that I'm only backup, so a lot of the time I just have to go "Oooooh, la la la la." My cousin Rosa once told me that if you mouth "Peas and carrots, watermelon" over and over, it looks like you're singing real lyrics, so I figure I can do that if I blank during the performance.

Val doesn't want the other girls to feel left out, so we spend the rest of Cabin Group having a talent show for everyone who's not singing karaoke. BaileyAndHope do an amazing series of soccer tricks that involves bouncing the ball off their knees and elbows and heads about thirty times before it hits the ground. Mei demonstrates how fast she can climb the huge tree outside our cabin. Petra does an absolutely terrible attempt at beat-boxing, which is so hilarious that she has to stop midway through because she's laughing too hard. Summer pulls out a pink notebook and reads us a sample from "Summer's Rules for Success," which includes advice like "'No' is never a final answer; it's a starting point for negotiations." I was sure Hannah wouldn't participate at all, but she gets up and shows us the clay skull she made in Arts and Crafts. It turned out great; the blood is really shiny.

"You guys are phenomenal," Val says when we're all done. "I have the most talented cabin in the entire camp. You ready to head to dinner? I think it's hamburgers tonight."

Roo wrinkles her nose. "*Ugh.* When are they going to learn that some people don't eat dead animals? I'm getting so sick of peanut butter and salad."

"Hang on," I say to Val. "Aren't *you* going to do a talent?"

"You get to see my stellar counseloring skills every day," she says. "What more could you possibly want?"

Part of me wants to keep what I know about Val's talents a secret; I love being the only one in the cabin who has heard her sing. But on the other hand, I really want to hear her do it again. So I say, "How about a song?"

"Hmm." Val pretends to consider it. "You guys really want that?"

There's a chorus of yeses, so she stands up. I wonder if she'll sing that "Stormy Weather" song again as a special tribute to me, but instead she picks something else, another slow, jazzy song about summertime that I kind of recognize. Her voice fills me up with so much happiness that I feel it like a physical pressure in my chest. It's almost not fair how amazing she is.

I suddenly don't care that "Chillin'" is probably the stupidest song in the history of the world. If it makes me the tiniest bit more like Val, I'm going to sing my heart out on that stage tonight.

We have half an hour between dinner and the competition to get ready. Petra puts sparkly silver and blue eye makeup on us to match our costumes, and Val does my hair in one of those cool braids that goes across the front like a headband. By the time she's done, I'm actually excited to perform; the idea of everyone in the camp watching me is pretty great. Mei promises to record a video with Roo's fancy camera so we can watch ourselves later.

When everyone's hair and makeup is almost done, Roo sends Lexi to her dresser to get our costumes. Lexi rummages around for a minute, then calls, "Are you sure they're in this drawer?"

"Dude, are you blind? They're right on the top."

"The spankies are here, but I don't see the dresses."

I go over to help, but Lexi's right—all I see are a bunch of T-shirts and a pile of days-of-the-week underwear. (Roo wears *days-of-the-week underwear*??) "Maybe you put them in a different drawer?" I say.

Roo sighs like we're the stupidest people in the universe. "Let me up," she says to Petra, and she comes over and nudges us out of the way. "I definitely put them in here this morning. They're probably—" She pushes the spankies to the side, and as the slinky metallic fabric unfolds, we see that there's a torn slip of notebook paper pinned to the butt of each pair.

CONSIDER
YOUR
BUTTS
KICKED

"Oh my god," Roo says, her voice trembling with fury. "Those little turds stole our costumes. How did they even *know* about them? Were they spying on our rehearsal?"

"I have no idea," I say, but all of a sudden I do. Josh was standing *right there* when I complained to Mackenzie about the costumes in archery on Monday. I didn't think he was paying any attention to us, but of course he was. In a prank war, you *always* have to be paying attention. How could I let myself slip like that?

"What are we going to do?" Lexi wails.

Roo starts moving toward the door. "I'm going over there. They're going to *pay* for this. I'm gonna take their stupid faces, and I'm gonna—"

Val puts a hand on her shoulder. "Hey, we don't have time for that right now. The competition starts in ten minutes."

"But those costumes don't *belong* to me! We have to get them back! My ballet teacher is going to kill me if anything happens to them!"

"Nothing's going to happen to them," Val says. "I'm sure they're hidden in the boys' cabin somewhere. I promise we'll go get them after the competition is over. But you don't want to miss your chance to sing, do you? You guys have worked so hard. Let's find you something else to wear, and then you can get up on that stage and show the Wolverines they couldn't ruin your performance with some dumb prank. Okay?"

"Fine," Roo grumbles, but she doesn't look happy about it.

By pooling everyone's wardrobes, we manage to find four pairs of black leggings and four red tank tops. The leggings I'm in belong to Petra and are a little long on me, but they're still way better than the itty-bitty ballet costumes. Honestly, it's hard to be too upset that the ugly sequin dresses are gone.

We get to the competition late and don't see the kids from Cottonwood or Chipmunk or Rabbit, but we catch the rest of the competition. Every other cabin just gets up onstage, stands in one place, and sings, and I realize for the first time how completely over-the-top Roo and Lexi and Ava have gone with all their choreography. I mean, I'm all for winning, but I can't help feeling a little resentful that I gave up so much free time

with Mackenzie to practice this ridiculous song about
air conditioners when it wasn't necessary. I search the
crowd for Josh so I can give him a death glare, but I can't
find him anywhere. He's probably too scared to show his
face after what he did.

Four girls from Maple do a pretty good rendition
of "Shake It Off," and then it's our turn. The emcee
announces us, and I try to catch Mackenzie's eye as I hop
down the steps toward the stage, hoping for a "good luck"
or a thumbs-up. But she's too busy congratulating her
own cabinmates to notice me. A girl with a long blond
ponytail slings an arm around her shoulders, and my
stomach twists as Mackenzie hugs her back. I didn't know
she was on hugging terms with anyone here besides me.

Concentrate, I tell myself.

We climb up onstage and strike our opening poses,
hips cocked and heads down, and I suddenly get a rush
of nerves. As much as I love being the center of attention, most of the people here at Camp Foxtail are still
strangers, and it's a little intimidating. But then, in the
moment of quiet before the music starts, Val shrieks, "Go
Willows! Those are my girls! Woooo!" and everything
feels okay again.

The opening chords play, and I lift my chin, beam at

the crowd, and give this insane song everything I've got. Ava grips her microphone and works the crowd like a real pop star, and Roo and Lexi and I spin and kick and "ooooh" in perfect sync. I don't mess up once, and when the song ends and a wave of cheering and applause washes over us, it feels fantastic. Even the counselors judging the competition stand up for us, though I'm pretty sure they're not supposed to show who their favorites are. I see a few camera flashes from the crowd, and I smile as big as I can, hoping these pictures will end up in the end-of-camp slide show.

The four of us bow, then wave at the crowd as we head toward the stairs on the side of the stage. The second we're on the ground, we crush into a jumping, screaming group hug. "That was perfect!" Lexi squeals. "We killed it, you guys! Take *that*, Wolverines!"

The emcee is actually announcing the Wolverines right now, but Roo talks right over him about how much the judges loved us, so I don't pay any attention. The boys and their failed attempt at sabotage don't matter right now, not when we've had such a stunning success. If they thought they were going to throw us off by stealing a few sequins, they're worse at pranking than I thought. We're going to win this competition *and* the prank war.

And then the entire camp bursts out laughing, and when I turn around to see what's so funny, my mouth drops open.

Four Wolverines are standing in front of the microphone, dressed in tiny ballet costumes covered in blue and silver sparkles. The skirts are shorter on them than they were on us, and several inches of boxer shorts hang out the bottom, spray-painted silver to mimic our spankies. The boys have blue and silver ribbons tied around their heads, and they're all preening and tittering and flipping imaginary ponytails over their shoulders. Josh is one of them, and when he catches me looking, he drops into a low curtsey. He's stuffed the top of his costume with balled-up socks, and one of them pops out and rolls across the stage, which makes everyone laugh harder.

And then the Wolverines' music starts playing, and things get worse. It's the same exact Squeegeez song we just sang, the one I idiotically mentioned right in front of Josh. The judges double over laughing when they realize what's happening, and Roo's eyes bug out so far that I'm worried her head might explode.

"They *were* spying on us," she sputters. "How *dare* they!"

"It's the only explanation," I agree, because I'm pretty

sure Roo would smother me with a pair of spankies if she ever found out what really happened.

"We need to get them back *immediately*," she says. "You sent that letter we wrote to Tomás asking for another prank idea, right?"

"Yeah, of course. I bet we'll hear back any day now. But if you want to do something before then, I can think up a prank without him. I actually have an idea that might—"

Roo cuts me off. "I don't think you understand how serious this is. We can't do just any old prank. We need help from a professional."

"Right, okay," I say. Mackenzie better hurry up with that letter.

As they sing, the Wolverines shake their hips so the sequin skirts swish back and forth. Their choreography is a mess, and all of them are off-key, but I guess that makes it funnier, because the entire camp is cracking up. When I look over at the rest of the Willows, I catch Val stifling a traitorous smile. It feels like a small betrayal, but I guess I can't blame her that much. If the boys were making fun of someone else right now, I would probably think it was funny too.

When the song ends, all four of them turn around,

lean over, and flip up their skirts, and everyone shrieks when they see the iron-on letters on their scrawny boxer-covered butts.

The letters spell out:

W-E-E-P, W-I-L-L-O-W-S!

CHAPTER 11

The Willows take second place in the karaoke competition.

The Wolverines take first.

Second out of twenty is great, and if we had lost to anyone else, we'd be thrilled. But losing to the Wolverines is absolutely infuriating. "This is *so* unfair," wails Lexi as we make our way out of the amphitheater, trying to ignore the Wolverines' jeers and laughter. "We worked *so* hard, and we were *so* much better than them. All they did is steal our song and our dresses and act stupid, and now they're getting all the attention!"

"Male privilege strikes again," Roo says. "My mom says girls almost always work harder and still get less respect, and it's *so true*." She shoots a death glare at Stuart, who's wearing one of the sequin costumes on his head as he dances in circles around Val and sings the line about the ice machine over and over. Val snatches the costume away and smacks him with it, which makes me feel a tiny bit better.

I spot the Maples ahead of us on the path, so I run to catch up. Mackenzie's laughing about something with that blond girl from earlier, and I touch her arm to get her attention. "Can you *believe* what the Wolverines did?" I say.

Mackenzie looks back and forth between me and the other girl, like she's not sure who to answer first. Finally she says, "Um, I have to talk to Izzy for a second. I'll meet you back at the cabin for you-know-what, okay?"

"Sure," the other girl says, and she jogs ahead to find her friends.

"What was that about?" I ask. "What's you-know-what?"

"Just cabin stuff. What were you saying about the Wolverines?"

It seems like it should be obvious what I was saying. "They stole our song! And our costumes! Can you believe they had the nerve to dig through Roo's drawer? Oh god, they probably went through *all* our drawers. They probably touched my underwear!" The thought of Josh looking at my underwear makes my face go pink. I guess he wouldn't have known which was mine, but still.

I expect Mackenzie to be outraged on our behalf, but she looks totally calm. "I mean, it's not really that unexpected, is it? You guys are in a prank war. It's not like they were going to leave you alone after the spaghetti thing."

"All we did was scare them, though. It was funny. Taking our costumes and making fun of us in front of the entire camp is totally different!"

"You didn't want to wear those costumes to begin with," Mackenzie says.

"That's not the point. The dresses didn't belong to Roo. They were from her dance school, and she has to return them, and now they're probably all stretched out. Plus, we would've gotten first place if they hadn't pulled that dumb stunt."

Mackenzie shrugs. "You still got second. And it doesn't really matter that much, does it? It was just a silly competition. And their dance *was* kind of funny."

Even though I thought the exact same thing earlier, her words still sting. "Are you taking their side?" I snap.

Mackenzie stares at me. "Um, obviously not. I'm the one thinking up ways for you to prank them, remember?"

"Shh!" I look around to see if anyone heard her, but

nobody's paying any attention. I lower my voice. "Okay, sorry. I know you're on my side. Speaking of that, do you think you could hurry up with that letter from Tomás? The Willows are really angry, and I want to start planning a way to get the Wolverines back, but they still won't listen to anything I say unless it comes from him."

A weird expression crosses Mackenzie's face for a second, but then she says, "Yeah, okay. I can probably give it to you tomorrow."

"That'd be great. And make sure nobody sees you writing it. Including that blond girl."

"That's Lauren," says Mackenzie. She sounds annoyed that I don't already know that, but how could I? It's not like she ever introduced us.

"Okay, but seriously, don't tell her, all right?"

"I'm not going to tell her," Mackenzie says. "This whole secret agent thing was *my* idea, remember?"

We're at the point where we have to separate to go to our cabins, and Lauren turns around and calls, "Mackenzie, come on!"

"See you tomorrow," she says.

"See you," I say, and she walks away.

She still hasn't congratulated me on our performance.

★ ★ ★

Mackenzie slips me the letter the next morning during Archery. It's sealed in an envelope with a made-up return address and everything, and the stamp even looks like it has a postmark over it. I have no idea how she did that; she's seriously a pranking genius.

"Thank you so much," I whisper to her. "You're the best. I'll volunteer to do mail call later and slip it in with the rest of the letters."

Josh is suddenly right next to us. "What's that?" he asks.

I scowl at him and stuff the letter into my back pocket. "I'm not talking to you, archrival."

He gives me an innocent smile. "Why? Didn't you like our performance last night?"

"Shockingly enough, I don't love it when people break into my cabin and steal from me. You certainly seemed to enjoy prancing around like an idiot, though."

"It's not 'breaking in' if the door is open. You should've hidden your costumes better if you didn't want them borrowed. And I'm pretty sure the judges enjoyed our performance too, Miss Second Place."

"At least our dance was original," I say. "We didn't have to resort to spying to think of something good. You only won because of *male privilege.*"

He ignores me. "So, what's in your pocket?"

"Nothing."

"It's clearly not nothing, or you would show me."

I pull out the envelope and hold it up. "It's a letter from my brother, okay? Will you leave me alone now?"

"If it's from your brother, how come *she* had it?"

"*She* has a name—it's Mackenzie. And she had it because there's a part where he said hi to her, so I let her read it." I'm pretty proud of how natural the lie sounds and how quickly I came up with it.

"I've known him practically my whole life," Mackenzie says.

Josh scratches his head, and his bright red hair sticks straight up on one side. "I heard your brother is some sort of prank master."

Man, word spreads faster here than it did at Camp Sweetwater. "Where'd you hear that?" I ask.

"I have my sources."

"Well, so what if he is? Why do *you* care?"

Josh shrugs. "I mean, I personally think it's cowardly to rely on your connections instead of thinking up pranks yourself, that's all. I was actually a little impressed by that spaghetti prank, but I guess I shouldn't have been, if it wasn't your idea."

I wish more than *anything* that I could throw the truth

in Josh's face, but obviously I can't say anything if I don't want it getting back to the Willows. Plus, if I'm honest with myself, I am relying on my connections. It's just that my connection is Mackenzie, not Tomás.

I shoot Josh my best sarcastic sneer. "Oh, I'm sorry, do prank wars have *rules* now? Because I was under the impression that all was fair in love and war. Not that there's any love here. *Only war.*"

"Listen, feel free to cheat if it makes you happy," Josh says. "We're going to beat you regardless."

"Shooters to the line!" shouts our counselor.

Before I pick up my bow, I stuff Mackenzie's letter deep into my sock, where I'm sure Josh won't be able to steal it.

I finally get to read the letter on the way to Horseback Riding, and it's absolutely perfect. Mackenzie has taken the prank we were plotting in Arts and Crafts and worked out all the details, and it's much funnier now than anything I could've thought up myself. I should do something nice to thank her; maybe I could plan a funny prank for her, like we always do for each other's birthdays. Last year she put a confetti cannon in my locker that went off when I opened the door, and I was picking gold glitter out of my hair for weeks. I got her back by standing on top of the breakfast table at Camp Sweetwater with a top hat and cane and singing a ridiculous song about how wonderful she was. The year before, Delilah helped me get hundreds of helium balloons with Mackenzie's face printed on them, and we crammed so many of them into our cabin that it was hard to move around. But I guess I don't really have to do anything for her now—Mackenzie said a well-executed prank is its own reward, and I can pretty much guarantee flawless execution.

We actually get to go on a real trail ride during Horseback Riding, and I get assigned a big black horse named Anna Sewell. Mei's on Drusilla again, and even though we're supposed to ride in a straight line, we end up riding side by side in places where the trail is wide enough. "You guys were so great at the karaoke competition last night," she says. "Your dancing looked so professional. I can't do that kind of thing at all."

I hadn't realized how much I'd missed hearing praise and reassurance from a friend until Mei's compliment slips into the gap Mackenzie's silence has left inside me. "Thanks," I say. "I'm happy with how it went, aside from the pranking thing. I wish Roo and Lexi and Ava had picked a different song, though. I can't get 'Chillin'' out of my head."

"Can I tell you a secret?" Mei says. When I nod, she whispers, "I actually like that song."

I start giggling. "Seriously? It doesn't make any sense. 'Baby, let me be the ceiling fan that brings your temperature down'? What does that *mean*?"

"I don't know, but it sounds so *happy*! I play it all the time at home. It drives my big sister crazy."

"Well, annoying your siblings is always a plus."

"Yeah, you know what I'm talking about." Mei's smile fades. "Do you miss your brother a lot now that he's away at college? My sister's applying to schools this fall, and she really wants to go to UCLA. That's all the way in California. I'm going to be so lonely without her."

"Yeah, I miss him sometimes," I say. "But he goes to University of Michigan, so he's not that far away. And I have a little sister, too, so I'm not lonely."

"Was it awful right when he left, though?" Mei asks. "I feel like it's going to be *the worst*."

"It was definitely sad, but then I got used to him being gone. We still talk. I'm sure you and your sister will too." Fictional Tomás is getting totally out of control. I had only ever meant for him to be a shadow looming in the background and giving me credibility. But now the Willows want to know all about him, the Wolverines are angry about him, Mei's trying to bond with me over him, and Mackenzie's pretending to *be* him.

"Your brother must be happy that you're carrying on the Cervantes' pranking legacy," Mei says.

I laugh. "That sounds so official."

"The prank war *is* official!"

"Do you think it's okay that he's helping us?" I ask. "It doesn't, like, violate the prank war rules or anything?"

"Prank wars don't have rules. The rule is, do whatever it takes to win."

I wonder if she would still think that if she knew about all the lies I've told the Willows. "Okay, that's what I thought," I say. "I'm only asking 'cause one of the Wolverines said it was cheating."

"They're probably jealous because our prank was so much better than theirs."

"Yeah, probably."

"Do you think Tomás will write back soon with another idea?" Mei asks. "I can't wait to get them back for what they did to you guys. That was *not* cool."

I smile and shift my leg so the paper crunches between my sock and my horse's side. "Definitely," I say. "I bet we'll hear from him any day now."

ALISON CHERRY

From: Izzy Cervantes <marshmallowmonster@gmail.com>
To: Mom <sarah.wyatt.cervantes@gmail.com>
Tues, July 19, 2016 at 2:46 PM

Hey Mom,
I bet you're surprised to be hearing from me by e-mail,
but don't worry, nothing's wrong. Val let me write this on
her phone because we couldn't wait days for a letter to
get to you. You know that ugly old fake-fur coat in the
basement that used to be Great-Aunt Roberta's? Can
you send it to me so I can cut it up for a crafts project?
Val says to ask you to overnight it, if you can. We need it
really soon.

I actually really like this camp, even though I miss Delilah
and my friends from Sweetwater. I performed in a karaoke
competition with three other girls yesterday, and we got
second place. The other day at breakfast, the Porcupines
caught their counselor with both his elbows on the table
while we were eating, which meant he had to stand on
a chair and kiss the taxidermy moose head right on the
lips. He did it, and a little piece of the fur came off IN HIS
MOUTH. It was sooooo hilarious.

146

Miss you! Let me know if you can send the coat. Val says she'll let me check my e-mail again tomorrow.

Love,

Izzy

CHAPTER 12

I find Mackenzie in the mess hall after breakfast the next morning so we can walk to Archery together. "The Willows *love* the new prank idea," I murmur to her as we head across the soccer field. "And they totally thought that letter was from Tomás. You did a really good job. I think that's exactly what his handwriting would look like, if he existed."

Mackenzie smiles. "Thanks. I spent a lot of time practicing."

I pull a new letter out of my pocket and slip it to her. "They wrote this yesterday during Cabin Group," I say. "I figure if you give me a reply on Monday or Tuesday, that'll seem realistic. Sound okay to you?"

"Probably. I'll try."

"Lexi wrote this one, too. Sorry about the way she dots

her *i*'s with little hearts. I know it drives you nuts when people do that."

Mackenzie wrinkles her nose. "How are you friends with those girls?"

It's weird that she's getting on my case about people she doesn't even know. It's not like I'm giving her a hard time about Lauren. "What do you mean?" I ask.

"I just . . . it doesn't seem like they have anything in common with us."

"Of course they do. They like pranks and swimming and stuff. Plus, they're nice. They like me."

"They seem . . . a little selfish," Mackenzie says.

"What? No they're not. Why would you say that?"

"I mean, they basically forced you to participate in that dumb karaoke competition. They didn't even ask if you wanted to do it."

"I *did* want to," I say. "It was fun. I'm glad they asked me."

"All right, if you say so."

Mackenzie's probably jealous because making new friends is easier for me than it is for her, but I can't exactly say that. "It doesn't matter," I say. "*You* don't have to be friends with them."

"Yeah, I guess I don't." She shoves the letter I gave her into her back pocket. "Anyway, do you want to go swimming during Free Time today, now that you're actually free again? They got a bunch of new inflatable rafts."

"Um," I say. "I do want to, but I kind of promised the Willows I'd start prepping for the new prank with them. We want to get back at the Wolverines as soon as possible."

"Oh," Mackenzie says. It's weird how surprised she sounds; she's the one who came up with this idea, and she of all people should know how much work it's going to take.

"Maybe you could come to our cabin and help? There may not be much for you to do, but the Willows probably won't mind if you're there."

Mackenzie toys with the earpiece of her glasses. "No, that's okay. I really feel like swimming. I think I'll see if Lauren wants to go with me."

I'm pretty sure my best friend has never turned down an opportunity to hang out with me, and it stings a little, but I try not to let it show. "Oh, okay," I say. "I guess you helping us might be kind of awkward, anyway."

"Probably."

A weird silence stretches between us for a few seconds, and then I say, "But you'll still write a new letter from Tomás, right?"

"Yeah, sure," Mackenzie says. "Whatever you want."

This whole conversation feels icky and wrong to me, and I'm relieved to see the archery range coming into view. "Your new prank is seriously amazing," I say. "I wish I could tell everyone it's yours, and I'm sorry we can't do it together. But seeing the prank succeed is the good part, right? So it'll all be worth it when the Wolverines totally freak out."

"Right, yeah," Mackenzie says.

She's the one who said that in the first place, but it doesn't seem like she believes it anymore.

As if to prove my point about how unselfish they are, Roo, Lexi, and Ava totally step back during the preparations for our new prank. None of them are that great at arts and crafts, and they suggest that Hannah, Bailey, and Petra take the lead. I want to be at the very center of the action again, but I try to follow Roo's example, even if it means I probably won't be the one who gets to wear the FOXY shirt this time. I comfort myself with the fact that I still get to walk from Sailing to the cabin with Val every afternoon, my tongue stained Popsicle-red.

It's pretty weird to see Bailey do anything without Hope glued to her side, but it turns out she's a talented artist, and she builds most of the frame for the prop we need out of chicken wire and cotton batting. The moment we leave for dinner each night, BaileyAndHope snap back together like magnets, and I want to point them out to Mackenzie and say, *See? People can do different things for a few hours and still be best friends.*

A package arrives from my mom on Thursday. Summer's doing mail call, and she brings it to me during Cabin Group. Inside is the beige faux-fur coat I asked for, a few more drawings from my sister, a striped shirt I forgot to pack, and a Ouija board with a card taped to it; I recognize my aunt Estella's loopy script on the front. I'm about to pull out the shrink-wrapped box and show it off to everyone, but Mei shoves it back down into the package before I can.

"Don't let Val see that," she whispers. "There was an *incident* in Poplar last year, and now we're not allowed to have them."

"What kind of incident?"

"This girl cut off another girl's hair in the middle of the night and blamed it on a ghost."

"Oh, wow," I say. "Okay. Thanks for the warning."

She gives me a conspiratorial smile. "Don't worry. We'll totally still use it. We just have to keep it secret."

As I'm covering the board with the shirt, a small envelope with my grandma's spidery handwriting falls out of the sleeve. Inside, tucked into a flowery greeting card that says *Una nieta es la rosa más dulce*—a granddaughter is the sweetest rose—is a photo of the actor who plays Juan Carlos on her favorite telenovela. On the last episode we watched before I left, he ran into a burning building to save a man he thought was his brother, but it turned out to be his enemy in disguise. As I requested, the actor's wearing normal clothes in the pictures. If I didn't know any better, I might think he was a supercute regular person instead of a TV star. I pray nobody else in my cabin has ever seen *Corazón de Hielo, Alma de Fuego*, but I'm pretty sure I'm safe. Only my Mexican friends at home have even heard of it, and most of them aren't allowed to watch it because it gets kind of racy sometimes.

Lexi comes up next to me and peers over my shoulder, and when she sees what I'm holding, she squeals like a tea kettle that's about to explode. "Is that Tomás? Omigod, let me see!" She grabs the picture out of my hand, and her eyes get huge. "He looks like a *movie star*! How did you not tell us he was this cute?"

I squirm. "I don't know. He looks normal to me."

The girls all crowd around to study the photo. "This man is not normal," Petra declares. "This man is superhuman."

"These are really professional," Roo says. "Is this, like, his headshot or something?"

"Yeah," I say, glad for an excuse. "He's been in a couple of commercials."

Val leans over Lexi's shoulder to look. "Oh, wow," she says. "He *is* cute. He looks familiar. Did he do a Verizon commercial last year?"

"Yeah, I think that was one of them." I *really* hope she doesn't suggest we go to the main office and look it up.

"Does he have a girlfriend?" Lexi breathes.

"He's dating, like, six different girls," I say. "He's a total player."

Lexi stares at the photo and sighs. I half expect her pupils to turn into cartoon hearts. "Can I keep this and hang it over my bunk?"

The idea of Lexi keeping the picture makes me nervous—for all I know, she might decide to carry it around to her activities, and someone else at camp might recognize the actor and bust me. "Eew, *no*," I say. "He's my *brother*. That's disgusting."

Lexi sticks out her lower lip. "It's not! He's not *my* brother."

"I know. But it's weird and gross to see you guys drooling over him. Just ask me if you want to see the picture again and I'll show you, okay?"

"Fiiiiine." Lexi gives the photo a dramatic kiss before she reluctantly hands it back, and everyone laughs. I tuck it into my drawer, and then I distract everyone by steering the conversation back to our prank.

Over the next two days, Hannah and Petra cut the fake-fur coat into pieces and sew it over the frame Bailey made like a skin. It's amazing to watch them work; I can barely sew on a button. When the construction part is finally done, Bailey adds some details with paint, and then we all crowd around to look at the finished product.

There on the floor sits the back half of a mountain lion, exactly like Mackenzie and I pictured. The coat is the perfect color for the fur, and the bone structure and pads on the feet are so realistic that I almost expect the end of its bottlebrush tail to twitch. It's absolutely perfect.

"Wow," I say. "This is fifty times better than anything I could've made. You guys did such a great job."

Bailey smiles and blushes. "Thanks," she says. "It was a really great idea."

Hannah lets out one of her evil giggles. "The Wolverines

are going to pee their pants," she says quietly, and everyone cracks up.

"So, who wants to be in charge of putting it in place later tonight during the campfire?" Val asks. She looks at Bailey, Petra, and Hannah. "You girls made it. You want to do the honors?"

Hannah shakes her head violently, and Bailey says, "I don't really want to miss the campfire, if that's okay."

"Me neither," says Petra.

"Izzy and I can do it," Roo says.

I feel like I should be annoyed that she's volunteering me without asking, but I *do* really want to put the mountain lion in place, and now I don't have to look greedy by volunteering myself. "Yeah, I'm happy to do it," I say.

"Perfect," Val says. "You girls are seriously the fiercest, most talented group. I'm not saying Tomás hasn't been a huge help, but you could *definitely* win this prank war without him."

"Down with Public Enemy Number One!" I shout, and everyone cheers.

We hide our creation on the back porch under a paint-spattered tarp we swiped from the Arts and Crafts lodge, and then we head to dinner. I detour past the Maple table on the way to ours and sidle up to Mackenzie, who's chattering away with Lauren.

"The crow flies at midnight," I say quietly.

Mackenzie glances up at me. "Cool, okay."

She's smiling and everything, but she doesn't look particularly excited, and I wonder if maybe she didn't hear me. "You know what that means, right?"

Her smile fades, and a crease appears between her eyebrows. "Yeah, of course."

"Oh, okay. I wasn't sure if . . . okay." I can't really bring up anything more specific in front of Lauren, so I just say, "I'll see you later, then."

"Good luck," she says, and then she turns right back to her new friend.

"Good luck with what?" I hear Lauren ask as I head back to the Willow table.

"Nothing," Mackenzie answers. At least she's not letting Lauren in on our secrets. Yet.

The campfire starts as the sun begins to go down, and all two hundred of us gather and sit on the huge concentric circles of logs arranged around the fire pit. Roo and I sit in the outermost ring so it'll be easy to slip away. As we planned, we wait until it's completely dark, and then we get up and tell Val we're "going to the bathroom."

Weirdly, she's sitting next to Stuart, who's holding a guitar by its neck like it's a strangled chicken—he hasn't actually *played* it all night, and I wonder if he even knows how. Maybe he thinks holding it makes him look cool. For a second I can't figure out why Val would get this close to him on purpose, but when she winks at me, I realize she's trying to keep him distracted while we execute our plan. I try to wink back, but I'm not very good at it, so it's more like a blink.

Roo and I jog across the soccer field by the light of a small flashlight, slip into Willow Lodge, and free the mountain lion butt from its tarp. Once we've got it, it's too risky to turn on our light again, so we carry it across the field in the dark. Roo does a perimeter check around the Wolverines' cabin, and when we're positive we're alone, we shove our creation under the three wooden steps that lead up to the door. In the pale light of the moon it totally looks like a real, live animal is sleeping under there. Roo and I quietly high-five, and then we return to the campfire, where everyone is in the middle of a rousing rendition of "Alice the Camel Has Ten Humps." It's hard to keep the goofy, excited smile off my face.

The campfire ends half an hour later, and flashlight beams crisscross the dark field as everyone heads back to their cabins. I walk with Roo and Lexi and Val, and we make an effort to stay right behind Stuart and the boys. I want to look for Mackenzie, but I don't want to draw attention to myself by craning my neck all around, so I just have to trust that she's watching.

Beans is the first to reach Wolverine Lodge, and when he spots the mountain lion legs, he gasps and bolts back toward Stuart. I'm actually pretty impressed; I think I would have screamed.

"There's something under the stairs," he hisses. "An animal. It's huge."

"*You're* a huge animal," Stuart retorts.

"No, dude, I'm serious. There's something under there." Behind his glasses, Beans's eyes are enormous.

Stuart's smirk falters a little. "What kind of animal?"

"It has a tail like a cat. A mountain lion, maybe?"

"I don't think there are mountain lions in Michigan anymore," Stuart says.

"Um, I'm pretty sure there are. Can you just come look at it?"

"Fine." Stuart approaches the cabin quietly, holding his flashlight high, and when the light hits the legs and tail, he freezes. For a second, I think he's figured out the mountain lion isn't real, but then he backs away.

"Counselors," he calls, and for once it doesn't sound like he's making a goofy joke. "We have a large wildlife alert. Get your campers away from Wolverine Lodge and inside your cabins with the doors shut immediately."

The counselors start herding terrified-excited kids toward the safety of their cabins, and Stuart turns to Val. "Can you take my boys to the Social Lodge? I need to call Animal Control and find Doobie."

Val nods seriously. "Of course. Willows, get inside and shut the door, quick quick quick. Wolverines, follow me."

We skitter into our cabin, and the second the door closes behind us, we all start laughing and talking at once. Lexi throws her arms around me. "This is going perfectly! Tomás is going to be *so* impressed! I can't wait to write him another letter tomorrow!"

Poor Mackenzie; she's going to have so much mail to answer.

The window by Lexi's and Petra's bunks has the best view of Wolverine Lodge across the field, and we all squeeze onto the beds and press our noses against the screens. But nothing interesting happens for a really long time, and eventually everyone starts to get antsy. BaileyAndHope move onto the floor and start a card game, and Petra picks up a magazine. I want take charge of the group, to keep this moment magical and exciting, but I don't know what to say to make that happen. Val would know. I wish so badly that she were here with us right now instead of in the Social Lodge with the stupid Wolverines.

Finally, after what feels like forever, Lexi hisses, "Someone's there!" and we all pile onto the beds again. Stuart's back, and in the light spilling from the windows of the boys' cabin, we can see that he's with Doobie (who's in pajamas) and two guys in uniforms. Both of them have guns, and seeing them sends a shiver up my spine.

"Are those cops?" asks Summer. "Are we going to get in trouble?"

"Those are forest ranger uniforms," Petra says. "My uncle's a ranger."

"So they can't get us in trouble?"

"Shh," Roo hisses. "I can't hear what they're saying."

Everyone shuts up, but we're too far away to hear more than an indistinct murmur of voices. Stuart points at the steps, and the rangers gesture for him and Doobie to back up. Then one of them raises his gun.

"Are they going to *shoot* it?" gasps Lexi.

"It's probably a tranquilizer dart," says Petra. "They wouldn't want to kill the mountain lion. I think they're endangered."

The ranger shoots his dart gun twice. Then he pauses for a minute, and when the mountain lion doesn't move (obviously), he approaches the cabin. He squats down in front of the stairs with his flashlight, then gestures for his partner to come over and look. The other guy checks out the situation and starts laughing.

"Oh man," I whisper. This is going to be so good.

The rangers stand up, and one of them reaches under the stairs and drags our creation out into the open. As he picks it up by its tail and holds it out for Doobie and Stuart to inspect, some of the stitches pop free, and the tail separates from the body. The way the legs and butt bounce when they hit the ground makes all ten of us scream with laughter, and I'm pretty sure Stuart hears us, because he looks straight across the field at our cabin. Then he shouts a whole *stream* of words I'm not allowed to say, which only makes us laugh harder. I don't think I've ever heard so many curse words in a row, including when my dad dropped a printer on his bare foot and broke two of his toes.

Petra grabs her stuffed tiger, which is lying next to her pillow, and holds it up by the tail. "Sir, ma'am," she says in a low, serious, imitation-forest-ranger voice, "I do believe you've been pranked."

CHAPTER 13

Bailey gets to wear the FOXY shirt the next day. She's closer to Val's size than I am, so it fits her a lot better, and the orange is nice against the tan of her skin. I try not to feel jealous, but it's pretty difficult when people keep telling her how good she looks. I know she did most of the work on the mountain lion, and she did an amazing job. But it's still a little hard to see someone else getting *all* the credit.

I wait till Val stands up to get more juice, and then I announce, "Willows, we need to celebrate *properly* tonight when Val's at her counselor meeting. A late-night dance party isn't going to cut it this time." I'm gratified when everyone looks up at me, like they're waiting for me to lead them.

I pause for a few seconds to build suspense, and then

I say, "My aunt sent me a Ouija board!" I hate to break camp rules behind Val's back, but if we're careful, she'll never find out. And if she does, I don't think she'd bother getting her favorite camper in trouble for something this silly.

"Oh my god, *yes!*" Lexi breathes. "There *have* to be ghosts at this camp, right?"

Roo nods and serves herself another pancake. "Definitely. There are probably tons hanging out in the woods."

"Plus, there's the Sea Witch," Petra says.

"The Sea Witch isn't a *ghost*," Ava scoffs. "She's a *Sea Witch.*"

"There's an old cemetery on the other side of the lake," Mei says. "It's not technically on camp property, but maybe the ghosts will hear us anyway."

"No offense, but we're not supposed to have Ouija boards," Summer says. "Won't we get in trouble?"

Roo rolls her eyes. "Summer, lighten up. It's a *toy*. Nobody's getting in trouble."

"Unless you're planning to cut off our hair," Petra says. "Then you'll definitely get in trouble." Near the end of the table, I see Hannah shudder. I hope she doesn't ruin what's supposed to be a fun game by freaking out.

"What should we ask the ghosts besides how they

died?" Lexi asks, but Val's almost back to the table now, and Ava shushes her and says, "We'll figure it out later."

The Maple table is already empty by the time we've cleared our trays. It's weird that Mackenzie hasn't waited for me to hear details about the prank, but I guess I can just tell her everything when I get to Archery. I relive the glory of last night inside my head as I walk to the range, and I'm so consumed by the memory that I nearly jump out of my skin when Josh appears right next to me.

"You look like an evil clown when you smile like that," he says.

"That's not my evil clown smile," I say. "That's my 'I'm winning the prank war' smile."

He gives me a creepy smile of his own. "Yeah, right. Wait till you see what we've got planned for you next."

He looks like he's hiding something, but I don't buy it. "You're totally bluffing. It took you guys *weeks* to get your act together enough to prank us last time. At this rate, camp's going to be over by the time you come up with a second prank."

He raises one eyebrow. "Is it? Or is that what we *want* you to think?"

"Whatever," I say. "You're not going to freak me out."

"If you don't want to watch your back, that's your call."

"Whatever it is, it can't possibly be as good as the mountain lion. You should've seen Stuart's face. Even Doobie thought it was real. Even the *rangers* did."

He shrugs. "I'm sure we could've fooled the rangers too if one of us had a big brother to make us a fake mountain lion."

"My brother didn't make that," I snap. "We did."

"Whatever you say." We're at the range now, and Josh strides off toward the arrow bin. "See you later, cheater."

"I'm *not*—" I say, but he's already stopped paying attention to me. Ugh, he makes me *so mad*.

Mackenzie comes up with two bows and hands me one, and I'm so excited to finally tell her every detail of last night that I'm able to put stupid Josh out of my mind. She doesn't seem quite as enthusiastic as I expected, so I keep making the story bigger and more ridiculous, and she finally laughs when I tell her about how the tail fell right off the body. "It was epic," I finish. "I can't wait to see what *Tomás* will come up with next. Do you think maybe he'll write to us again soon? Like Monday, maybe?"

I just spent, like, five minutes telling her how incredibly well her prank went, but she still looks kind of annoyed. "Maybe. I bet *Tomás* wishes he could actually be there to take credit for some of this stuff."

"I thought *Tomás* said he didn't care," I remind her.

"I guess he did," she says. The counselor calls her to the shooting line, and she doesn't bring it up again when she comes back, so I guess that conversation is over. But when it's time to switch activities, she barely says good-bye to me before taking off.

I try to put Mackenzie out of my mind; sure, she's a little annoyed right now, but I'm sure this will work itself out. And I've got other things to worry about, like the fact that it's the last day of round two activities, which also means my last Popsicle run with Val. As I help fold sails and coil ropes at the end of class, I glance over at her to see if she looks downcast, too, but she's acting pretty normal. What if these walks don't mean as much to her as they do to me? What if Val has special end-of-week-two stuff to take care of today, and she didn't think to tell me? What if we've already *had* our last Popsicle run and I didn't know?

But when everything's done, Val slings her towel around her neck and asks if I'm ready to go, just like always. I nod, relieved that I still have fifteen whole minutes left with her.

Unfortunately, it turns out it's impossible to enjoy something great when you know it's the last time you'll ever get to do it. Val talks about how well we pulled off the mountain lion prank and how angry Stuart was and how she wonders what Tomás's next idea will be, and I know her enthusiasm should make me happy and proud. But all I can think is, *This is the last time Val and I will ever pass that tree,* and, *The Popsicle I'm about to get is probably the last one I'll have at camp.* It makes me miss half of what she's saying, and I'm furious at myself for ruining this before it's even over. There are still so many things I want to ask her and tell her, and every step we take decreases the time I have left to do it, and all the words get caught in my throat so that I can't say anything at all.

Val bumps my arm with her freckly elbow. "You're quiet today. Everything okay?"

"Yeah," I say, but it doesn't sound very convincing.

I guess it's obvious to her, too, because she says, "What's going on, Iz?"

I don't want to tell her how much I'll miss our walks. It'll make me sound clingy and needy, and I don't want her to give me special attention because she thinks I'm weak and need to be coddled, like Hannah does. So instead I say, "It's no big deal. I'm just sad camp is half over already, and I don't really like my week three activities. I have to do *fishing.* I wish I could do sailing with you again instead."

She puts her arm around my shoulders and pulls me in for a squeeze. Our hips bump, and I kind of step on the edge of her foot, but she doesn't seem to mind. "I'll miss having an activity with you, too," she says. "But I run Sailing during Free Time some days, so you can always come by then."

"Maybe," I say. "But Mackenzie usually wants me to spend Free Time with her, and she doesn't like sailing. She gets seasick." I have this sudden flare of resentment—why do I always have to worry about what *Mackenzie* likes? I should be able to do whatever I want during Free Time, whether it's the ropes course or sailing or dumb karaoke rehearsals. If I'm having fun, she should be happy for me instead of acting weird and sulky and holding me back.

But as soon as I think *that*, I start feeling guilty. Mackenzie's my best friend. Her feelings should be more important to me than any camp activity, and it's not her fault she's not brave and adventurous like I am. I've never minded making sacrifices for her before. What's wrong with me?

"Well, I'm sorry you don't like your activities for next week, but there's still lots of stuff to look forward to," Val says. "Our overnight's in a week and a half. Have the other girls told you about Sandpiper Village? It's so cool. We'll swim in the river and grill hot dogs and make s'mores, and there's a rope swing and a hammock and a big hill that's perfect for stargazing."

I picture myself lying on top of a hill between Lexi and Roo, staring up into the night sky as Val teaches us the constellations. "That sounds like so much fun," I say. "I can't wait."

"And Color Wars is coming up too. I'm running the Blue Team. I really hope you'll be on it with me."

"Blue's my favorite color," I say. My favorite color is actually red, but when I picture Val trying to pull strings to get me on her team, it temporarily switches. "Maybe I could be one of your captains, even. Roo said it's always the people who are the best leaders, right? I've basically been leading the prank war."

"And you're doing an amazing job," Val says, which makes everything start feeling brighter again. "We take all kinds of things into account when we're choosing captains, but leadership is definitely part of it. Some of the girls who have been here longer might have a better shot at it, but you never know. We'll just have to see what happens next week." She shoots me a secretive smile, and it feels like a promise that she'll put in a good word for me. She's obviously not ready for our quality time together to end either.

We get to the kitchen, and Danny reaches into the freezer and pulls out the giant box of Popsicles as soon as he sees us coming. "Hey, ladies," he calls. "What color do you want today? Red again?"

I smile at Val to show her I understand the wordless message she was trying to send me. "Actually," I say, "I think I'm in the mood for one of those blue ones."

CHAPTER 14

Mackenzie finds me at the end of Cabin Group and asks if I want to go to the lake during Free Time. I feel guilty about spending so much time away from her lately, so I head toward the dock, even though there's a trail ride I wanted to go on with Mei. But she acts superweird the whole time we're swimming. I try to start a conversation about what we should do for our next prank, but she doesn't seem to want to talk about it, and she doesn't want to help think up questions for the Ouija board, either. She keeps staring at me like she's waiting for me to do or say something specific, but I have no idea what. I'm pretty sure she's still annoyed about how much time I spent on karaoke rehearsals and the latest prank, but it's not like I can do anything about that now. I offered to let her help us make the mountain lion, and she didn't want to. But I decide to be a good friend and not confront her about how strange she's acting. She probably needs more time to cool down, and then things can go back to normal.

That evening as we're walking back from our all-camp activity—building a contraption that will keep an egg unbroken if it's thrown off the roof of the Social Lodge—Roo says, "So, Val, what time is your counselor meeting tonight?" Lexi starts giggling like crazy, and Ava has to elbow her to shut her up.

"It's from nine thirty to ten fifteen," Val says. "I'll be back for Cabin Chat, but you guys should have plenty of time with your Ouija board before that."

"Oh maaaaan," Petra whines.

"How did you know about that?" asks Summer. She sounds terrified that we're going to be punished.

Val raises one eyebrow. "I know about everything. Nothing gets by these eagle eyes."

"You're not going to take it away, are you?" I ask. "My aunt Estella gave it to me." I was certain she wouldn't get me in trouble, but all of a sudden I'm not totally sure. What if she thinks I've betrayed her trust and it makes her like me less?

"Of course I'm not going to take it away," she says. "You guys are old enough to play with a toy. Ouija boards are great. Actually, if you wait till I get back, I'll do it with you."

"OMG, seriously?" Lexi says.

"Seriously. I'm only twenty-one, you know. I'm not exactly an old fogey yet." She smiles at me, and I smile back. I should never have doubted her.

While we're waiting for Val to come back from her meeting, Roo and Lexi and Ava and I squeeze onto Roo's bunk and look at her pictures from the day. She has one of Josh at the climbing wall, and even though he's probably adjusting his harness, it really looks like he's scratching his butt, and we spend, like, five minutes laughing at it.

"That guy is so annoying," I say after we've finally calmed down. "He's constantly acting like he's better than me and accusing us of cheating in the prank war."

"Maybe our next prank should target him," Ava says. "We could help you take him down a notch."

"We could ask Tomás for suggestions," Lexi says.

"Nah," I say. "I can handle him myself. Thanks, though."

Roo looks at me long and hard, head tilted like she's figuring something out. Finally she says, "I'm glad you came here this summer instead of your old camp."

It's so unexpected that for a second I have no idea what to say. Roo doesn't exactly dole out compliments right and left. "Thank you," I finally manage. "I'm glad too." And I realize I'm not lying. I love Camp Sweetwater, but this is exactly the right place for me now.

"You should be bunking over here with us," Roo says.

I almost laugh, but I stop myself in time when I see that all three of them look serious. "My bunk is fine," I say. "It's like twenty feet away."

"These are the *best* bunks, though," Lexi says. "The breeze is better over here. Plus, you could talk to us late at night if you can't sleep."

"You should swap with Petra," Roo says.

I really like bunking with Mei, and I'm about to say so, but then I remember the day Roo and Lexi and Ava told me I should sing karaoke with them, how they said they were "offering me an opportunity." It seems like maybe this is the same kind of thing. If I don't switch beds, will they stop letting me lead the prank war?

"That doesn't really seem fair to Petra," I say carefully.

"She won't care." Ava turns around and calls, "Petra, do you mind switching bunks with Izzy?"

Petra looks up from playing cards with Summer and shrugs. "Not really."

"I don't want to steal your bunk," I say.

"It doesn't matter. It's not like I care where I am when I'm sleeping."

"Oh," I say. "Um, I guess it's okay, then."

Lexi squeals and claps. "Yaaaay, we're gonna be bunk-mates! I wish you had a purple sleeping bag with stars to match ours. It would look so cool if all four of our bunks were the same."

I actually prefer my yellow one, but I nod anyway. "When should I move my stuff?"

"Right now," Roo says. "We still have time before Val comes back." I can totally picture her running a huge company and ordering a billion employees around when she grows up. She'll probably plaster her office with those posters that have people climbing mountains and inspirational quotes about perseverance.

I hop off Roo's bunk and go over to my own, where Mei is sprawled on her bed with a book. I almost ask what she's reading, but when she looks up, I start feeling ridiculously awkward. "Um, did you hear that?" I ask.

"Yeah," she says. "So you're moving?"

"Do you mind?"

"You should do whatever you want." Mei's voice doesn't sound cold, exactly, but it certainly doesn't sound as friendly as usual. She's so nice that she's probably not capable of sounding meaner than this.

"Okay," I say. "I'm sorry. I really liked bunking with you."

"It's fine." Mei looks back down at her book, and I'm pretty sure it's a signal that the conversation is over. I wish there were a way to make everyone happy at the same time, but really, I'm doing this for the good of the cabin. We'll never win the prank war if someone else is in charge.

I move my stuff over to the other side of the room. I know my new bunk should feel like a victory, but it doesn't. Everything just looks weird and different from over here.

I'm transferring my last load of clothes to Petra's dresser drawers when Val comes back from her meeting. "Who's ready to summon some spirits?" she calls.

Lexi bounces on the bed. "Yay, it's time! Get the board, Izzy!"

I reach for the box and start tearing off the plastic. "Ooh, it's a brand-new one," Val says. "You know Ouija boards are especially potent the first time they're used, right?"

"That's not true," Roo says. "I have an old one at home, and it works fine."

"Oh, it's definitely true. You can hear the spirits way

more clearly when it's brand-new," Val says. "Go ahead and take it out of the box, Iz."

I set the board in the middle of the floor, and all the girls squeeze into a tight circle around it. There's barely room for everyone, even when Hannah decides to sit out. (What a surprise.) I end up shoulder to shoulder with Lexi on one side and Petra on the other, near the word NO and the drawing of the moon. The word YES and a sun are on the opposite side, near where Val's sitting, and the alphabet and numbers one through nine are printed across the center. At the bottom of the board, where Roo's crouched on her knees, is the word GOODBYE, which seems kind of ominous. I set the little plastic piece in the center, near the letter G, like my cousin Rosa did the only other time I've used a Ouija board.

"Ooh, hang on a second," Val says. "I forgot something." She gets up and pulls three fat candles in glass jars and a book of matches out of her bag. She arranges them in a triangle around us and lights them. "This always works better if it's dark," she explains.

"Where did you get those?" asks Petra at the same time Summer says, "No offense, but aren't candles against the rules?"

"They've been sitting in the main office for, like, two

years. I think someone gave them to one of the admin ladies as a gift, but she obviously doesn't want them. And I promise I'll take full responsibility if we burn down the cabin, Summer." Val wrinkles her nose as an overwhelming smell of vanilla starts to fill the cabin. "Ugh, it smells like a Bath and Body Works threw up in here. But I guess it's better than nothing."

"Turn off the lights," Roo urges. Val does, and creepy flickering shadows fill the cabin. It makes the chemical cupcake smell totally worth it.

"All right, *now* we can get down to business." Val squishes back into her spot between Ava and Mei. "Hannah, are you sure you don't want to join us? It's really fun, I promise."

Hannah shrinks farther back into her bunk and shakes her head. She's hugging a pillow to her stomach like she thinks it'll help her ward off evil spirits. It's weird how she likes creepy stuff like skulls and blood, but she can't handle anything that's remotely unpredictable or startling. I know I should probably feel bad for her, but I kind of want her to just deal with it for once. If she starts crying, Val will have to get up to comfort her and everything will be ruined.

"So, we all put our fingers on the little plastic piece, right?" I ask, to start things off.

"It's called a planchette," Summer says. Of course she would know that.

We all reach out, and Val says, "Rest your fingers on it very lightly. Barely touch it. We need to give the spirits total control."

"Do you think there are actual ghosts at this camp?" Lexi asks. "Like, for *real*?"

"What if there's one inside the cabin right now?" asks Hope.

"What if it's a boy ghost and he's been watching us change all summer?" says Petra.

"Eew!"

"Is everyone ready?" Val asks, and we nod. "Okay, all together now. Ouija, are you there?"

"Ouija, are you there?" we chant. My heart starts beating faster as I wait for the planchette to move, but nothing happens.

"Again," Val says.

"Ouija, are you there?" we repeat. Finally, on our fourth time, the planchette seems to tremble under our fingers, and then it swoops across the board to the word YES.

Lexi shrieks and pulls her fingers back like she's been burned. "This is freaky," she says.

"God, Lex, don't be such a baby," Roo says. Lexi bites her lip and reaches for the planchette again.

"Who has a question for the spirits?" Val asks.

"Hi, ghost," I say. "What's your name?"

The planchette immediately starts moving, slowly but surely, toward the letter section of the board. We all say the letters aloud as the little plastic piece travels from place to place.

"A-N-N-I-E."

"Phew, it's a girl ghost," Petra says.

"Petra, you're totally moving it," Ava says.

"I'm not! I'm barely touching it! I'm *channeling*. You're touching it way more than I am."

"Are you kidding? My fingers are hardly on it at all!"

"It wasn't any of us, it was Annie," Mei says.

"This is dumb," says Summer, but she doesn't sound sure.

"Annie, were you a camper at Camp Foxtail?" asks Hope. The planchette swoops over to the word NO.

"Are you dead?" Lexi asks, and the planchette moves over to YES.

"Um, obviously she's dead," Ava says. "She's a *ghost*."

"I just meant—"

"Annie, were you *murdered*?" I ask before Lexi and

Ava can start fighting. The planchette moves over to NO.

"Aw, man," Roo says.

"Seriously?" says Summer. "You're *disappointed* someone wasn't *murdered at our camp?*"

"She wasn't a camper! I bet she lived here when there were, like, log cabins and stuff. She was probably eaten by a bear or something."

"Annie, were you eaten by a bear?" asks Summer, and the planchette remains firmly on NO.

"How did you die?" asks Val.

The planchette does nothing for a second, and then it lurches back toward the letter section of the board. "T-R-E-E," it spells out.

"She was killed by a *tree?*" Roo asks.

"Maybe it fell on her," says Summer.

"Or she fell out of it," says Lexi. "Oh my god, Mei, you shouldn't climb that tree outside our cabin anymore. What if it was *that* tree? It might be haunted. She might make it kill *you*, too."

"Ghosts don't kill people," Mei says.

"But what if she's lonely and she wants more dead people around?"

There's a sudden snapping sound outside, and everyone gasps. "What was that?" squeaks Bailey.

"Probably a twig breaking," says Val. "I bet there's a raccoon or something."

"It's the tree!" Lexi hisses. *"It's coming for us!"*

It doesn't even make any sense, but I get goose bumps anyway, and a bunch of the girls squeal. "Lexi, shut *up*," Ava says.

"Does anyone have another question for Annie?" asks Val. "We're running out of time. Spirits usually don't hang around for long. The board makes it easier for them to talk to us, but it's still pretty hard."

"Annie, can you go haunt the Wolverines for us?" I ask. A bunch of the girls laugh, but then we hear another sound outside, louder than the first. It sounds like a branch hitting the side of our cabin, but there aren't any trees close enough to touch it.

"Shh!" Summer hisses. "There's definitely something out there."

Even Roo looks genuinely scared now. "We shouldn't have asked Annie to do something for us. Ghosts don't like that. Now she's going to punish us."

"Is that true?" Ava asks. She's looking up at Val, and for the first time, her perfectly put-together mask drops and she actually looks like a thirteen-year-old kid.

"No, it's not true," Val says. "But it does sound like

there's something out there. Keep your fingers on the planchette while I check it out, okay?"

Before she can get to her feet, there's this horrible ghostly sound *right* outside the window near where my old bunk is. It's halfway between a shriek and a howl, like how werewolves usually sound in movies. All the hair stands up on my arms.

"Omigod, omigod, omigod," whimpers Lexi.

"It's okay," Val says. "Guys, you know the Ouija board's not real, right? It's only—"

And then Hannah starts screaming like someone's amputating her feet with a dull, rusty saw. She's pretty far outside the circle of candlelight, but her eyes are so wide I can see the whites all the way around from here. She looks like she's seen an actual ghost.

And when I follow her trembling, pointing finger, I see the white specter glowing softly in the dark as it rises up from beneath the window ledge.

We all shriek and scramble away from the board. Regardless of what Val says, it's obvious the Ouija board *is* real, because we just summoned a spirit, and it's *right there*.

"Guys . . . ," Val says. But we're not listening anymore, because now there are glowing white shapes rising up in front of *all* the windows. The howling sound suddenly seems to be coming from everywhere at once, coupled with other ghostly noises: creaking doors, clanking chains, a faraway child crying. When I glance over at the tree closest to the cabin, there's yet another ghost nestled in the branches, and that freaks me out more than anything. What if it's Annie? What if she's coming to get us after all?

Petra's foot hits the board, and the planchette goes flying and skids under Roo's bunk. Now that nobody's touching it, I feel like the ghosts should disappear, but they don't; they keep rising higher. Somewhere in the back of my mind, I vaguely recall my cousin telling me that if you don't end a Ouija session by saying good-bye to the spirits you summon, they'll haunt you for-ever. The specter in the tree suddenly swoops down, closer to the cabin, and my heart tries to leap straight out of my chest.

"Guys!" Val shouts over our screams. "It's okay!" She flips on the light, and we all go quiet as the white shapes come into focus.

They're not the spirits of dead people coming back to haunt us. They're a bunch of ratty old bed sheets draped over the heads of mops and brooms and lit from below by flashlights. Some of them aren't even white, now that I'm seeing them more clearly—one of the sheets is pale blue, and another has a pattern of tiny yellow butterflies.

And crouched right outside our windows, holding up the ghosts and laughing so hard I can see their back teeth, are the Wolverines.

Dear Tía Estella,

Thank you so much the Ouija board. Please
don't be offended that I'm sending it back.
It's not because I don't like it or because it
doesn't work—we tried it out last night, and
we summoned the spirit of a girl named Annie
who died when she fell out of a tree. (Or
maybe a tree fell on her? We're not positive.)
The thing is, these boys played a prank on
us while we were using it, and one of the
girls in my cabin got so freaked out that she
refused to come back inside while the Ouija
board's still here. I told her I'd get rid of
it, but I'm not sure you're supposed to throw
out a Ouija board, and I'm scared to try
in case something horrible happens. Maybe
you're supposed to bury it? Anyway, I figured
you would know what to do. I hope the spirit
we summoned doesn't haunt YOU, but you're
probably safe, because how would she know
where you live? Unless she reads the address
on this package, I guess.

Other than that, things are good here. I've made a bunch of new friends, and I learned to sail a Sunfish. My mom told me about the party you had to celebrate Tío Joaquin's promotion at work—congratulate him for me, okay? Did you make the sweet tamales I like? Will you make them again when I get back?

Hug Rosa and Julio for me, and I'll see you in two weeks.

Te amo,
Izzy

CHAPTER 15

I desperately need to talk to Mackenzie the next day; none of us expected the Wolverines to retaliate so quickly, and I need another prank idea from her right away. Fortunately, I already asked her to have another letter ready by today or tomorrow, and she's never failed to come through for me before. It would be great to have something new to present to the Willows during Cabin Group this afternoon. I feel a whole new level of responsibility now that I'm bunking with Lexi and Roo and Ava.

The weird thing is that I can't find Mackenzie anywhere. I don't see her at breakfast or lunch—both of which Stuart spends waving white napkins in Val's face while making ghostly howling sounds—and she's not in any of my new activities, even though I thought we were supposed to have Nature together. I figure she'll come find me during Free Time, but she doesn't show up to ask if I want to go to the lake. I put on my swimsuit anyway and go over to Maple to look for her, but the only people there are three girls braiding each other's hair, and none of them have seen her. (*What* is with the Maple girls and hair braiding?) She's not at the dock or the archery range or under our favorite tree. I even check the infirmary, but the only person in there is a boy from Owl with poison ivy all over his face. What if something happened to Mackenzie and she had to go home or to the hospital, but nobody thought to tell me because I'm not in Maple?

When she's not at dinner, I start to get seriously worried, and Val promises we can find Doobie at the all-camp activity—a carnival in the Social Lodge—and ask if anything happened to her. But when we get there, I immediately spot Mackenzie across the room. She and Lauren are playing this game where you try to eat powdered-sugar doughnuts hanging from the ceiling on strings without using your hands, and she certainly doesn't look sick or injured. I push through the crowd to get to her, past the flour blow and the sponge toss and the station where you throw darts at balloons. I almost get distracted by the dunk tank; Stuart's sitting on the tiny seat above the water and belting out "Ninety-Nine

Bottles of Beer on the Wall" at the top of his lungs. It's hard to resist joining Val in line to lob baseballs at the lever that would make him fall in. But my aim is pretty bad, and I don't want to embarrass myself in front of her.

When I finally manage to get to Mackenzie, her cheeks are bulging with doughnut like a chipmunk, and she's doing the silly victory dance we made up together last year when our team won the Sweetwater Olympics. It's bizarre to see her doing it without me. Her face and shirt and the lenses of her glasses are all dusted in powdered sugar, and when a counselor hands over her prize—a plush elephant—she hugs it to her chest and smears it with sugar too.

And then she sees me, and all the happiness seems to drain right out of her, which doesn't make any sense at all.

"Hey," I say cheerfully. "Did you win?"

"Yeah," she says, but she doesn't smile. She hugs the elephant tighter.

"Awesome. Hey, did you check if those doughnuts are dairy-free? 'Cause sometimes—"

"I checked, okay?" Mackenzie snaps. "God, you're worse than my *mom*."

I'm not sure I've ever heard Mackenzie sound this fierce, including the time she caught Brian Scarponi cheating off her math test. Usually she seems to want me to take care of her. Usually she seems to need it.

"Oh," I say. "Okay. Sorry. Where were you all day? I looked everywhere for you."

Mackenzie tries to cross her arms, but the elephant makes it awkward, so she drops her hands to her sides. "My counselor's in charge of the carnival," she says. "Lauren and I helped her set up."

"I thought something happened to you. I was really worried. I even went to the infirmary to see if you were there."

Her eyes narrow behind her glasses. "Why? Do you *need* something from me?"

"What? No. I just wanted to hang out. That reminds me, though, I did want to talk to you about something. Can we go outside for a minute? It's kind of important."

Mackenzie looks over her shoulder at Lauren, and I assume she's going to tell her she'll be right back. But then she turns to me and says, "Actually, not right now. Lauren and I were about to go play the basket-shooting game."

"It'll be quick," I say. "We can shoot baskets after. It's just . . ." I'm pretty sure it's loud enough that nobody can hear us, but I lean in and lower my voice anyway.

"Did you hear what the Wolverines did last night? We were using the Ouija board my aunt Estella sent me, and those little jerks put sheets on brooms and raised them up outside the windows—"

Mackenzie cuts me off. "You know what, Izzy? I don't really care what the Wolverines did."

"It was so scary, though! It really looked like there were ghosts, and we were *totally* freaking out, and—"

"Just *stop!*" she shouts. "All you ever talk about is your stupid prank war!"

I feel like I've been slapped. Mackenzie has definitely been acting a little weird toward me lately, but I had no idea she was this angry. I didn't know she was *capable* of getting this angry.

"The prank war's not stupid," I say. "You don't think that."

"Don't tell me what I think," she snaps.

I hold up my hands in surrender. "Okay! Calm down. What's with you tonight? Are you mad we did the Ouija board without you? I didn't think you were interested in it, and anyway it was a cabin activity, so you couldn't have—"

"It's not about the Ouija board!" Mackenzie's full-out yelling now, and everyone lined up for the doughnut game is looking at us. "Can you seriously not think of *anything else* you were supposed to do yesterday?"

I think back through my day. Breakfast, Archery, Horseback Riding, lunch, Sailing, Popsicles with Val, Cabin Group, swimming with Mackenzie, dinner, egg drop, Ouija board, bed. I can't think of anything I missed. We didn't have any prank preparations to do, and I don't remember Mackenzie asking me for any favors I forgot.

"Can you please tell me?" I beg. "I'm really sorry for whatever it is, but I don't know what I did."

Mackenzie's face scrunches up, and I realize with horror that she's trying not to cry. "Yesterday was my *birthday*," she says, and her voice wobbles. "Lauren remembered, and she's only known me two weeks." She looks down at her wrist, and I notice for the first time that she's wearing a bracelet I've never seen before. It's made of intertwined strings of turquoise and purple beads, Mackenzie's favorite colors. A birthday present. From *Lauren*.

I am officially the worst person *ever*. Of *course* that's why Mackenzie was acting so weird yesterday; she was waiting for me to wish her happy birthday and do my traditional birthday prank. I should've covered the grass in front of her cabin with plastic lawn flamingos wearing party hats. Or decorated the horses with blankets that spelled out a birthday message and made the counselors parade them around in a circle when she got to Horseback Riding. Or even just had Val's friend in the kitchen make her a special ChocoNanaFlufferNutter Delight covered in candles and made everyone in the mess hall sing to her.

"Oh my god, Mackenzie, I'm *so* sorry," I say. "I got mixed up about what day it was, and there was all this other stuff on my mind . . ."

"Yeah, *super*important stuff like your Ouija board and your stupid rivalry with some boy. I thought you were supposed to be my best friend, but it's obvious what actually matters to you."

How does she not get that the prank war is a big deal, a time-honored tradition that goes way, way back? It's not just a rivalry with *some boy*. Nine other girls and Val are all counting on me to take the Wolverines down. But that's not the most important part of this argument, so I say, "That's ridiculous. Of course you matter to me."

"Really? 'Cause it doesn't seem like it, unless you need me to help you with something. Otherwise it's like, 'Mackenzie? Who's that?'"

"I don't—"

"Ever since we got here, you've been a total show-off, parading around in your stupid FOXY shirt and practicing your dumb karaoke dance moves, and I'm *sick* of it. There's more to life than making everyone think you're popular and important, you know."

That stings, and I stare at her. She never minded when I was popular and important at Camp Sweetwater. Is she bitter because all that attention isn't rubbing off on *her* this time?

"Mackenzie—" I start.

"Whatever. Why don't you go hang out with your *new* friends?" She spins around and starts pushing through the crowd toward the door. She collides with a guy doing the cakewalk, and he yells, "Dude, watch it!" at her retreating back. I can't see her very well through the crowd anymore, but I think I see her whip off her glasses and swipe a hand across her eyes.

"Mackenzie, wait!" I start to chase after her, but I've only gone about three steps before Lauren grabs my arm. She looks slight and delicate in her flowy flowered shirt, but her grip is surprisingly strong.

"I don't think she wants to talk to you right now," she says.

I twist away. "Stay out of this! It's none of your business. And you have no idea what she wants. She's *my* best friend."

"Oh yeah? Then maybe you should start acting like it," Lauren says. And then she pushes past me and strides toward the door after Mackenzie, like she has more of a right to chase her than I do. I've known Mackenzie since we were in preschool, and fourteen days ago, Lauren was an anonymous stranger. How could she think Mackenzie would want her over me?

But Lauren's out the door now, and she makes a beeline for Mackenzie, who's huddled on the ground with her back against our favorite tree, her knees pulled up to her chest and her face buried in her stuffed elephant. I watch through the window as Lauren sits down on the ground and wraps both arms around my best friend. Mackenzie's not a touchy-feely person—hasn't Lauren picked up on that?—and I wait for her to pull away. But instead, Mackenzie puts her head on Lauren's shoulder and keeps crying, and Lauren strokes her hair like she's done it a million times.

At least Mackenzie still thinks I'm worth crying over, but that's not really much of a comfort.

As I'm standing there with my nose pressed to the screen, wondering if I should go outside and try again to explain myself, someone taps my shoulder, and I whirl around. There's Roo, carrying her camera in one hand and an inflatable turtle in the other. Lexi and Ava are right behind her. "Hey, we're about to get some cotton candy," Roo says. "Want to come with?"

I turn back to the window, where Lauren's rubbing Mackenzie's back and saying something that's making a small smile creep onto my friend's face. She's right—Mackenzie doesn't want me right now. She wants the shiny new person who hasn't had time to make any mistakes yet. Roo and Lexi and Ava are the ones who actually care about me. They're not perfect, but they like me, and they respect me, and they probably don't expect me to be flawless, unlike *some* people.

"Sure," I say.

Lexi links her arm with mine, and we head off to cram our faces full of sweet, sugary fluff.

CHAPTER 16

Mackenzie and I haven't been in a fight since we were eight and couldn't agree on who was going to be which Pokémon character for Halloween. That fight ended the next morning when I offered to share my Fruit Roll-Up, and by the time we were done licking our sticky fingers, we were ready to play on the jungle gym together like nothing had ever come between us. I cross my fingers that she's not any better at holding grudges now.

We're both waiters at breakfast the next morning, and I rush through setting the table and retrieving pitchers of orange juice and water so I can talk to her alone before everyone else gets here. When I approach the Maple table, she's busy laying out forks and knives. I give her my most sheepish smile and say, "Hey."

"Hey," she mumbles, but she doesn't look up. I guess

she's going to make me work for this, but I'm willing to do whatever she wants. I'm so ready for everything to go back to normal.

"I'm really, really sorry about forgetting your birthday," I say. "I totally screwed up. When we get home, I'm going to get you the best present, and I'm going to—"

"I don't want a present," Mackenzie says. "That's not the point."

"Yeah, I know. I'm going to get you one anyway, though. Do you want to hang out during Free Time today? We can do whatever you want. Swimming or a trail ride or whatever." I hold my pinkie out like a white flag of surrender, but she still doesn't look at me.

"I have plans with Lauren today," she says.

"Maybe tomorrow, then?"

Mackenzie nudges a fork two millimeters closer to a plate with the tip of her finger. "I'm not free then, either. Don't you and Roo have superimportant boy bands to talk about or something?"

I sigh. "Come on, Mackenzie. I said I was sorry." I'm about to remind her that I need her help thinking up a new idea from Tomás—she should be flattered to know she's important and necessary. But then I remember all the stuff she said yesterday about how the prank war is stupid and how I only talk to her when I need something, and I swallow the words back down. I can wait a few more days if I have to.

"Hi," says Lauren's voice right behind me, and Mackenzie finally looks up. I hadn't noticed other people were starting to arrive. "You okay?" she asks, like Mackenzie could possibly need protection from *me*.

"Yeah, thanks." Mackenzie turns to me and says, "See you," which obviously means *go away*.

Fine, I think as I storm back to the Willow table. *I don't need her anyway. I can plan another amazing prank by myself.* But I'm not totally sure that's true.

I try to get a seat next to Val at breakfast—she always makes me feel better—but Petra and Mei snag the spots on either side of her while I'm busy fetching platters of bacon from the serving station. Instead, I claim the spot across from Roo, who raises her camera and takes a picture of me as soon as I sit down. I should be used to this by now, but I'm already annoyed, and for some reason her sneak-attack photo makes it worse. I hold my hand up in front of my face. "Can you not?" I snap.

She takes one more photo of my hand-covered face, probably to prove that she doesn't have to listen to me. "What's with you this morning?"

I sigh and stab my bacon. "Sorry. It has nothing to do with you. Mackenzie and I are in a fight."

"Who?"

"My best friend in Maple. You've met her. The girl with the purple glasses?"

"Oh, her," Ava says, like she's remembering a really bland cracker she once ate.

"I don't get why you're even friends with her," Roo says. "She doesn't seem that interesting."

"She's just shy, she's actually really—" I start, but then I stop myself, because why should I defend Mackenzie when she's refusing to speak to me? "You know what, never mind."

"Don't worry about her," Roo says. "You have us to hang out with now."

Lexi nods. "Yeah."

"Right. Thanks." But it doesn't make me feel any better. Having other people to hang out with isn't the point. I want them to tell me it'll blow over, that Mackenzie and I will still be best friends. But they don't seem to care at all if my friendship with her ends in a flaming pile of wreckage.

Nothing goes right for me all morning. It turns out Mackenzie's in Nature with me after all, but she spends the whole time pretending I'm not there and talking with this girl from her cabin. It's unbelievably hot and humid, so I'm dripping with sweat within the first ten minutes, and then I get a bunch of burrs stuck in my hair. In soccer I wipe out while failing to score a goal and end up with grass stains down the entire left side of my favorite shirt. Lunch is "Mexican Fiesta," which means hard yellow taco shells filled with ground hamburger meat, packaged orange cheese, iceberg lettuce, and watery, bland salsa. It's like no one who works in the kitchen has ever tasted actual Mexican food, and the whole thing makes me grouchy and homesick. All I want to do is curl up with my grandma and a big plate of her spicy enchiladas and watch *Corazón de Hielo, Alma de Fuego* while she pets my hair.

And then it's time for stupid *Fishing*, which of course I have with stupid Josh.

I gather my rod and bait from the bored-looking counselor-in-charge, who seems way more focused on his car magazine than on teaching us anything, and sit down at the far end of the dock. I managed to bait my hook fine yesterday, but today I feel so gross already that impaling a worm seems extra disgusting. As I'm trying to psych myself up to do it, Josh comes up behind me and looms over my shoulder. I was really hoping he'd leave me alone for once, but everything else has gone wrong today, so it figures this would too.

"Squeamish, nemesis?" he asks cheerfully. "Do worms scare you as much as ghosts? Are you going to scream?" He flails his hands around and demonstrates a falsetto shriek.

I try to think of a snappy retort, but all I can come up with is *Your MOM's scared of worms and ghosts*, which doesn't seem particularly clever. "Can you please get off my case for one hour? Is that too much to ask?" I say instead. I'm trying to sound ferocious, but it comes out kind of sad and tired.

Josh's expression changes, and I think for a second that he's actually going to leave. But instead he sits down next to me on the sun-scorched dock. "You okay?" he asks, and weirdly enough, it doesn't seem like he's trying to make fun of me. It sounds like he actually wants to know.

"Bad day," I say. "Whatever."

"You want me to bait that hook for you?"

"I can do it myself."

He shrugs. "Yeah, I know. But you obviously don't want to, and it doesn't bother me." He holds out his hand. "Come on, give it here."

I look at him closely, trying to figure out if this is some kind of trick. I know I'm never, ever supposed to let down my guard around a Wolverine. If I give him the worm, he'll probably drop it down my shirt or something; plus, I'm pretty sure I'm supposed to be an empowered girl and bait my own fishhook. But I don't have the energy to think too hard about Josh's motives right now, and letting someone else skewer a worm for me one time probably isn't going to ruin feminism.

I hand him the hook, and three seconds later he gives it right back, expertly baited.

"Thanks," I say. "That was really fast. Do you fish a lot or something?"

"Yeah," he says. "My grandpa has this boat, and he likes to take me and my brother out." He looks at the way I'm awkwardly holding my rod. "I take it you don't fish a lot?"

"I hate fishing," I say. "I have no idea how I ended up in this activity."

"I think they throw the preference forms out and assign everything randomly. I specifically said I didn't want Arts and Crafts, but I've still got it next week. I got a D in art last year. I can barely draw a stick figure."

"At least you don't have to kill anything in Arts and Crafts."

"I'm so bad with a pencil, I probably *will* kill someone," he says, and I smile against my will. "Anyway, you don't have to kill anything either, except the worm. If you catch a fish, throw it back."

"It'll still hurt the fish, though. And I don't know how to get the hook out."

"I can show you."

I want to say, *Why are you being nice to me?* But I'm afraid that if I call attention to it, he'll remember we're supposed to be enemies and go back to taunting me. Plus, I actually don't mind this side of Josh. I almost feel like I'm making a new friend.

"Hey," I say. "Thanks for not ratting us out about having a Ouija board."

Josh shrugs. "The Ouija board rule is so stupid. We don't want to get you guys in trouble or anything. We just want a fun prank war."

"Yeah, us too." I swallow hard. "That was a pretty decent prank, actually."

Josh grins. "I know."

"How did you even know we were going to use the Ouija board that night?"

"Seriously? You think I'm going to reveal my sources to *you*?"

I shrug. "Fair enough."

We cast our lines and sit in silence for a minute, and then he asks, "So, what's bad about today?"

I remind myself that I probably can't trust him. Who knows if he's being genuine right now? Maybe he's trying to lull me into a false sense of security, and then he'll use everything I tell him against me. But the weird thing is, I kind of want to tell him anyway, even if letting down my guard is a betrayal of my cabin. Roo and Lexi and Ava are great, but they clearly don't care about my friendship with Mackenzie. Mei probably isn't into having deep conversations with me either after the whole bunk-swapping thing. If Val and I were still doing our daily Popsicle runs, I'd ask her what she thinks about the situation, but I never have time alone with her anymore. Josh is sitting right here, basically a captive audience, and unlike everyone else, it seems like he's willing to listen.

"I'm in a fight with my best friend," I say.

"That girl from Archery?"

I nod. How weird is it that he remembers Mackenzie, when my actual friends didn't seem to know who she was?

"What's the fight about?" he asks.

I obviously can't tell him the parts that have to do with the prank war, so I keep my explanation simple. "She's mad I forgot her birthday."

"Seriously? That's a dumb thing to fight about."

"We usually make a big deal out of each other's birthdays," I say. "We do funny surprise birthday pranks and stuff. I can see why she's upset."

"Why don't you just say you're sorry?"

"I did, a bunch of times. She's still mad, though."

Josh's eyebrows furrow like he's trying to understand a really hard math problem. "But . . . why is she still mad if you apologized?"

"Because it's more complicated than that. And besides, sometimes people stay mad no matter what you say until they're ready to forgive you. Hasn't that ever happened to you?"

Josh scratches the back of his neck. "Not if I said sorry. Isn't that the entire point of saying sorry?"

How does he not understand this? Don't all humans understand this? Maybe boys aren't as complicated as girls. When the boys in my class fight, they usually yell and shove each other for, like, thirty seconds, and then someone breaks it up and makes them apologize, and two minutes later they're talking about video games again.

"Do you have any sisters?" I ask.

"What? No. Why?"

"I guess maybe it's a girl thing,"

He nods slowly. "Girls are weird."

I think about the strange power dynamics that seem to be going on between Roo and Lexi and Ava and the way they offered me an "opportunity" before the karaoke competition, like they wanted to go into business with me. I've never seen boys do anything like that.

"Yeah," I say. "Girls are super weird."

"Wait till Friday night," Josh says. "All the girls in the camp are gonna go *insane*."

"How come?"

"Color Wars is this weekend, remember? Captains get chosen at the campfire on Friday. Do you know about the Sea Witch thing?"

"Yeah. A counselor dresses up and kidnaps one of the captains, right?"

"Right, and then they announce the rest of the captains and split everyone into teams, and all the girls freak out. Some of the guys, too, but mostly the girls. Some of them cry because they're happy, and some of them cry because they're upset, but basically *all* of them cry. Stuart was the Sea Witch last year, and the girl he 'kidnapped' got so excited she accidentally elbowed him in the face and gave him a black eye."

I seriously doubt the girls are as bad as he's making them sound; if I get chosen as a captain, there's no way I'll cry or punch someone. But that's not what catches my attention. "Is Stuart always the Sea Witch?" I ask.

"He's done it the last couple of summers, and I think he's doing it again this year," Josh says. "I don't know why he likes it, honestly. Tromping through the cold lake in the dark wearing a dress doesn't sound very fun to me."

"No, that doesn't sound fun at all," I say, but my mind is spinning now. I suddenly remember this old Mexican legend my grandma told me about Devil's Alley, a street everyone was afraid to walk down because the devil appeared there every night. The only way to keep him from terrorizing the town was for everyone to leave offerings of gold, which always disappeared by the morning. But then one day, two guys got suspicious that it was someone dressing up as the devil and stealing everybody's stuff. So *they* dressed up as devils, too, and they scared the pants off the first fake devil, who never stole anything again.

Ever since we heard the Sea Witch story in Arts and Crafts, Mackenzie and I have been trying to think up a prank we could do at the Color Wars campfire. Now that I know Stuart is the one dressing up as the Sea Witch, I suddenly know exactly what it should be. And the best part is that I didn't *need* Mackenzie to think of it. This idea is 100 percent mine, which proves I can handle the prank war on my own after all.

Josh is going to freak out when he discovers how much he just helped the Willows.

Dear Mom, Dad, Lina, Tomás, and Abuela,

Things at camp are all right, but my
activities aren't nearly as good as last week.
Fishing is the absolute worst. It's sooooooo
boring, and I swear there aren't actually
any fish in the lake, because not a single
person has caught anything. Also, I don't
think the counselor who runs Nature actually
knows anything about nature. Three girls got
poison ivy yesterday because he didn't warn
them what it looked like. I wish I could do
last week's stuff again.

Lina, Mom told me you got first place in
the long jump at your camp's field day.
Congratulations! I was always the long jump
champion too. We have Color Wars starting
Friday night, which I think is a lot like Field
Day, except it goes on for the whole weekend.
I'm really hoping I'll get chosen to be one of
the captains. I know you're not ready to go
to sleepaway camp yet, but when you are, I
think you'd like this one. We can go together,

and all the younger kids will think you're the coolest because you're my sister.

Mom, you know that green wig from my Halloween costume last year? Would you find it and send it to me? I think it's on the second-to-top shelf of my closet. The fake-fur coat was a big hit. Sorry I keep making you send me random stuff, but you don't mind, right? Riiiight? ☺

Abuela, thanks for the update on "Corazón de Hielo, Alma de Fuego." I can't believe Marianna turned out to be Federico's stepmother AND stepsister at the same time! Are Luz and Umberto STILL in the desert? How are they not dead? Hasn't it been, like, three weeks since they've had water?

Love you guys, and I'll see you in less than two weeks!

Izzy

CHAPTER 17

During Free Time, I sneak off on my own, find a secluded spot near the horse barn, and try to write a fake letter from Tomás. It's much harder than I thought it would be, and it takes four drafts before I'm able to replicate the sloppy boy handwriting Mackenzie did in her first letter. I sketch out my new prank idea, but I leave a few parts out so I can pretend to come up with them on the spot and impress the Willows. The finished letter looks decent, so I seal it in an envelope, address it to myself, buy a stamp at the Trading Post, and do my best to draw convincing postmark lines. It's not nearly as good as Mackenzie's letters, but hopefully nobody will look too closely.

I volunteer for mail call again that afternoon, and everything goes according to plan. All the girls crowd around me when I show them the letter during Cabin Group. "Read it out loud," says Roo.

I do, and everyone is *super*excited about the new prank. "I think this is his best one yet," says Ava, and Val nods in agreement, which makes me really happy. It's nice to hear that my solo pranks are more impressive than Mackenzie's. I almost wish I could just tell everyone I thought it up on my own; I'm getting sick of giving so much credit to Fake Tomás when I could be showing Val how much of a leader I *really* am. But I'm still not positive the girls would take me seriously without Tomás's authority behind me. What if I told them the truth, and it made them lose respect for me altogether? I have too far to fall at this point to take that chance.

"How did Tomás know Stuart was going to be the Sea Witch?" Roo asks.

Somehow I didn't anticipate that question. "I told him," I say. "I suggested that the Color Wars campfire might be a good place for a prank because we can humiliate the Wolverines in front of the entire camp, like they did to us."

"But . . . how did *you* know about Stuart?"

"I found out from Josh," I say. "That redheaded kid."

Roo wrinkles her nose. "Why were you talking to him? Are you guys *friends*?"

"No!" I say. "Obviously not. I *pretended* to be friendly so he'd let his guard down, and then I weaseled the information out of him." It makes me feel guilty to say that when Josh was so nice to me the other day, but if the Willows find out I actually kind of like him, they'll never trust me again.

"Good," Roo says. "'Cause he's the enemy, you know."

"Of course," I say. "I would never betray you guys like that."

The week goes by much faster now that I have something to focus on. We work on our Sea Witch prank during Cabin Group every day, and whenever I start to think about Mackenzie, I force my mind back to ways we can make the prank scarier. Why should I waste energy imagining what she and Lauren are doing or what horrible things they're probably saying about me? She's the one who's in the wrong. If she can't accept that people make mistakes sometimes, maybe we *should* take some time apart until she calms down and sees that I'm right. I already tried to apologize to her twice. Now it's her turn.

Even fishing is a little better now that I have Josh to talk to. We can't have our normal rivalry because neither of us ever catches any fish, so we compete at other things instead. Josh can throw stones farther than I can and hold his breath for longer, but I'm better at undoing knots quickly and keeping a straight face while he tries to make me laugh. I actually kind of look forward to seeing him every day, but when he asks me to have a race on the ropes course with him during Free Time on Thursday, I immediately say no. Hanging out during an activity we *have* to attend is one thing, but choosing to be in the same place on purpose is a step too far. The Willows would never forgive me if they thought I was seeking him out on purpose.

By Friday I'm starting to think Josh might be right about how seriously everyone takes captain announcements for Color Wars. Summer and Lexi don't eat any lunch or dinner because they're too nervous, and Roo, who's certain she's going to be chosen, eats only protein because she needs to "fortify herself for leadership." I'm glad I'm in charge of all the important parts of the prank tonight, 'cause I'm pretty sure nobody else would be able to concentrate. Of course, I'm still holding out hope that *I'll* be one of the captains—if it were totally up to Val, I'm pretty sure I would be. But I know it's not a guarantee, since most of the other counselors barely know me and only twelve kids in the entire camp get picked. So I try not to think about it too hard and focus all my energy on taking down Public Enemy Number One. Winning the prank war is way more important than Color Wars.

As soon as dinner's over, I start getting ready. I put on my bathing suit, then slip on the Sea Witch costume we've made. The base is a lightweight gray gown Val found at a thrift store when some of the counselors went into town for supplies. We've altered it so it has a raggedy, calf-length hem in front and a long, shredded train in the back that looks like tendrils of seaweed. Bailey painted the dress so it looks moldy and gross, like it's been decaying in the water for ages, and the sleeves are all ripped up and covered in fake seaweed as well. Roo twists my hair up into a bunch of tiny buns, and Val helps me bobby-pin on the green wig, which Hannah has wrapped into chunky sections with green thread so that it looks like snakes. Then Hannah and Petra do my makeup: a base of green waterproof paint on my face and hands, dark hollows around my eyes, and a few disgusting fake wounds. They top it off with fake blood trailing from the corners of my mouth and one of my eyes, like Hannah's clay skull.

When we're finally finished and I peek in the mirror, I almost gasp at my own reflection. I look *terrifying*. Roo brings out her camera, and I do all kinds of scary poses for her, including one where Val's screaming as I pretend to bite her neck. That one's going to be a big hit at the end-of-camp slideshow. I'm totally going to blow it up and hang it on my bedroom wall at home, too.

"Ready?" Val asks me. "You've got everything you need?"

I'm nervous all of a sudden, but I nod. "All I need is a lake, an audience, and Public Enemy Number One."

"You're a champ, Izzy. I can't wait to see this go down. Remember not to go into the water until Paige gets there, okay?"

I sigh. "I really don't need a lifeguard watching me. The water's only, like, three feet deep where I'll be."

"I know, but we can't take any chances. Your safety's really important to me. I'd watch you myself, but I have to be there for the start of the Color Wars ceremony or everyone will get suspicious."

"Yeah, okay." It's a little annoying, but it *is* nice that she cares so much.

"You're going to be amazing," Val says. "I'd give you a hug for luck, but you're kind of gross right now." We air-high-five instead.

Val promised there would be at least half an hour of regular campfire songs before the Sea Witch story, so I wait till it gets darker before I head toward the lake. I'm antsy and excited and can't sit still; I've been in charge of the other pranks, but this is the first one that's up to me and *only* me. If something goes horribly wrong, the Willows will have no one else to blame. I catch myself wishing Mackenzie were here to calm me down, but I push the thought away. She made it perfectly clear that she didn't want anything to do with this "stupid" prank war.

When the sun finally goes down, I put on Val's giant black hoodie over my costume, pull up the hood to hide my face, and tuck in all the green tendrils of my wig. I wrap the long train of my dress around and around my wrist so I can walk, and then I slip out of the cabin and go over to the lake. I can hear the sounds of singing as I draw near the campfire—they're starting "Show Me the Way to Go Home." But I turn before I reach them and head toward the dock, which is about fifty feet away on the other side of a small grove of trees. The other Willows told me that the "Sea Witch" always comes from that direction. I creep down the path as silently as I can, careful not to step on any twigs or crunchy leaves.

I slip out of my hoodie and shoes and stash them behind a tree. When Paige the lifeguard finally arrives and flashes the secret signal Val arranged—three quick flashlight blinks—I unwrap the train of my skirt and let it trail behind me as I slip into the water. I dunk my whole body under to get my dress and wig wet, and then I crouch behind one of the dock's pylons and wait for Stuart. Paige gathers up my clothes and waits behind the tree, so silent and still that it's easy to forget she's there.

When I planned this prank, I had assumed the waiting would be the easy part. But it turns out time passes really slowly when it's dark out and you're wet and cold. The temperature of the lake has never bothered me before, but it feels way chillier now than it ever does during the day, especially with this clammy wig sticking to the back of my neck. I wish I could jump up and down to warm up, but I have to stay perfectly still—the rest of the campers aren't that far away, and they might hear me splashing. They've launched into another song now, the one about making a purple stew, and I can't stop thinking about how delicious a hot bowl of stew would taste right now. After a couple more minutes I start to shiver, and I clench my teeth together so Stuart won't hear them chattering when he arrives.

Just as I'm considering climbing back out and waiting on the bank, I hear footsteps crunching down the path. I hold my breath, pray that I don't have a sudden urge to sneeze, and peek around the edge of my hiding spot. Stuart props his flashlight against a tree trunk, strips down to his boxers, and pulls on a long black dress and a messy dark wig. His costume isn't nearly as detailed or scary as mine. Finally, he grabs the flashlight, turns it off, and slips into the water.

I crouch behind my pylon, my eyes locked on him like a lion that's ready to pounce on its prey. *Game on, Wolverines*, I think.

And then, right on cue, silence falls over the campfire, and I hear Doobie's voice, low and creepy. "Now it's time for a grisly tale, a story that has terrified Foxes young and old since the beginning of time . . . the story of *The Sea Witch!*"

Everyone hisses, and Doobie starts telling the story Mackenzie and I heard during Arts and Crafts our first week here. This version is much longer and includes lots more gory details, and I picture Hannah trembling. Stuart rubs his arms to keep warm, and I lurk quietly ten feet behind him.

"The Sea Witch's spirit could be lying in wait inside anyone at all," says Doobie. "It could be any counselor, any camper. During the day, there's no way to know the difference. She could be next to you at any moment. She could be on your soccer team. She could be eating spaghetti next to you in the mess hall. She could be lying above you in your bunk bed.

"It's only at night, when she enters the lake, that she takes on her true form: a haggard, filthy, terrifying monster, ready to drag unsuspecting campers to their watery doom!"

This must be Stuart's cue, because he turns on his flashlight, points it up at his face like he's telling a ghost story, and starts making growling sounds as he splashes toward the campfire. I slip out from behind my pylon, duck down low in the water, and follow him. I try to glide silently along like an alligator, but it's surprisingly hard to move in this dress, even with the hem ripped short in front. The long train keeps snagging on stuff— seaweed, probably—but fortunately, Stuart's doing this weird, shambling zombie walk, and he's splashing so much that he doesn't hear me.

A bunch of campers gasp and squeal as Stuart starts climbing the upward slope of the bank, revealing his waist, then his hairy thighs. His free hand is curled into a Sea Witch claw, ready to "kidnap" the first Color Wars captain, and the mass of kids seems to cringe away and lean forward at the same time, sparking with anticipation.

When I'm sure he has everyone's rapt attention, I let out a long, shrill, wild scream.

A bunch of campers shriek along with me, sure it's part of the show, but I can see from the way Stuart freezes that he's confused, like the thief in Devil's Alley. This isn't how things are supposed to go; *he's* supposed to be the only scary thing in the lake right now. The other counselors know it too, and a bunch of them half stand, ready to leap up and protect their campers. Stuart glances back over his shoulder and scans the dark water, but his eyes have adjusted to the firelight, so he doesn't see me right away.

I decide to give him some help.

I surge out of the water with another deadly shriek and rush toward Stuart with both green-painted hands extended, my face twisted into a hideous expression. His eyes bug out under his ratty wig, and he stumbles a few more steps toward the shore. When I'm close enough, I take a flying leap and land on his back, piggyback style. He lets out a shout of genuine terror and drops his flashlight in the water as I wrap my seaweed-covered sleeves around his neck and lock my legs around his waist. As I poke my head over his shoulder and let out another piercing shriek, I see a camera on the bank flash once, twice, three times. Good old Roo—always there to capture the most dramatic moments.

Stuart spins around and bats at my legs for a few seconds before he loses his balance, and we both crash into the shallow water. The shouts of the camp grow muffled as the lake closes over my head, and for a second I'm afraid he might fight back by holding me under. But when I come up for air, he's fleeing toward the campfire, his black Sea Witch dress hiked up and clinging to his legs and his wig askew so that it covers one eye. It's supersatisfying to see his face without its trademark smirk. I was planning to chase him a little longer, but he looks so ridiculous that I can't keep it together, and I just stand there in the water and laugh.

"Oh my god," I gasp. "I got you! I totally got you! You were *so scared! Willows rule! Wolverines drool!*"

The rest of the Willows pump their fists in the air and take up the chant, and as the other campers slowly realize what's happening, they all start laughing their heads off. Stuart smiles and tries to act like he knew it was me the whole time, but he's obviously shaken. Even Doobie is holding her hand over her heart like I gave her a good scare. My friends and Val stand up on their log and scream the Willow cheer, and I chant with them as I climb out of the water. One tiny boy reaches out to touch my dripping, seaweed-covered sleeve as I pass, and I hold up my hand for a high five. He slaps my palm, his eyes wide with wonder, and then stares at the smudges of green paint on his fingers like they're magical.

"Who *is* that?" I hear someone say as I dance past a group of Magnolias.

"That's Izzy Cervantes," her friend answers. "She and her older brother are both pranking *legends*."

Part of me wants to look for Mackenzie; we're not speaking, but I still want her approval, and I *know* she'll love this prank. But then I remember what her face looked like when she said I'd become a huge show-off, and I decide it's probably better not to try to find her in the crowd. I don't want anything to spoil this moment. So instead, I glance over at the Wolverines and scan the group for Josh. He'll be *furious* that I trounced them so badly based on the information he gave me, and I know his defeated expression will make my victory sweeter.

But when I catch his eye, he actually *smiles*. It's almost like he's impressed with what I've pulled off, even though we're enemies, and it's actually even better than the anger I was hoping for. I smile back.

CHAPTER 18

When I finally reach the Willows, all the girls lean in to tell me how great I did. I sit down in the place of honor that Lexi saved for me between her and Roo, and Val wraps me in a huge, cozy towel and helps me unpin my wet wig. Even in my soaked costume, I feel warm and flushed with accomplishment.

I ask Roo if I can see her pictures, and when she hands over the camera without making sure my hands are dry, I realize for the first time how tense and distracted my friends are. I was too focused on taking Stuart down to remember that the most important part of *their* night—captain announcements—hasn't happened yet. I kind of wish I'd been able to do my prank at a time when people could fully concentrate on how awesome it was.

Nobody else seems interested in the pictures, but I

scroll through them anyway. There's one of me on Stuart's back where it looks like I'm about to eat his head, and he's holding up both hands and screaming. For a second I actually think, *I can't wait to show this to Tomás,* before I remember my older brother isn't real.

Doobie climbs up on top of a log and whistles with two fingers. "All right, everyone settle down," she yells, and the whole camp goes quiet. "It's time for the moment you've all been waiting for. Emissaries of the Sea Witch, please approach and collect your anointing tools."

I have no idea what that means, but everyone else goes *insane.* On the log in front of me, a girl from Poplar clasps her hands like she's saying grace and starts going, "Oh please oh please oh please oh please." I glance over at Lexi and Summer, and even in the firelight, I can tell they look a little green. Next to me, Roo is completely motionless, tension radiating off her.

Val, Stuart, and four other counselors make their way over to Doobie, who's holding a plastic bucket. Each of them reaches inside and pulls out two water balloons—the "anointing tools," I guess. Val has blue balloons, so I guess they indicate who's leading which team. When the counselors hold them up in the air, they catch the light of the fire and glow like jewels.

"We are the emissaries of the Sea Witch," they say together. "She speaks through us and guides our hands toward captains who are brave and true."

"Valerie," Doobie says "Which two campers has the Sea Witch chosen to lead your team?"

Val starts walking around the fire pit, so smoothly it's almost like she's in a trance, and everyone follows her with their eyes, mouths slightly open. She stops in front of a girl from Oak with light brown skin and giant dark eyes. "Amira Roy," she proclaims, and the girl gasps and covers her mouth with both hands. "The Sea Witch has chosen you as one of the two leaders of the Blue Team. Do you accept this task?"

"*Yes,*" Amira breathes, and a tear slides down her cheek.

"By my hand, the Sea Witch anoints you," Val says, and *sploosh*, she drops the water balloon right on Amira's head. Amira screams, and her friends hug her and cheer.

"Please join the Master of Ceremonies," Val says, and Amira gets up and scurries over to where Doobie is standing with the other five counselors. Doobie drapes a blue lei around Amira's neck, and she fingers the fabric flowers gently, like they're made of glass.

Val continues around the circle, second water balloon held high, and heads right toward us. My heart starts pounding, and for a few seconds I allow myself to hope that she really *is* going to choose me after all. Maybe it doesn't matter that I'm a new camper; maybe she was able to convince the other counselors that I can handle the responsibility of being a captain. On our last Popsicle run, she basically said she was going to put in a good word for me.

But Val passes right by me and stops to my left. "Lexi Silverman," she says, and then I don't hear any of the rest of her speech, because Lexi's laughing and sobbing and screaming, "Yes yes yes yes!" When the water balloon explodes over her head, she springs up and throws her arms around Val, then runs over to the counselors and tackle-hugs Amira. I've never even seen Lexi *talk* to Amira before, but I guess cocaptainship makes you into instant friends. I try to be happy for her, but my heart aches a little bit despite my best efforts. If I can't be captain of Val's team, I don't really want to do it at all.

Roo clearly doesn't feel the same way; next to me, she starts cracking her knuckles one by one. "Don't worry, you've still got a chance," I whisper to her.

"*Obviously,*" she snaps back, and I wish I hadn't said anything. "Hang on to my camera so the water balloon doesn't get it wet, okay?" I wonder if she's really as confident as she sounds, but I tuck the camera under my towel, just in case.

The counselor who's leading the green team goes next, and he drops water balloons on a girl from Poplar and a guy from Coyote. Then comes Stuart, who "anoints" Bloody Mary and the boy from Porcupine who told me the Sea Witch story. Mackenzie's friend Lauren is chosen as one of the purple team's leaders. Every time another camper is anointed, Roo flinches, and I can see her counting down in her head: four more chances, three more chances, two more chances.

The red team's counselor goes last, and when she walks straight toward us with her final balloon, it seems like Roo was right to be confident all along. But she stops in front of Summer instead, who starts happy scream-sobbing like Lexi did. When the water balloon explodes over her head, Hannah clutches her hand and sympathy-cries, and I see more tears breaking out all around the campfire as other campers realize they no longer have a chance of being captain. Some of them are totally hysterical, and the Cottonwood counselor has to lead two of her sobbing campers away from the circle. Josh wasn't kidding about how many tears there were going to be tonight. When I catch his eye across the circle, he makes a face like, *Told you*.

Roo is sitting incredibly still beside me, and I'm almost afraid to look at her, but I sneak a glance. "It's okay," she says, but instead of meeting my eyes, she stares very fixedly at something about six feet in the air. "There's always next year." I think about trying to comfort her, but she obviously doesn't want to cry in public, and tears always come way more easily when someone's being nice to you. So instead I hand her camera back, and she takes it, raises it to her eye, and starts clicking away. She looks grateful to have something to hide behind.

"Captains!" shouts Doobie. "Place your right hands over your hearts, raise your left hands in the air, and repeat the Captain's Oath after me."

The twelve lei-draped captains raise their hands and repeat:

"I solemnly swear to be honest and square
And to guide my whole team with a hand that is fair.
In my color I'm dressed, I'll be put to the test,
And I'll show the whole camp that my team is the best!"

Doobie lets everyone scream and cheer for a while, and when the hysteria finally dies down, she hands the captains colored envelopes containing their team rosters. Lexi and Amira read their list of names first, and it's strange to hear Lexi sound so authoritative. She's always so willing to let Roo and Ava take the lead; this is the first time I've seen her try to be something on her own. I've just decided she'll probably do a really good job, when she says my name. Val winks at me from where she's standing behind Amira, and it takes everything I have not to squeal and clap and bounce up and down. I'm the only other Willow on the Blue Team, and I'm sure Val must've rigged this somehow so we could have some quality time together. She probably didn't want me to be captain because it takes so much time and effort. This way, we'll get to enjoy Color Wars together without anything getting in the way.

I spent the first few weeks of camp hoping Mackenzie and I would end up on the same team for Color Wars, but when Lexi doesn't call her name for the Blue Team, relief floods through me. Honestly, I'm way more likely to have fun if I don't have to deal with her drama and her weird grudges. Now I can pretend she's not here for the next two days, and I can focus on having fun with Val and my team. Mackenzie is assigned to the Red Team with Josh, and I try not to feel smug that she won't be with her new BFF, either. Maybe having nobody to hang out with all weekend will give her some perspective and she'll finally apologize to me.

When all the names have been read, Doobie tells us to

break into teams for a quick meeting before bed. I rush over to Lexi, who squeezes me tightly. "I'm so glad you're on my team!" she says. "Amira, this is Izzy. She's *the absolute best.*"

Amira grins at my green face and wet dress. "You were the Sea Witch? That was *amazing.* Definitely the best prank I've ever seen."

"Thanks," I say. "It was so much fun. Freezing cold, but fun."

"Izzy and her supercute older brother have thought up *all* our pranks. That's why the Wolverines are losing so badly." Lexi turns to me. "You'll help us run the Blue Team, right?"

"Of course," I tell Lexi. "We're going to make this the best Color Wars ever."

CHAPTER 19

When we get to the mess hall for breakfast the next morning, it has been transformed. Instead of individual tables, there are six huge team tables draped in colored tablecloths, and there's an enormous scoreboard hanging next to the stuffed moose head. It looks like camp crossed with *Harry Potter*. Lexi and I head toward the Blue Team table and take the two seats right in the center, across from Amira. I hope Val will sit with us, but she moves down to the end where some nervous little kids are sitting, and she has them all giggling within minutes. She's seriously the best counselor in the entire world, and I'm so proud to be her friend.

I know I shouldn't care, but I look around the dining hall until I find where Mackenzie's sitting. She's wearing her favorite red shirt that's faded from the time her mom accidentally washed it on hot with all the white sheets and dyed everything pink. Since she doesn't have any friends on her team, I expected to find her sitting alone at the end of the bench and picking at her breakfast, but instead she's chatting with a pair of twin girls from Poplar. As I watch, she says something that makes them laugh, and I feel a weird pressure in my chest. Since when is Mackenzie so good at talking to strangers?

I turn away; she doesn't matter right now. "What's the schedule for today?" I ask Lexi and Amira.

Lexi consults her official blue clipboard, which she's decorated with curly blue ribbons from Arts and Crafts. "We're making our team banners right after breakfast," she says. "And then we have swimming relays, and after lunch we have soccer against the White Team and softball against the Yellow Team, and tonight is all-team capture the flag." I'm relieved we don't have any one-on-one games with the Red Team today.

"Our banner should have tons of glitter," Amira says. "Then it'll be supersparkly in the sun and catch everyone's attention."

"I think we should—" I start to say, but a chorus of screams and whoops from across the room cuts me off. When I turn around, everyone from the Red Team is standing on their benches. They wait until everyone's looking at them, and then they shout:

"Through your thoughts we softly tread,
Spreading fear, inspiring dread!
Hiding under your warm bed,
Lurking, silent, overhead.
Think we're sweet like gingerbread?
Better watch your back instead.
We will get inside your head
And take you down, cause we're TEAM RED!"

"Impressive," calls Doobie, who's dressed in a hideous rainbow shirt and pants that include all six colors. "Score-keeper, give the Red Team ten points." The Red Team cheers, and everyone else groans. "You all want points, get to work and be as clever as the Red Team."

"Ugh," mutters Amira. "That was annoyingly great. There's no way I can come up with something that good."

"Me neither," says Lexi.

"I'll work on it," I say, but I'm more irritated than they are. I'd recognize a Mackenzie-written cheer anywhere. She always used to write the cheers for our Sweetwater Olympics teams, and we always won prizes for them. My suspicions are confirmed when everyone at the Red Team table starts high-fiving Mackenzie; one girl I don't know gives her a hug. It's been awful not having her as an ally this past week, but it feels even worse to have her actively working against me.

When breakfast is over, we spend an hour on our banner, and I start to feel a little better. Val writes out "We will leave you black and BLUE" in bubble letters, and Amira draws a giant pair of crossed swords on one side and a boxing glove punching a cartoon guy in the face on the other. The younger kids go nuts with glitter on the whole thing, and I know it's dumb, but seeing everything so sparkly kind of cheers me up. Glitter improves pretty much every situation.

By the time we're done, the banner looks fantastic, and the day only gets better from there. I swim the front crawl in the last leg of our relay, and even though my teammate was pretty slow with her backstroke, I manage to pull ahead at the very end and put us in second place. Our White versus Blue soccer game is interrupted when two little boys wearing nothing but underwear and purple paint streak across the field, but their team leader intercepts them, and we end up winning. I've hated softball ever since I got hit in the face with a ball last year during Sweetwater Olympics, so Lexi and I sit that one out and work on our cheer while our team battles Stuart's. Captains—and honorary captains—get special privileges.

I'm trying to think of more rhymes for the word "blue" when I idly glance up and see something really weird across the field. Val and Amira have been in the dugout area for most of the game, psyching up our batters, but now Val's standing a little ways off with Stuart. She's laughing, so I assume she must be teasing him about how badly his team is losing. But then he slings an arm around her shoulders. For a second I think he's going to put her in a headlock or something, but it doesn't turn into anything but a friendly side-hug. She doesn't hug him back or anything, but she does tip her head toward his for a moment so that her forehead grazes his jaw. Then Stuart lets go, and Val starts cheering for a girl from our team who hit a double, and everything is normal again.

The whole thing only lasts about five seconds. If I had looked up a moment later, I would've missed it. But I *didn't* miss it, and I can't wrap my mind around what I just saw. Why on earth would Stuart and Val be acting friendly? He's on the other team, not to mention that he's superannoying *and* he's Public Enemy Number One. And then something horrible occurs to me: He's probably trying to lull Val into a false sense of security so he can weasel information out of her, like I did to Josh before the Sea Witch prank. I bet she's too smart to fall for something like that, but just in case, I figure I should say something later. She could lose the whole prank war for us if she lets her guard down and reveals some crucial piece of information to the one person who's always looking to take us down.

Someone starts shouting in the other dugout area across the field, and when Lexi and I look over, we see Roo yelling at one of the kids on her team because he's holding his bat incorrectly. "What is she *doing*?" I say. "She's not even a captain."

"She can get really intense sometimes," Lexi says.

"Is she like this at home, too? How do you and Ava deal with it all year?"

"No, she's . . . It's not . . ." Lexi glances at me sideways. "Okay. If I tell you something, do you promise to keep it to yourself?"

"Sure," I say, and my heart speeds up. I love it when people trust me enough to tell me secrets.

Lexi leans closer and lowers her voice. "Roo's not the most popular girl in our class. She really *wants* to be, but there's this other girl, Sienna, and everyone's completely obsessed with her for some reason. They're always falling all over themselves to dress like her and tell her how pretty she is and do whatever she wants, which I think is kind of weird, honestly, because she's not *that* amazing. But she goes to stay with her grandparents in Colorado every summer, and being free to boss everyone around for four weeks gives Roo a serious power trip."

Everything suddenly makes so much more sense: how much Roo seems to care about everything here, how she saw me as a threat when I first took over the prank war, how angry she is that she didn't get to be captain. I never realized how similar the two of us are. I bet Roo has that ticking-clock feeling in her chest that I sometimes get, counting down the days until she has to go back to real life, where nobody thinks she's that special.

"Oh," I say. "Wow. Yeah. I can totally see that."

"Seriously, though, you can't tell anyone. She'd kill me if she knew I'd said anything. Nobody knows except Ava and me."

"I won't tell." We both watch Roo throw up her hands and stalk away from the younger camper, who immediately runs to his captain for comfort. "Does it bother you, the way she acts here?"

"It can be a little much sometimes, but she really seems to need it. And we know it's going to end when we get home, so we just deal with it."

"But if she's always the ringleader here, and Sienna's in charge at home, then you never get a turn."

Lexi smiles. "I'm getting a turn right now," she says. "So . . . what else rhymes with 'blue'?"

The cheer we come up with isn't Mackenzie-level clever, but it's pretty solid, and we debut it right after dinner:

> *"If you try to break Team Blue,*
> *We'll spring back like we're bamboo!*
> *Toss you in a witch's brew,*
> *Eat you for dinner like a stew!*
> *So respect us, it's our due,*
> *Or we'll bite you like a shrew,*
> *Kick you with a steel-toed shoe,*
> *And jump away like a kangaroo!"*

Screaming it out loud makes me realize that it doesn't actually make a ton of sense. But the little kids love it, and it must be basically okay, because Doobie shouts, "Scorekeeper! Ten points to the Blue Team!" I'm still a little embarrassed that it's not as good as Mackenzie's cheer, though. I sneak a glance at the Red Team table to see if she's reacting to it at all, but she has her back to me and doesn't turn around.

The rest of the evening is dedicated to an epic six-way capture the flag game. In order to win, you have to hang on to your own flag *and* capture two other teams' flags. We're allowed to hide our flag anywhere on the camp property as long as it's out in the open, and we decide to dangle ours from the roof of the horse barn, a little too high for someone to jump up and grab it. We station guards in front of the building, including Sadie Pasternak, who's known for her piercing shriek. Then we split up into teams to hunt for the other flags.

"I'll take the youngest kids," Val says. "We'll search the area around all the cabins and the main field, if that sounds okay."

"I can go with you and help," I say quickly before Amira and Lexi ask me to head up a different search party.

Val looks surprised and pleased. "Thank you, Izzy," she says. I feel a tiny bit guilty letting her think I'm doing this out of the kindness of my heart, but I really need to talk to her, and I can't figure out another way to get her alone.

We gather the five smallest kids and head off toward the cabins. They run ahead and start searching right away, but I hang back with Val. The sun is getting lower in the sky, splashing slanted golden light across the grass, and as we walk quietly together, it actually feels kind of like our Popsicle runs. For a second I consider asking if she wants to sneak off and grab some Popsicles right now, but we can't exactly leave in the middle of an important game.

"You know we probably won't find any flags around the cabins, right?" I ask instead. "This is way too central and easy to ambush."

Val smiles. "I know. But the little kids don't, and it's easier to keep an eye on them in a wide open space." There's some shrieking from the direction of Cottonwood Lodge, and I spot the youngest two girls chasing each other around and around it. They look so ridiculously tiny to me. It seems impossible that Mackenzie and I were ever that small.

"It's really nice of you to help me," Val says. "But if you want to go search for real, it's totally fine. I can handle these guys, and it seems like a shame to waste a great strategic mind like yours."

"Maybe in a little while," I say. "I actually wanted to talk to you about something first, though."

"Sure, what's up?"

I take a deep breath and plan my words carefully. I don't want to sound like I'm accusing her of anything when really I want to protect her and the Willows. "I saw you with Stuart earlier at the softball game," I start.

She smiles. "We totally kicked their butts, huh?"

"Yeah, but . . . I saw you two talking, and you looked, like, really friendly with him. And he's supposed to be The Enemy."

"I mean, technically all the other teams are the enemy, but Color Wars is just for fun, right? It's not like I'm going to have a serious fight with Stu over a softball game."

Stu? This is exactly what I was afraid of. He's already gotten in her head, and it's up to me to save her before it's too late. "Yeah, I know," I say. "But I was actually talking about the prank war."

Val shrugs. "Neither of us is really in prank war mode right now. We've got too much other stuff to deal with. We can pick that up again on Monday."

I can't believe she's brushing off the prank war like it's something we can take a break from. How does she not understand how critical this is? *She's* the one who told us it was an important, time-honored tradition.

"I'm always in prank war mode," I say. "And we completely humiliated Stuart yesterday with the Sea Witch thing. I'm sure *he's* not taking a break because of Color Wars. He and the Wolverines are probably plotting new ways to take us down right this very second!"

"I think they're probably focusing on capture the flag right this very second," Val says. "Don't worry about it, okay? I promise we'll think of new ways to take them down, too, right after Color Wars is over. Oh, by the way, Lexi asked me if we could print out some of Roo's Sea Witch photos in Doobie's office and send them to Tomás. I think he's going to love them, don't you?"

Val clearly doesn't understand what I'm getting at, so it looks like I'm going to have to be blunt, even if it hurts her. "It's just . . . here's the thing. I know it might seem like Stuart is your friend, but he's not. You might think he's acting friendly and nice because he likes you, but he doesn't really. He's trying to get you to drop your guard and tell him stuff he can use against us. I know because I did the exact same thing to Josh, and that's how I got the information we needed for the Sea Witch prank. We all have to be careful who we talk to."

I expect Val to look surprised or maybe a little wounded, but her expression softens, almost like she feels sorry for me. "I don't really think this is the same thing, Iz."

"I don't want you to get hurt, that's all. I'm trying to protect you."

She puts an arm around my shoulders. "That's really sweet, but you don't have to worry about this, okay? It's not your job to take care of me. It's *my* job to take care of *you*."

"We can take care of each other," I say. "That's what friends do."

"And I'm so glad to have you on my side," she says. "God knows I wouldn't want to go up against you. You make a formidable opponent."

Her words send a rush of happiness through me, and I snake my arm around her waist and give her a squeeze in return. But in the back of my mind, underneath where all the joy is bubbling and fizzing around, I can't help feeling as if I haven't really gotten through to her at all.

CHAPTER 20

The most important part of Color Wars is the steeplechase, which starts in the early afternoon on Sunday and lasts for hours. It's a race with thirty different parts, and figuring out which team members are going to do which elements requires some serious strategic planning. Our team's in second place after capture the flag last night and our water polo game against the Purple Team this morning, and if we win the steeplechase, we'll pull ahead of the Yellow Team and take the all-camp title. It's a lot of pressure, and I think Lexi and Amira are feeling the full weight of their cocaptain responsibilities, because they lean on me to help them make decisions more than usual. But I don't mind, and by the time we've locked down the final schedule, we're all superexcited. Lexi gives our team a rousing pep talk, and then Amira leads the Blue Team cheer, which leaves us all so pumped up I think we might explode.

I'm doing the very first leg of the race—kayaking across the lake—and the entire camp gathers at the dock to see us off. Just when I think this whole thing couldn't get any more exciting, I see that Josh is kayaking for the Red Team; that ought to give me that extra burst of speed I need to come in first. He catches my eye as I'm securing the bright blue Active Racer sweatband around my head and raises one eyebrow at me. I respond by doing that thing Stuart did to Val on our first day—pointing two fingers at my eyes and then at him like *I'm watching you*—and he half smiles and looks away. I wonder if what I said to Val last night was really true. Is he always thinking about ways to take me down? Or is it possible for rivals to be friends?

But I can't think about that now. I need to focus. I put on my sunglasses, partially because the water is bright but mostly so I'll look cooler and more intimidating to the other racers.

The six of us climb into our kayaks, and Val gets ready to push me off. "Make us proud, Iz," she says into my ear, and I promise I will. As Doobie climbs up on the dock and raises her official whistle to her lips, I grip my paddle, concentrate on the white flags on the opposite shore, and tell myself I can do this. My entire team is behind me on the dock, waving our banner and screaming my name, and it makes me smile. I love being a crucial part of something so important.

The whistle blast shrieks through the air, and we're off.

I fumble a little right at the beginning, and a girl from the Green Team pulls to the front of the pack. Josh starts out in front of me too, but once we get into deeper water, I find my rhythm and push ahead of him. It's easier to concentrate once I can't see him, and I focus hard on closing the gap between Green Team girl and me. The sun is warm on my shoulders, the breeze plays with my hair, and even though I'm nervous, it feels great to push my muscles to the limit. About two-thirds of the way across I finally pass the Green Team girl, and I hear her make a frustrated sound. A hundred more yards . . . now fifty . . . now twenty . . . and then I'm coasting up onto the opposite bank, and my teammate, a boy named Baxter, is grabbing my hand and helping me out of the boat. I whip the Active Racer sweatband off and slip it around the bike helmet he's wearing, and he hops onto a mountain bike and takes off. "Thanks!" he calls as he heads toward the trail that will take him back around the lake and up to the tennis courts.

"*Go Blue!*" I shout after him, and then I collapse with my hands on my knees and try to get my breath back. My arms are burning, and I know I'll barely be able to lift them tomorrow, but it's totally worth it. I'm only sad the rest of my team isn't here to congratulate me.

And then I look up and notice that Mackenzie's standing ten feet away with another mountain bike, waiting for Josh to hand her the Red Team's Active Racer sweatband. It's exactly the right event for her; she's superfast on a bike.

I give her an awkward nod and say, "Hey," because it seems weird not to acknowledge her at all.

"Hey," she says back.

The Green Team girl's kayak pulls up to the shore, and her teammate snatches her sweatband and tears off on her bike without exchanging a single word. Kayak girl comes up next to me and starts massaging her biceps. "Oh my god, my arms hurt so much," she says.

"Mine too," I tell her.

"You're Izzy, right?" she says, and I nod. "I'm Christina. You dressed up like the Sea Witch the other night, right?"

"Yeah," I say.

"That was *so* funny. My entire cabin was laughing about it all night."

"Thanks," I say. "I'm glad you guys liked it. It was really fun."

I sneak a look at Mackenzie, wondering if she's annoyed that everyone in camp is freaking out over the prank I thought up without her. But she's not paying attention to me, because Josh's kayak has pulled up on shore, and she's running over to get the Red Team's sweatband.

I suddenly don't want to deal with either of them, so I turn to Christina and say, "Come on, let's go watch the rest of the race." We take off running down the path before Josh is fully out of his boat, and I try not to watch Mackenzie as she speeds by me on her bike and rounds the corner.

By the time we get to the tennis courts, panting and sweaty, the Green and Blue teams are both in giant circles, holding hands and passing hula hoops over their bodies one at a time as quickly as they can. Val is in the middle, jumping up and down and cheering, and when she sees me, she smiles and gives me a huge thumbs-up. "Seven more people!" she shouts. "Four ... three ... two ... one ... you did it, guys! Okay, everyone let Lexi through! Robbie, you're on deck to eat peanut butter and jelly sandwiches in the mess hall, and then Rachel and Destiny are up for the three-legged race!"

Lexi puts on the sweatband, grabs a tennis racket, and sprints onto the nearest court. There's a bucket of tennis balls ready and waiting, and she starts serving them to a waiting counselor one after the other. I had no idea she could even play tennis, but she's got a seriously powerful arm.

Amira comes up and tackle-hugs me. "I heard you came in first with the kayaks! Nice!"

"Thanks," I say as Lexi hits another ball across the court. "Man, she's really good at this."

Amira looks at me, surprised. "Well, yeah. She goes to tennis camp every summer before this."

"Oh," I say, and I realize for the first time that I know basically nothing about Lexi. I've always just thought of her as part of the Roo-and-Ava package deal.

"Are you ready for the fire building?" I ask. Amira's doing the last, most important leg of the race, which one of the two captains always takes. If I were her, I think I'd be freaking out right now.

"Yeah, I think so," she says. "Nervous, though. I wish I could've practiced last night, but my counselor wouldn't give me any matches."

Lexi whacks her final ball across the court and then thrusts the Active Racer sweatband into the hands of tiny Robbie, who's waiting right behind her. "Good job," I tell her when she jogs over, cheeks bright pink with exertion.

"Thanks. Come on, let's go cheer Robbie on while he stuffs his face." She beams at me, and when she takes off running, I follow her. I've never seen her look so confident; being captain totally agrees with her. I can see why the counselors chose her instead of Roo.

Robbie eats the two peanut butter and jelly sandwiches faster than I would've imagined was possible; I'm pretty sure he swallows them whole, like a snake. Rachel and Destiny trip and fall during the three-legged race, which costs us some time, but only the Green Team manages to pass us. Then we dash off to the ropes course, where the object is to pass five team members through shoulder-high sections of the giant rope spiderweb without touching any of the ropes. That takes a while, since everyone's so hyper that it's hard for them to go slow and steady. The Green and Red teams are here, too, and everyone's screaming their team cheers at once, so the woods are total chaos. But Lexi and Val coach our team through the exercise, their voices calm and soothing. I try to keep Mackenzie out of my sight line; every time I spot her, I have memories of holding hands with her and screaming for our team during Sweetwater Olympics. It's a lot easier to have fun when I can pretend she's not here.

The race goes on for hours. A girl named Tricia roller skates to the infirmary, where she retrieves a sugar cube. She hands it over to Josh's cabinmate Beans, who dashes to the horse barn, feeds it to one of the horses, and then rides him around the ring three times while belting out the Foxtail anthem. Megan from Poplar has to carry a raw egg on a spoon all the way from the horse barn to the dock, and when she drops it most of the way there, she has to go all the way back to the beginning and start again. She cries through the entire second round, especially when the Red Team passes us, but we're able to make up the time during the Mermaid Swim; Anna-Marie from Oak has no trouble swimming out to the raft and back with her feet tied together. One of our youngest girls does twenty cartwheels across the main field, pukes in the bushes, and then does twenty more in the other direction. There's crab walking and pogo-sticking and croquet-ball hitting, and there's even a part where Kim from Magnolia has to peel ten ears of corn and ten bananas.

By the time we get to the final event, our team is in second place behind Green, and I've been cheering and singing for so long that I basically have no voice left.

But I don't let that stop me, and my entire team screams for all we're worth as we run up the hill to where the captains will build their fires. There are six little pulley systems rigged up on a flat stretch of ground. At each station a rope runs through two low hooks above the tiny pit where the fire will go, then extends about six feet in the air, where it loops over a third hook. Rubber duckies painted each of the team colors hang from the ends of the ropes and dangle over buckets of water. The winner of the steeplechase will be the one who burns through their rope first and causes their duckie to splash down into the water.

Amira kneels by her box of supplies, a fierce look of concentration on her face. The Green Team's captain, Kaitlyn, is already working on building a teepee out of small sticks, and Amira starts doing the same thing. "She can do this, right?" I shout to Lexi over the screaming. I only sort of know how to build a fire, so I can't really tell if she's doing it right.

Lexi nods. "She's a Girl Scout," she shouts back. "She does this all the time. I think. That's what Girl Scouts do, right? Besides selling cookies?"

Amira adds a few crumpled balls of newspaper to her pyramid, and then she grabs a match from her box. It takes her about five tries to light it, and when it blows out immediately, she fumbles for another one with shaking hands. *"Go, Amira!"* I scream. *"You've got this!"*

A cheer goes up from the Green Team, and to my dismay, I see that Kaitlyn's pyramid is burning bright. A bunch of the little kids on our team are already crying, too overwhelmed to keep it together, and Lexi turns around and leads them in another round of Blue Team cheers.

And then, there it is: a tiny flicker of flame. "It's lit!" I scream, and our whole team goes crazy. At the exact same time, Kaitlyn's fire goes out, and she shouts a word I'm *positive* she's not allowed to say. I don't know how Amira's keeping it together with all this hysteria around her, but she looks totally calm and focused now. She crouches low and blows gently onto the tiny flames, and they start to grow. Very carefully, she starts adding larger sticks to her pyramid, and soon she's got a steady blaze going. When the fire climbs up one of the bigger sticks and touches the rope for the first time, Lexi grabs my hand and squeezes so hard it hurts, and we jump up and down and scream together.

Kaitlyn manages to ignite her twigs again, and the Green Team starts shrieking. My ears will probably be ringing for days. I keep my eyes locked on Amira's fire as it blackens the white cotton rope and starts to eat away at the fibers, as if my laser stare will make it burn faster. I pray for a well-timed gust of wind to slow Kaitlyn down; it would be so terrible to get this close to victory and have it snatched away.

And then it happens. Amira's rope snaps, and her bright blue rubber duckie splashes down into the water. We've won the steeplechase. We've won *all of Color Wars*.

Amira springs to her feet, pumps her fists in the air, and lets out a victory scream, and we all pile on top of her, shrieking and hugging and jumping around. I don't think I've ever been this excited in my entire life, including the time my dad got us a kitten for Christmas.

I squeeze Lexi's shoulders on one side and Val's waist on the other, and as I feel them squeeze me back, I realize my cheeks are wet. I've become one of Josh's crazy girls who cries at Color Wars, and I don't even care.

CHAPTER 21

We gather back around the campfire for the Color Wars closing ceremony as the sun begins to set. The sky over the lake is a gorgeous wash of pink and orange with the occasional golden-edged cloud, and it's so beautiful it's hard to force my eyes back down to what's happening at ground level. The cicadas whir in the trees, singing us a victory song. It's like nature's trying to congratulate us on our win.

To kick things off, we all stand, put our hands over our hearts, and sing the Foxtail anthem. The Red Team goes up to the front first to receive their bronze medals, which are strung on red ribbons, and Mackenzie spends the whole medal presentation giggling with one of the twins from Poplar. I have to work hard to push down the annoyance that bubbles up in my chest. When the Green Team goes up to receive their silver medals, I almost feel bad for them; Kaitlyn's eyes are so puffy and red that I'm pretty sure she hasn't stopped crying since Amira beat her at fire building.

But it's hard to feel *too* bad, because then it's our turn.

We make our way up to the front, and I plant myself in the middle of the group between Lexi and Amira. Doobie brings out the box of gold medals, strung on satiny blue ribbons, and Val helps her hang one around each of our necks. I'm right in the center, so I'm not sure whether I'll get Val or Doobie, but Val gets to me first, and I feel like it might be on purpose.

"Thank you so much for all your help, Izzy," she says in a low voice as she slips the ribbon over my head. "You were a truly indispensable team member."

I'm pretty sure she didn't any anything like that to the rest of the team. I wonder if they mind that I'm clearly her favorite.

When she moves on to the next person, I pick up my medal and inspect it more closely. There's a fox head stamped in the center, and around it in loopy script, it says *Camp Foxtail Color Wars: First Place*. Roo is moving along the edge of the fire with her camera to her eye, and when I raise my medal and smile at her, she snaps a picture. I couldn't feel more like a champion.

Everyone sits back down, and the six counselors who led the teams produce torches and light them in the fire, then move to stand behind the captains. Doobie gives a short speech about their incredible leadership, team spirit, and graceful acceptance of defeat, which is actually kind of funny since Kaitlyn is crying again. Lexi looks radiant. When Doobie finishes her speech, she says, "Captains, please follow your counselors down to the water," and the entire camp falls silent. Nobody coughs or fidgets, and the only sounds are the crackling of the fire and the captains' footsteps as they form a procession down to the lake. I picture myself in that procession next year; now that everyone has seen what an amazing unofficial captain I am, there's no way I won't be chosen as one of the twelve best leaders in the camp.

Each pair of captains climbs into a canoe, and the counselors sit behind them and hold their torches aloft. And then, as the captains start to paddle, the counselors begin to sing. The song doesn't have any words I can understand—it's either nonsense syllables or another language—but it's haunting and sweet, almost unearthly. Val's gorgeous voice floats above the others, and even though it's still pretty warm outside, listening to her gives me goose bumps all down my arms. We watch the canoes cross the lake in complete silence, and when they reach the opposite shore, the torches all go out in perfect unison. Color Wars is over.

When the campfire ends and the captains have returned to our side of the lake, almost everyone heads to the mess hall for cookies and hot chocolate. But because we're the winning team, we get our own special treat: pizza in the Social Lodge next door. Dinner was only a couple of hours ago, but I'm already starving again, probably because I spent the entire day running around screaming. The whole Blue Team must feel the same, because everyone descends on the pizzas like a herd of velociraptors. I push my way over to the pepperoni, which is disappearing fastest, and grab a slice. Pepperoni is Val's favorite, too, but I don't see her anywhere, so I grab an extra plate and take a piece for her. We have to look out for each other, like we talked about, because that's what friends do.

"Izzy, over here!" Lexi shouts from across the room, where she and Amira have claimed the squishy green couch with the fewest springs sticking out of it.

"Have you guys been on your overnight to Sandpiper Village yet?" Amira's asking when I join them. "We did ours last week, and it was soooo fun. I almost set Sadie's hair on fire with a flaming marshmallow."

"Ours is on Wednesday," Lexi says. "It's going to be the *best*. Last year Roo and Ava and I slept out under the stars instead of in our tent, and we got a million mosquito bites, but it was so worth it. You should do it with us this year, Izzy."

"Definitely," I say.

"We carved our initials into this giant tree by the lake on our first overnight when we were ten, and every year we sit in the exact same order and take a picture by it," Lexi says. "I've got all the pictures framed in my room at home. Here, look, I'll show you the one from last year." She looks around to make sure nobody's watching, then pulls her phone out of her back pocket and scrolls through her photos till she finds the one she wants. There she is with Roo and Ava, sitting on the ground by the base of a huge oak tree with their arms around each other. Lexi's hair is much shorter, and Roo has different glasses. All three of them look incredibly happy and relaxed. I wonder if they'll let me be in the photo this year.

"You can look at some of the other pictures," Lexi says. "Sandpiper Village is so beautiful. It's seriously the best part of the entire summer."

I swipe through some of the photos. There's Lexi on

the rope swing, Summer setting up a tent with Hannah, BaileyAndHope swimming in a stream with Petra and a girl I don't know, who must be Juliet. Lexi's not kidding about how pretty Sandpiper Village is; there are giant trees on one side of the campsite and wildflowers all along the banks of the stream. There's even a gazebo.

I hand back the phone. "I can't wait to see it in real life," I say. "Hey, do you guys know where Val is? I got her some pizza, but I don't see her."

"I think she went into the storage room," Lexi says. "She's probably getting more napkins or something."

"Cool. I'll be right back. Save my spot." I know I could wait for Val to come out—it'll probably only be a minute. But I want one more second alone with her before Color Wars ends for good, to thank her for letting me be an honorary captain. And if I'm honest, maybe I'm hoping to snag a few more compliments about what a fabulous unofficial leader I was.

The light is on in the storage room, but the door is shut most of the way. "Val?" I call as I pull it open. "I got you some pizza. There's room on the couch if you want to come hang out with—"

And then I stop and stare, because my brain can't process what I'm seeing.

Val's in the storage room, like Lexi said. But she's not getting more napkins. She's pressed up against the wall next to the door, both arms around a boy, and she's kissing him furiously.

And the boy is Stuart. Public Enemy Number One.

The plate of pizza falls out of my hand, and the cheese hits the floor with a wet slap. Val and Stuart immediately pull apart, like that'll somehow erase what I've seen, and Stuart yells, "Get *out*! What are you *staring* at?"

"Don't yell at her," Val says, but I don't hear anything after that, because I'm too busy running away.

All this time, Val made me believe she was my friend, the one person I could absolutely trust at Camp Foxtail. She took me on special secret Popsicle runs and told me secrets about her family and her love life and pulled strings to get me on her team for Color Wars. She never made me feel like I had to prove myself to her, unlike everyone else, including Mackenzie. I thought I totally understood her. But now that I've seen her wrapped around Stuart, that illusion crumbles into a million tiny pieces.

Since the day I got here, I've been plotting and scheming and working so hard to help Val *beat* Stuart, to help the Willows beat the Wolverines, because I thought everyone cared about this prank war as much as I did. I thought we were all taking it seriously. And now it looks like Val isn't even on our side. Who knows how long she's been cozying up to Stuart behind out backs? For all I know, she's been lying to us since the very beginning.

I think back on the conversation Val and I had yesterday, when I told her Stuart was trying to manipulate her. I thought I was so special, looking out for her feelings, and I thought she cared about *my* feelings in return. But now that I know she's an enemy-loving traitor, I don't know what to believe. What if she sneaked out of the cabin after we were asleep last night and told Stuart all about our conversation? What if they laughed together about how stupid and naive I was to try to protect her from him? What if they've been laughing about things I told her in confidence *all summer*?

I was so sure Val and I had a special bond. And now it turns out I don't really know her at all.

The last thing I want to do is cry. But finding out someone you trust has betrayed you is like having a hole punched in your chest, and I'm so worn out from this weekend that I can't hold my tears back. I wipe them away quickly; when Val follows me out here, I'm going to have to look strong and confront her. But I wait, and I wait, and she doesn't come, even though she *has* to know how much she hurt me. So I give up and let the flood-gates open.

There are a bunch of kids sitting in the grass in front of the mess hall, and I'm relieved when I spot Mackenzie among them. She doesn't see me at first because she's too busy laughing about something with Lauren. But I walk right up to them, and her eyes widen when she notices I'm crying. "Hey," she says. "Are you okay?" For once, she actually sounds like the normal old Mackenzie, not Lauren's new Mackenzie.

"Not really." I wipe my eyes and sniffle. "Can we talk for a minute?"

"Yeah, okay." She turns to Lauren. "I'll be right back."

Mackenzie and I don't speak until we reach the big oak tree where we used to sit and plan pranks, back before everything fell apart. Then she asks, "What's going on?"

"I caught Val and Stuart kissing," I blurt out, and saying it out loud is enough to trigger a fresh flood of tears.

I wait for Mackenzie to comfort me, but she just stands there with her eyebrows scrunched together. "Um, okay . . . ," she says. "Why do you care?"

"Seriously?" It seems like it should be obvious.

"Do *you* like him or something?"

"What? *Stuart?* No! God!" I can't believe she would

consider that possibility. How is she this out of touch with my feelings after one week?

"Sorry, I just . . . I don't really get what the big deal is."

"She's not supposed to like him!" I shout. "He's our *enemy*, and I thought she was on *our* side, but now she's obviously not, and the entire prank war is ruined!" My nose is running now, but I don't have any tissues, so I wipe it with the back of my hand.

"Did Val say you have to stop pranking them?" Mackenzie asks.

"No. That's not the *point*."

"Then . . . sorry, but I still don't really get what the point *is*."

"The *point* is that I was taking this prank war seriously 'cause she made it seem like *she* took it seriously, and then it turns out this whole thing was a huge joke to her! She's been lying to us this entire time so we'd keep thinking up pranks for her!"

"I mean, technically, you've been lying to her this whole time too," Mackenzie says. "She still thinks Tomás is real, right?"

"I should've known you'd take her side," I snap. "You're as much of a traitor as she is."

Mackenzie blinks at me. "What? How am *I* a traitor?

What does this even have to do with me? All I did was help you!"

"Yeah, until you decided you weren't getting enough credit and you ditched me!"

"Are you serious?" Mackenzie's eyes are bugging out of her head now. "*I* ditched *you*? I did all your dirty work and wrote your stupid letters from 'Tomás,' and I never complained about any of it, including when you started backing out of our plans every time someone more popular made you a better offer! And you couldn't even be bothered to remember my birthday!"

"I apologized for that, like, *fifty times!*" I shout back. "What do you want me to do, get down on my knees and beg you for forgiveness?"

"You apologized *twice*, and then you literally never tried to talk to me again!" Mackenzie's starting to cry now too, and she shoves her hands up behind her glasses to wipe her eyes. "I had every right to be mad, and you gave up on me after two seconds, like it didn't even matter to you if we were friends anymore!"

"You obviously don't care if we're friends either, now that you have *Lauren* to hang out with! You're with her, like, *every second*. It's *Lauren Lauren Lauren* all the time. Remember when I offered to let you help with the mountain lion prank, and you turned me down to go swimming with *her*?" We're being loud enough that Lauren can probably hear us from where she's sitting, but I don't care.

"This isn't about the prank war!" Mackenzie yells. "Not everything is about the stupid prank war, okay? I started hanging out with Lauren because I was sick of sitting around by myself and waiting for the popular girls to dump you so you'd notice I existed again!"

"Roo and Lexi and Ava are my *friends*! They're not going to dump me! They actually respect me, unlike *some people*!"

"If they respect you so much, why did you need to make up a fake older brother to get them to listen to your ideas?"

"Fake older brother?" says another confused voice.

I seriously didn't think tonight could get any worse. But when I turn around, Roo, Lexi, and Ava are standing right behind me.

CHAPTER 22

"What are you guys doing out here?" I ask, like that's the most important question right now.

"It was too hot in the mess hall. We needed some air," says Ava.

"I saw you run out of the Social Lodge, and you looked upset, so I came out to see if you were okay," Lexi says.

I glance at Mackenzie like, *See? My new friends* do *care about me.* But she's looking over her shoulder toward the mess hall. She's probably trying to figure out how long she has to stand here before she can go join her *real* friend again.

"So, is it true?" Roo asks.

This is probably the worst possible moment to try to explain myself to her. She's spent the whole weekend furious about not being a Color Wars captain, and I'm sure she's not feeling very forgiving. "Is what true?" I say to stall a tiny bit longer.

"Come on, Izzy. Do you have a brother or not?"

"I do," I say, and it's not a lie.

"Then why did she say your brother is fake?"

Mackenzie meets my eyes, and hers are steely. If I don't tell them the truth, it's clear she's going to do it for me.

"My brother's not fake," I say. "But, um . . . he's four years old."

Lexi's eyes widen. "Then who was that in the picture you showed us?"

"Some actor," I say. "His name is Raul something. He's on this telenovela my grandma likes."

"Where were the letters coming from? Who thought up the pranks?" I swear Roo has grown six inches since we started this conversation, and I take a small step back.

"Mackenzie and I wrote the letters," I say. "We thought up the pranks together."

"It was mostly me," Mackenzie says. For someone who accused me of being a show-off, she's pretty interested in taking credit all of a sudden.

"It was both of us," I say. "And the Sea Witch prank was all mine, after Mackenzie decided she was too good for the prank war and refused to keep helping."

Roo and Lexi and Ava stare us down, and for a second, I allow myself to imagine that they'll be impressed by the truth. After all, coming up with professional-quality pranks by myself is way cooler than relaying them from my "brother." But then Roo says, "So . . . you've been lying to us the entire summer."

"I wasn't *lying*," I say. "I mean, okay, I guess I kind of was. But I only did it so you guys would listen to me! I tried to suggest pranks to you on the first day, and you shut me out and told me I didn't know how anything worked around here!"

"Because you *didn't*," Roo says. "You'd gotten here three seconds ago. The rest of us have been coming here since we were eight. We weren't going to let you walk in and take over."

"I didn't want to take over! I just had better ideas than you! You *admitted* they were better when you didn't think they were mine! Roo, you're the one who was talking about how boys get more credit than girls for the same ideas, right? Isn't this exactly the same thing? You wouldn't let me suggest stuff, but when the pranks came from Tomás, who's a *boy*, you were totally willing to listen."

Roo looks at me like I'm a squashed cockroach on the bottom of her shoe. "We didn't take Tomás's ideas seriously because he was a *boy*. We took them seriously because you told us he was a Wolverine."

"I don't see why it matters where the pranks came from," I say. I'm trying to sound confident, but it kind of comes off like I'm begging. "They were pretty genius either way, right?"

"What *matters* is that we thought we could trust you, and we clearly can't," Roo says. "If you've been lying about this, who knows what else you've been lying about? How do we know you're not working for the Wolverines?"

"Yeah, how else would they have known about our dance costumes? Or the Ouija board?" Ava says. "Seems awfully suspicious. We've seen you acting friendly with that redheaded guy."

"Don't try to deny it," Roo says. "I have pictures."

It's very possible Josh really *did* learn about the dance costumes from me, but it's not like I told him on purpose. "I'm not working for them!" I snap. "I've been ridiculously loyal to the Willows! If anyone around here is a spy, it's *Val*!"

"Val?" Roo says. "What are you talking about?"

"I caught her making out with Stuart in the Social Lodge tonight," I say. "I thought she was on *our* side, but she's not. She's a traitor." Roo's eyes bug out with rage, and for a second I think I've gotten through to her. "I can help you think of more pranks if you want to keep going without her," I say in case this is working. "I can—"

She cuts me off. "Just because *she* defected too doesn't make what you did any better. We don't need either of you. We can take down the Wolverines without your help." She turns and walks away.

Lexi and Ava follow her, and I run after them. "Come on, guys. Give me another shot. I only lied to you for the good of the cabin, and I promise I won't ever do it again!"

Lexi stops for a minute and looks back at me, clearly torn. If she were by herself, I think I could convince her to give me a second chance. But when Roo says, "Lex, come *on*," she shrugs and turns to go.

"Sorry, Izzy," she says quietly. When it all comes down to it, being part of the group is more important to her than doing what she believes in. She can't afford to lose her friends either.

It hurts to know that if I were in her place, I'd probably do the same thing.

Tears prick my eyes again—I can't believe I have more tears left in my body. I automatically turn to Mackenzie for comfort; maybe now that she's seen how horribly my new friends treated me, she'll feel like we're even. But she's not there anymore. She's across the lawn with Lauren, headed back into the mess hall.

I spin around and start walking fast. I have no idea where I'm going; I just want to be far, far away from here as quickly as possible. But my eyes are blurry with tears, and I've only gone a few steps before I slam directly into someone in the dark.

"Oof," says a familiar voice. "Oh man, I'm so sorry. You okay?" He grabs my elbow to steady me, and I realize it's Danny from the kitchen.

"I guess," I mumble.

"Wait, I know you," Danny says. "You're one of Val's Popsicle girls."

I didn't know it was possible to feel worse than I already did, but *one of Val's Popsicle girls* sticks me straight through the heart. I thought I was *the* Popsicle girl. But everything else about her has turned out to be a lie, so I guess it only makes sense that this would too. Getting Popsicles wasn't a special thing she did with *me*; it was probably just a thing she always did, and I happened to be in the right place at the right time. It shouldn't hurt this much to hear, not after all the other things I've been through in the last ten minutes. But it still does.

"Hey, are you crying?" Danny asks. "What's the matter?

Do you want a Popsicle to cheer you up? I can get you one as long as you eat it in secret."

"No thanks," I say. I want nothing to do with Popsicles or secrets or sailing or flip-flops or sunshine or anything else that would remind me of the supposedly happy times Val and I had together.

"Well, okay," Danny says. "I'm going to clean up the pizza stuff. You know where to find me if you change your mind. I hope you feel better."

"Thanks," I say.

I find a big tree out of range of the mess hall lights, and then I sit down in the damp grass, wrap my arms tight around my knees, and bury my face in them. It was nice of Danny to say, but I know I'll probably never feel better again. My best friend hates me. My new friends hate me. My counselor betrayed me. I've been kicked out of the prank war. And for the first time since I got to camp three weeks ago, I am totally, horribly, 100 percent alone.

I'm not sure how long I sit there, wallowing in my misery. When the counselors call us in for the night and everyone starts making their way back to their cabins, I don't move. Nobody sees me as they tromp out of the mess hall and the Social Lodge, laughing and screaming random lines of

Color Wars cheers. I sit perfectly still, hoping Mackenzie or Roo or Lexi will relent and come looking for me, but nobody does. One by one, cabin doors slam shut, and the shouts and laughter die out.

It's silent for a little while, and then I hear the bang of one last screen door. "Izzy?" calls Val's faraway voice. "Where are you?"

I consider keeping quiet and staying out here all night; it would show her—and everyone else—when they saw me all wet and cold and cast out on the hard ground in the morning. There's something kind of tragically wonderful about that image. But the thing is, after everything else that's happened tonight, I'm not convinced anyone would care. By now Roo and Lexi and Ava have probably told everyone in camp that I'm a liar and a fake, and all my former friends have probably turned against me. Plus, I'm not actually willing to be that uncomfortable until morning just to make a point.

"Izzy?" Val shouts again, and this time, I call back, "I'm here."

The beam of her flashlight sweeps over the grass, and then comes the soft slapping sound of her flip-flops as she approaches. "Hey," she says when she gets to me. She's already wearing her plaid boxers and the T-shirt she sleeps in, which means she didn't realize I was gone until everyone was changed for bed.

"Hey," I say.

"I'm glad I found you. I didn't know where you'd gone."

"Well, here I am."

"It's time to come back to the cabin, okay?"

"I don't want to go anywhere with you."

Val's quiet for a minute. "Look, about what you saw earlier in the Social Lodge—"

"I don't want to talk about it."

She sighs and kicks at the grass. Even her blue toenail polish annoys me now, despite the fact that two hours ago I was planning to ask if I could borrow it. "Okay," she says. "But . . . you looked really shell-shocked back there, and I wanted to check in with you about it."

"You wanted to *check in with me*?" I'm suddenly angrier than I've been all night. "You're not going to say you're *sorry*?"

I expect Val to look remorseful, but instead she seems confused. "I can see you're upset, Iz, but I'm not sure what I should be apologizing for."

"*Seriously?* You kissed *Stuart!* You're supposed to be on *our* side!"

"There are no sides," Val says gently. "We're all just trying to have fun."

There definitely *are* sides; this whole summer was supposed to be Willows vs. Wolverines. She's the one who *told* me about the sides.

"You can't be part of the prank war if you're going to keep seeing him," I tell her. "How are we supposed to take the whole Public Enemy Number One thing seriously when we know you're probably telling him everything we say?" It feels kind of great to throw all Roo's accusations in her face.

Val looks genuinely surprised. "Izzy, I wouldn't do that. That would take all the fun out of it."

"It's too late," I say. "You lied to us. We want you out." She doesn't need to know I've been exiled for lying too. I want to hurt her as badly as she's hurt me.

Val's quiet for a minute, and then she says, "Listen, I heard about the whole Tomás thing. I know you're probably embarrassed, but I wouldn't worry too much about it. I really think the girls will get over it."

My cheeks flame in the dark. It's *so* unfair how she can see through me all the time. "I'm not embarrassed," I snap. "How did you find out about that?"

"I heard the girls talking. Listen, I think you've done

such an awesome job planning pranks on your own, and—"

"I don't want to talk about this, either," I say. If she had praised me earlier today, I would've lapped up every word, added it to my list of proof that we had a special bond. But now her compliments sound hollow. If Val thought I was the least bit special, she wouldn't have misled me like she did. I didn't realize how much space she was taking up inside me until all those parts emptied out at once.

Val deflates. "All right," she says. "We don't have to talk about any of this right now. Just come back to the cabin, okay? It's time for lights-out."

"Fine," I say.

We walk back in silence. I can hear the other Willows talking and laughing in their bunks as soon as we get close, but as soon as I pull open the door, everything goes quiet. Val heads straight into the bathroom, and I walk over to my bunk above Lexi's. It's already occupied by Petra in her horse-printed sleeping bag.

"No liars allowed over here," hisses Roo.

I don't bother answering; anything I could say would only make things worse. Cheeks flaming, I cross the cabin to my old bunk. All of my stuff has been pulled from the dresser and tossed haphazardly onto the mattress: clothes, shoes, my damp swimsuit. My picture of the Virgin Mary is lying upside down in a pile of underwear, and someone ripped down my drawings from Lina and Tomás so quickly that the tape tore the corners off. As I try to gather some of it up, a hoodie and some shirts fall out of my arms and land on the bottom bunk.

"Sorry," I whisper to Mei, but she just turns over and pretends to be asleep.

Dear Mom, Dad, Lina, Tomás, and Abuela,

I can't **WAIT** to come home on Sunday.
Everything about this camp is AWFUL,
including ALL THE PEOPLE. I HATE THEM
AND I AM SO, SO READY TO LEAVE.
I am **DEFINITELY** not coming back here
next year. If you won't let me go to Camp
Sweetwater, I won't go to camp at all.
EVERYTHING IS TERRIBLE.

Love,
Izzy

P.S. We won Color Wars. That part wasn't
as bad. BUT EVERYTHING IS
TERRIBLE NOW.

P.P.S. I'm not sick or dying or anything.

CHAPTER 23

Nobody wants to sit with me at breakfast the next morning. I end up at the very end of the table like Mackenzie always did our first week here, next to BaileyAndHope, whose conversation is so filled with inside jokes they might as well be speaking another language. Hannah sits across from me, but she has clearly been told not to talk to me, because she keeps opening her mouth to say stuff, catching herself, and stuffing food into it instead. When I glance over at Roo, she raises her camera and snaps a candid picture of me. Right after she clicks the button, I realize I have a smear of hot sauce next to my mouth.

I know this isn't the *worst* possible situation—there are only seven more days of camp, and then I never have to see these people again. I once saw on TV that you could go

three times that long without *eating*, and it's not like I have
to suffer through that. All I have to do is lay low. But it's still
pretty awful being treated like I have the plague when I was
basically a camp hero yesterday. It was sad enough knowing
I'd have to go back to boring real life in one short week—
without my best friend, this time—and now I don't even
have those few remaining days to feel special and in charge.
It makes me wish I'd never come here in the first place.

New activities start today, and I head off to Rock
Climbing in a terrible mood. Mei's ahead of me on the
path, and she looks like she's going to the same place, but
I don't call out to her. After last night, it's pretty clear she
doesn't want to talk to me any more than the other girls
do. Mackenzie's counselor Eleanor is in charge of the rock
wall, and I wonder if she's heard Mackenzie complaining
about me.

I grab a harness, and I've almost got it all the way
cinched up when someone comes up right behind me
and says, "Hey."

At first I don't bother to turn around; nobody could
possibly be talking to *me* right now. But then the voice
says. "Izzy. Hey."

It's Josh. Of *course* it's Josh. Why does Josh have to be
everywhere?

"Hi," I say.

He grabs a harness of his own and starts putting it on. "I never got to talk to you after the Sea Witch thing on Friday," he says. "I know I'm supposed to be mad at you, but that was freaking *hilarious*."

"Thanks," I say, and I smile for what feels like the first time in weeks. Friday night seems like it was *forever* ago.

"Better enjoy resting on your laurels now, because when we strike back, it's going to be epic."

"The prank war's pointless now, Josh." I pull the last strap on my harness into place with more force than necessary, and it squeezes around my thigh.

"Um, no it's not. We still have an entire week of camp left. Your prank was great and all, but it doesn't mean you won."

"Didn't you hear?" I say. "Val and Stuart are, like, *dating* or something."

Josh's eyes widen. "Wait, what? Since when?"

"I don't know. I caught them making out in the Social Lodge last night."

"*Ugh.* Seriously? How are we supposed to trust them now? They're probably telling each other everything we plan."

"I know!" He's on the wrong side, but it's still the right reaction, and it's pretty gratifying.

"I need everyone's eyes over here!" calls Eleanor. "I know you're all eager to get up on the wall, but first we need to talk about the most important thing: *safety*. Now, this is a carabiner . . ."

Josh edges closer to me as Eleanor drones on about all the stuff we already learned in Ropes Course. "We could keep the prank war going anyway," he says in a quieter voice. "We could do it in secret, without them. I mean, you guys would have the advantage now, so it wouldn't really be fair, but it would be better than quitting while we're behind."

"We don't have an advantage," I say. "What are you talking about?"

"Well, we wouldn't have an adult helping us get supplies and stuff, and you guys would still have your brother."

I consider keeping the myth of Tomás alive, but gossip spreads fast enough here that I know he'll find out regardless. "No, we wouldn't," I say. "Tomás doesn't exist. I made him up."

A crease appears between Josh's eyebrows, which I notice for the first time are the same red as his hair. "Why would you make up something like that?"

"Because when I first got here, none of the Willows believed I was actually good at pranking. Nobody trusted me, and they wouldn't let me suggest stuff, even though my ideas were way better than theirs. So I told them I had a brother who used to be a Wolverine so they'd take me seriously." I shrug. "It was dumb, I know."

I wait for the same expression of disgust and betrayal to cross Josh's face that I saw on Roo's last night. But instead he says, "So . . . you came up with all those pranks yourself?"

"My best friend helped with the spaghetti and the mountain lion. The Sea Witch thing was all mine."

"Whoa," Josh says. "I hate to say this, but that's really impressive. We thought for sure you guys were kicking our butts because you had outside help."

A tiny smile creeps across my face. "Nope. We're just better than you."

"Well, now we really have to finish this off. My pranking genius against yours, no brothers, no counselors. You up for it?"

"You'll have to talk to Roo," I say. "The Willows all hate me now that they know I lied. Nobody's speaking to me."

"Even though you said you were sorry?"

"I *didn't* say I was sorry. I'm *not* sorry. I wanted to win the prank war, and I did what I needed to do to make that happen. They should be thanking me for everything I did for them, and instead I've lost every single one of my friends. I don't see how that's supposed to be fair."

Josh is quiet for a second. "I don't know. Maybe you should—"

"I need two volunteers to start us off!" calls Eleanor, and I raise my hand high; I'm ready to be done with this conversation. She calls on me, and I make my way to the foot of the wall, where I clip her belay rope onto my harness. But of course, since the universe hates me, the other person she chooses is Josh. "Go ahead whenever you're ready," she says to me.

I jam the toes of my sneakers onto the first footholds and pull myself up as fast as I can, trying to get a head start on Josh so he won't be able to lecture me. But he catches up quickly, and soon we're eye-to-eye again. "You haven't, you know," he says.

"I haven't what?"

"Lost all your friends."

There's a tricky spot coming up above me, and I take a minute to decide between an orange handhold and a red one. I grab for the orange, miss, and reach for the red instead. "You didn't see the Willows last night and this morning," I tell him when I'm securely braced again.

"They moved all my stuff to another bunk without asking me. And Mackenzie's still not talking to me either, even though I've apologized to her like a million times."

Josh grabs a green handhold and pulls himself up higher. "Yeah, but . . . we're friends, right?"

I think about it. I've spent all this time denying that Josh is my friend. But if I'm honest with myself, I don't talk to him because I need to extract information for our pranks. I talk to him because he always notices when I'm upset and asks me what's wrong. He listens to me talk about my problems. He baited my fishhook when I was having a bad day, and he's actually pretty funny sometimes. Sure, he's annoying and competitive, and his advice is so boylike that it couldn't possibly be useful. But he's also the only person at camp who's always been nice to me. If Val's going to make out with Stuart in the supply closet, I'm allowed to hang out with whoever I want, including someone who's supposed to be The Enemy.

"Yeah," I say. "I guess we're friends."

Josh smiles, and for the first time all day, I actually feel pretty decent.

"Race you to the top," he says.

We race. And when he wins, it doesn't even bother me that much.

CHAPTER 24

For the next few days, all the Willows talk about is our overnight in Sandpiper Village. Before everything fell apart, I was so excited about swimming in the river and roasting marshmallows and stargazing with Val on the big hill. Even sleeping outside with Roo and Lexi and Ava and getting a million mosquito bites sounded like an exciting adventure. But now that everyone's avoiding me, the overnight just feels like one more thing I have to get through before I can go home. If Roo has anything to say about it, I'll probably be sleeping outside by myself while the rest of them huddle together in the tents and laugh at me. None of the Willows have spoken to me directly since Sunday night, and every time Mei or Lexi or Hannah looks like they're about to slip, Roo distracts them. I keep waiting for Val to step in and do something, but she doesn't seem to notice I've become a total outcast. And it's not like I'm going to *ask* her for help after everything she's put me through, so I keep my head down and tough it out alone.

During Cabin Group on Wednesday, Val goes to the kitchen to pick up our hot dogs and s'mores ingredients, and Roo and Summer retrieve the tents from Doobie's office, spread them out on the floor of the cabin, and count the pieces. The tents give off a musty, moldy smell, like they were packed up and stored wet, but nobody seems to care. I don't think I've ever seen Roo so excited—she usually keeps her emotions under control pretty well, but today she twirls and skips around the cabin and keeps hugging everyone (except me, obviously). It seems like it would be really fun to be her friend right now.

As soon as Free Time ends, we pile into a big white van with a picture of a fox on the side. There are enough room for all of us to fit comfortably, but Roo and Lexi and Ava make everyone cram into the first three so that I'm sitting alone in the back. It's kind of a relief, honestly. If I'm behind them, maybe they'll forget about me for a little while.

"I call first turn on the rope swing!" Roo sings as we bump along the dirt road.

"I call first turn in the hammock," Ava says.

"We should do our picture with our tree right away, while it's still light," says Lexi. "Will you take it, Summer?"

We make a left off the road and roll into a small gravel lot, where another white Foxtail van is already parked. "Val, this is the wrong turnoff," Petra says. "Sandpiper Village is farther down."

Roo looks out the window and snorts. *"Catfish Hole?"* she says. "Ha-ha, very funny. Let's get back on the road."

But Val turns off the van and takes off her seat belt. "It's not a joke. I thought we'd try something different this year."

"What?" Roo gasps. *"Why?* You said we were going to Sandpiper Village!"

"This place is a dump," Ava says. "Everyone hates Catfish Hole."

"No offense, Val, but it's true," Summer agrees.

"It's perfectly nice," Val says. "There's a fire pit and a stream and woods. What else do you need for an overnight?"

Roo's voice is rising now, edging toward hysteria. "Um, a hill where you can actually see the stars? A rope swing? Water that's not full of *mud and catfish?*"

"And we need to take our tree picture!" Lexi whines.

"There are lots of trees here," Val says. "I can still take your picture."

"It can't be some random tree! It has to be *our* tree!"

"I don't get why we—" Roo starts.

And then Stuart comes around the corner, smiling and waving. "Oooooh, baby!" he shouts with this weird cowboy drawl. "Here comes my *woman*!"

Roo looks livid now, even madder than when she found out Tomás was fake. "Oh no," she says, her voice low and deadly. "No no no no no. You brought us here so you could hang out with your *boyfriend*?"

Val's cheeks flush bright red. "He's not—that's not why," she says. "I thought it would be cool for you to get to know the Wolverines better. Overnights are more fun with more people."

"The Wolverines are our *enemies*," says Summer. "We're not supposed to get to know them. We're supposed to take them down."

"That's a game, though," Val says. "We're not enemies in real life. They're really nice boys. You'll see."

Roo looks like she might cry. "The overnight is my favorite thing in all of camp," she shouts. "You already ruined the prank war. I can't believe you're ruining this, too!"

She just accused Val of ruining the prank war. *Val.* Not me. I have to work hard not to smile.

"Try to have fun, okay?" Val says, but Roo is already out of the van and storming away. Val goes after her, but she stops when Stuart slips an arm around her and says something I can't hear. When she nods, he kisses the side of her head, and I have to look away.

Convincing Val is clearly a lost cause, and it's not like we can drive the van ourselves, so we pile out and gather our stuff in silence. The Wolverines don't look much happier with this situation than we are, but they don't seem surprised to see us. I wonder how long Val has been plotting with Stuart to bring us here.

"Some of you can take the tents over to that flat stretch of ground and start setting up," Val calls. "Everyone else should start collecting firewood with the Wolverines so we can roast some hot dogs and marshmallows!" Usually her bouncy enthusiasm is infectious, but tonight none of us are buying it, and it falls flat. Mei and Summer grab the tents and trudge off without looking at her.

I spot Josh collecting wood near the creek, so I head over to help. This place definitely isn't as nice as the pictures I saw of Sandpiper Village, but at least there's one person here who doesn't hate me. "Hey," he says. "How's it going?"

I pick up a thin branch and start stripping the leaves off. "Terrible. Everyone's still giving me the silent treatment. And we were supposed to be at Sandpiper Village tonight, but Val brought us here instead."

"Seriously? Sandpiper Village is eight thousand times better. You can actually *swim* there."

I look down into the creek and shudder. The water is sluggish and brown; anything could be hiding in there. "Yeah. She made up some ridiculous excuse about how we should be *bonding* with you guys. She obviously just didn't want to be away from her boyfriend for a whole night."

"Stuart's acting like an idiot too," Josh says. "When we found out you guys were coming tonight, we started planning a prank, and he told us we couldn't do it. He said 'we should 'hang out with you guys and have fun.' Like 'hanging out' could possibly be more fun than pranking."

"Love ruins everything," I say.

"Seriously."

I glance at Val and Stuart, who are sitting by the fire pit. They're not doing anything but talking, but it still makes me furious to look at them. I swipe at a pile of dead leaves with my branch. "Ugh. They make me want to vomit. We should prank *them*. They deserve it way more than you guys do."

Josh looks up. "We could, you know. That's a really good idea."

"Nobody's going to listen to us. The rest of your cabin hates the Willows, and the Willows hate me." It's so depressing to think how far I've fallen. Five days ago, *everyone* listened to me around here.

"We don't hate the Willows," Josh says. "Especially not you. I told the other guys about how you came up with the spaghetti and the mountain lion and the Sea Witch, not Tomás, and they've spent the whole week talking about how we should recruit you to our side."

"Really?" I say. It feels great to know that there are still *some* people at Camp Foxtail who respect me.

"Yeah. So what do you think? Should we take the counselors down a notch?"

I tally the people I might be able to sway. Hannah's an easy sell, and I'm pretty sure I could convince Mei and Lexi, too. But none of them would team up with me against Roo's orders. Everyone knows how dangerous it is to be on her bad side, especially after watching her shut me out this week.

Is it possible I could turn Roo around? She's still furious at me, but right now, she's *way* angrier at Val. If I offer her a chance to get revenge for our ruined overnight, maybe I could draw her back in, and everyone else might follow.

"I'd need to talk to Roo," I say.

"So talk to her," Josh says, like it's no big deal.

I spot her at the edge of the woods on the other side of the fire pit, collecting sticks with Lexi and Ava. "I don't want to go alone," I say. "Will you come with me?"

"What, to be your bodyguard? Are you that scared of her? She's tiny."

"You don't know her. She looks cute and small, but she's like a hurricane mixed with an alligator mixed with your school principal."

"Eh, I've dealt with worse," he says. "You haven't known true terror until you've smelled Bloody Mary's socks. Let's go."

Josh and I skirt around the fire pit, where Stuart is taking his guitar out of its case. I'm afraid he's going to call us all back so we can have a dumb sing-along, but instead he starts singing to Val in this supershowy way. It sounds kind of like an acoustic version of the Squeegeez song we sang for the karaoke competition. His guitar playing is awful, and I'm pretty sure all the chords are wrong, but Val stares up at him with this sappy smile on her face anyway. It's sickening.

Roo glances up at Josh and me as we approach. "Oh great, it's the traitor and her boyfriend," she says. "What do *you* want?"

I feel my face go pink; what if Josh thinks I told everyone we're dating? "He's not my boyfriend," I say quickly. "He's . . . Josh. He and the Wolverines want to help us get revenge on Val and Stuart for ruining our overnight and the prank war."

"Hi," Josh says. Lexi smiles and waves. Roo and Ava don't even look at him, but Josh seems totally unaffected by all the tension in the air. Do boys not have the same awkwardness sensors as girls?

"Get revenge how?" Roo asks.

"We want to prank them," I say. "All of us together. We'd love your help thinking up something good." Josh and I could obviously plan a prank by ourselves, but asking for her help seems like the best way to get her to drop her guard. If I were in Roo's shoes right now, that's probably what I would want.

"Why should we trust either of you?" Roo asks. "You're as much of a traitor as Val, and this guy is our enemy."

"I'm not your enemy," Josh says. "I was your rival, but that's not the same thing. And now Val and Stuart's stupidity is making all of us suffer. Izzy says Val kept you guys away from Sandpiper Village so they could sit there making goo-goo eyes at each other, and Stuart told us we should stop pranking you guys, because apparently his love life is more important than *fun*. Don't you want to get back at them?"

We glance over in time to see Stuart tucking a piece of Val's hair behind her ear. I've never understood why girls think that's romantic. If my hair's bugging me, I can fix it myself.

Roo seems to be wavering, but she's still not quite ready to give in. Part of me wants to tell her to forget it and walk away; I'd rather deal with the silent treatment for a few more days than beg. But another part remembers my conversation with Josh on Monday, when I told him I wasn't sorry for what I had done, that it was the Willows' problem if they couldn't accept that I lied to help them win. It was for a good cause, but I really shouldn't have tricked them like that. Maybe they would've come around and let me plan pranks if I had waited a few days for them to get used to me. I never even tried to be patient with them, and maybe they do deserve an apology for that.

I take a deep breath and try to swallow my pride.

"Listen," I tell them. "I just want to say . . . I shouldn't have lied to you about having an older brother. I was so excited when I found out about the prank war, and when you guys didn't let me be in charge right away, I got upset. I really wanted you to like me and think I was cool, like the girls at my old camp. And then when you did, I didn't want you to *stop* thinking I was cool. I never thought you'd find out the truth. I just thought we'd win the prank war, and that would be it."

Roo and Lexi and Ava are staring at me now, but they don't say anything, and I'm not sure if I'm making sense or getting through to them. But it's not like things can get worse than they already are, so I forge ahead.

"Basically, what I'm trying to say is that I'm really sorry. I can totally see why you're mad at me. But I promise I'm never going to lie to you again, and I *really* think we should prank Val and Stuart, and it would be much more fun if you guys did it with me. So can you maybe forgive me? It only has to be for five more days, and then you can go back to hating me again as soon as camp's over, if you want."

Nobody says anything for a few seconds. And then, to my surprise, Lexi says, "Okay. I forgive you."

Being Color Wars captain must've done something to her; I've never heard her express an important opinion without looking to her friends for approval first. I guess Roo and Ava are pretty surprised too, because they stop gaping at me and gape at her instead.

"What?" Lexi says. "It's not that big a deal. She didn't hurt anybody. She's a good friend, and she's loyal—you guys should've seen how hard she worked to help us win Color Wars. And she comes up with the best pranks. She should've apologized sooner, but now she has, so I don't see why we have to shut her out. This silent treatment thing is getting exhausting."

After a few seconds, Ava shrugs. "Yeah, whatever. I'm fine with it if you guys are."

Roo looks over at Stuart and Val again. A few feet away from them, two of the Wolverines are having a sword fight with sticks and shouting insults at each other in bad British accents, but neither counselor is paying any attention. It's like the rest of the world doesn't exist for them anymore.

When Roo turns back to us, there's a new resolve in her eyes. "Tell me what you have in mind," she says.

CHAPTER 25

We can't exactly call a full Willows-Wolverines meeting right in front of Stuart and Val, so Josh rounds up the Wolverines who are best at pranking—Beans, Groucho, and Bloody Mary—and Roo, Lexi, Ava, and I meet them at the edge of the woods. I expect that the boys will take some convincing, but they're into the idea of a combined prank right away, and they seem excited to be doing it with *me*, specifically. The way they're looking at me kind of makes me feel like a rock star again.

My instinct is to come up with a killer prank myself and assign everyone the roles I think they'll be best at. But I'm pretty sure Roo won't stick around if I'm remotely bossy, so I ask if anyone else has ideas. Lexi has a few that are surprisingly decent, and so do Josh and Beans, and pretty soon Roo starts chiming in too. Once we have a basic framework, we agree to tell the rest of our cabins what's going on, then reconvene to put the final touches on the plan after s'mores. I feel like I'm floating as we scatter and I head off to find Mei, my designated outreach person. After three days of being completely alone, it is so ridiculously nice to be part of something again.

I find Mei looking for marshmallow-roasting sticks behind the girls' tents. When she sees me coming, she automatically glances around to make sure nobody's watching. But as soon as I tell her Roo sent me and explain our plan, she starts looking a lot more relaxed and happy. "I'm definitely in," she says. "Val and Stuart totally deserve to be pranked. And I'm, um . . . I'm glad Roo's not going to freak out if I talk to you now."

I smile at her. "Me too."

"Should we go see if they're ready to start the fire? If we're stuck here at stupid Catfish Hole, we might as well make the most of it and eat as many s'mores as possible."

It would be so easy to slip back into my friendship with Mei like nothing happened, but I don't feel quite right about that. "Hang on a second," I say. "I just wanted to tell you that I'm really sorry I lied to you about Tomás." I repeat everything I said to Roo and Lexi and Ava, and it comes out smoother this time. Maybe apologies get easier with practice. Maybe Josh was actually onto something.

"I honestly didn't care that much about the prank thing," Mei says when I'm done. "The stuff you came up with was really good."

"Thanks," I say.

"But . . . I was kind of mad anyway when I found out." Mei looks down at the branch she's holding and peels off some of the bark, like she doesn't want to make eye contact with me. "Remember when we talked about my sister leaving for college, and you made it seem like you knew what I was going through? I felt like a total idiot when I found out you didn't really."

Oh. It never occurred to me that *those* lies had hurt anyone. "Wow, I didn't mean it that way at all," I say. "I'm really sorry. And I obviously don't think it's idiotic to be sad about your sister leaving. That's how you're supposed to feel."

"I know. But I trusted you and told you personal stuff, and I thought you trusted me back. But then it turned out you were lying the whole time."

"I do trust you," I say. "Can we try again? I could tell you something personal now. Something juicy and embarrassing. Would that help?"

A smile tugs at the corners of Mei's mouth. "Maybe. It's definitely worth a try."

I think for a minute, and then I say, "Okay, here's one. Do you know what a telenovela is?"

"Like those soap operas in Spanish?"

"Yeah, exactly."

"There's this lady in the retirement community where my great-aunt lives who's always watching those. They seem really stupid."

"They are. But here's the thing. There's this one called *Corazón de Hielo, Alma de Fuego*—it means 'Heart of Ice, Soul of Fire.' I watch it every single day with my grandma. I tell everyone she makes me, but I actually watch it even when she's not home. I've really missed it while we've been here. You're the only one besides my family who knows."

Mei laughs. "What kind of stuff happens on it?"

"Right before I left, there was this guy named Rodrigo who had amnesia, and he fell in love with his evil ex-wife all over again because he didn't remember who she was. They were on a cruise ship, and he was chasing her all over the place trying to declare his love to her, and she fell overboard and got eaten by sharks."

"Whoa," Mei says. "That's . . . umm . . ."

"Ridiculous, I know," I say, and she laughs again. "But I don't care. There's something weirdly addictive about it."

"So, you speak Spanish?" Mei asks.

"I speak it okay, but I understand it really well. My grandma lives with us, and she's from Mexico, so she speaks Spanish most of the time. I pretty much always answer her in English, though."

"I do the exact same thing when my parents speak Mandarin to me! It drives them nuts. They're making me go to Chinese school on Saturdays so I can get better." She wrinkles her nose. "Maybe I should find some Chinese soap operas for practice."

I laugh. "Maybe."

"Well, anyway, your secret's safe with me," Mei says. "By the way, I'm glad you're bunking with me again. Petra thrashes around when she sleeps."

"I'm glad too. I never should've switched in the first place."

Mei smiles, and just like that, we're friends again.

Stuart and Val let us stay up really late eating marshmallows, and by the time the campfire burns down to embers and ashes, we have a solid prank plan for tomorrow. Unlike our other pranks, it barely requires any preparation, and we'll be able to gather everything we need during the day tomorrow with no problem. It's not the most cohesive plan, since it's a mix of all our ideas, but I kind of like that about it. I like that it belongs to all of us.

Val mostly hangs out with Stuart until it's time to go back to our tents. As we walk across the grass with our flashlights, she finally says, "I really hope you guys had fun tonight even though we're not at Sandpiper Village."

Petra shrugs. "It was okay, I guess."

"I didn't know coming here would upset you so much," Val continues. "I should've asked you first. But I'm really proud of the way you rose above the whole prank war thing and bonded with the Wolverines."

Lexi and I exchange a look like, *if you only knew.* "We'll get over it," she says. A few of the other girls agree, and Roo manages a halfhearted "I guess." It's a lot easier to forgive someone when you know she's about to get what's coming to her.

If Val realizes we're not being sincere, she doesn't let on. Maybe she knows this is the best she's going to get. "You girls are fantastic," she says. "Sleep well, okay?" She unzips the flaps on the larger tent and slips inside.

The girls start filing into the tents—Roo and Lexi and Ava take the smaller one, and everyone else goes into the big one. I hesitate for a moment, not sure who to follow. But then Lexi sticks her head back out and says, "Izzy, there's room for one more in here, if you want." It's not exactly the same as sleeping out under the stars with them or being in the tree photo. But as I duck through the nylon tent flap and unroll my sleeping bag next to hers, I finally start feeling like part of the group again.

The next morning we eat cereal around the blackened remains of our fire, then head back to camp in time for our first activities. We spend the day gathering supplies and trying to act normal so Val won't suspect anything. When it's time for bed, we put on our pajamas like always, but I notice people are wearing things that are slightly less ratty and stretched out than usual, since we're planning to be up and about again in a few hours. Summer even borrows a pair of pajama shorts from Roo instead of wearing her signature pink ruffled nightgown. I'm worried Val might wonder about the change, but she doesn't seem to notice any of the little details around her these days, unless they're details of Stuart's annoying face.

I expect it'll be hard to fall asleep, knowing I have to wake up again at one in the morning, but I drift off surprisingly fast. It doesn't seem like any time at all has passed before Roo's standing beside my bunk and shaking my foot. Silently, I slide out of my sleeping bag and help her wake everyone else. The Willows put on their shoes and head out single file through the back door, since the front one always creaks. Before I leave, I grab my flashlight and the bag of supplies I stashed under my bunk, then tiptoe back to check on Val. She's sleeping peacefully with one arm flung over her head, and she looks so innocent and vulnerable that I almost want to call the prank off. I force myself to remember that she's a traitor, that she brought this on herself.

Wolverine Lodge is straight across the big field from our cabin, but we don't want to cut across the grass in case someone spots us from their window. Instead, we walk along the dirt path that loops around the backs of all the cabins. Hannah trips over a root as we pass Cottonwood Lodge and lets out a squeak, and Summer grabs her arm and shushes her. Honestly, I'm pretty impressed she and Summer were on board with this plan at all—Summer hates breaking the rules, and Hannah hates the dark and doing anything risky. Either they're afraid to disobey Roo after what happened to me, or they've actually loosened up a little bit over the last few weeks.

I hear the boys' feet crunching down the path long

before we run into them; they're not being nearly as sneaky as we are. We meet up behind the infirmary, which is at the turn in the path, and I find Josh, who's carrying his own sack of supplies. He's wearing a faded Foxtail T-shirt and plaid flannel pants, which cover a lot more of him than the shorts he wears during the day, but it's still kind of embarrassing to see him dressed for bed. I wonder if he feels the same about seeing me in my red boxer shorts. My dad would totally freak out if he knew I was talking to a boy in my pajamas in the middle of the night.

"Did you get out without Stuart hearing?" I whisper.

"Yup. You could back a garbage truck into the side of the cabin and he wouldn't wake up. How was Val?"

"She was totally out when we left," I say. "She's a pretty sound sleeper, but her feet are ticklish, so don't touch them or she'll wake up. And be sure to go in through the back door, 'cause the front door creaks. Did you get all the supplies you need?"

"We're all set," says Josh. "You?"

"Yeah. Oh, but . . . one more thing. Um, my bunk is the first one to your right when you walk in from the porch. I'm on the top. Yellow sleeping bag. Can you . . . would you mind taking that one for tonight?" It feels kind of weird to ask *Will you please sleep in my bed*, but I'm pretty sure most of the Wolverines don't shower very often, and I'd rather know where my sleeping bag has been.

"Sure," Josh says. "Mine's second on the right when you come in the door. Red sleeping bag. You're welcome to it if you want."

"Thanks," I say. "Good luck."

"You too." Our shoulders brush as we squeeze by each other on the narrow path, and it makes my skin tingle.

We walk the rest of the way to Wolverine Lodge, and I distribute the supplies outside the front door: a satin sash for Roo; a bottle of hair gel for Ava; a Sharpie for Bailey; a bottle of hot pink nail polish for Lexi, and a paler pink for Petra. I keep the giant container of silver glitter for myself and load Summer, Hannah, and Mei up with silly string and rolls of toilet paper.

"Ready?" I whisper.

Everyone nods, and we tiptoe up the steps of the cabin and inch the screen door open. My heart is beating quickly; it's a heady, exciting feeling to be out here this late, playing a prank that wasn't okayed by any adults.

The first thing that hits me when I set foot in Wolverine Lodge is the smell—sweaty socks, unwashed skin, and a strong note of body spray. I'm also pretty sure someone has illegal food, because I hear the scritching sound of mice in the walls, but I try not to think too hard about it. I am *so* lucky I'm a girl. It's really dark, but it's easy to pinpoint Stuart's location by the chainsawlike snores coming from the front right corner of the cabin. We tiptoe in that direction, and when Roo turns on her flashlight to scope out the scene, we find him sprawled on top of the covers in a pair of ratty Superman pajama pants and no shirt.

We get to work.

Soon Stuart's hair is sticking straight up and coated in silver glitter, as are all the clothes in his dresser drawers. He's sporting an impressive pink Sharpie mustache, which curls up at the ends like it's been waxed. Draped across his chest is a pink satin pageant-style sash that says LOVELORN SAP in purple letters, and the nails on his hairy feet and his left hand are painted pink. (His right hand is wedged between the mattress and the wall, and we can't get to it without waking him up.) His bed frame and dresser are crisscrossed with a web of pink and green silly string, and the exposed beams in the ceiling are decorated with long tendrils of toilet paper. Though Stuart almost wakes up a bunch of times, especially when Bailey's drawing the mustache, he miraculously sleeps through the whole thing.

I give the girls a thumbs-up, and we pack our supplies and climb into the boys' bunks. I make sure to get to Josh's before anyone else and wriggle into the red sleeping bag. A couple of the Willows make quiet gagging sounds and whisper about how nasty their beds smell, but Josh's just smells musty, like his sleeping bag has been in a basement closet. I lay my head on his pillow and try to concentrate on how hilarious it's going to be when Stuart wakes up tomorrow morning.

It's way less embarrassing than thinking about how Josh is probably in *my* bunk, smelling *my* smell, right this very moment.

CHAPTER 26

None of us get much sleep, and we're already awake and waiting when the sun peeks over the horizon the next morning. Josh's bed is directly across from Stuart's, so I have a clear view of him, and I'm glad to see that his sash hasn't fallen off during the night. Stuart's unpainted hand is hanging off the bed now, and I think about getting up and applying a quick coat of polish, but I don't want to risk waking him. I hear a creak from across the room as Roo slips out of her bunk and pads toward the bathroom with her camera in hand. She's planning to sit under the sink and wait for Stuart to catch a glimpse of himself in the mirror, then take a bunch of reaction shots. I'm impressed by her dedication to her art. I don't think I'd be willing to sit on the floor of the boys' bathroom for any reason.

We don't have to wait long before Stuart starts to stir. Through slitted eyes, I watch as he reaches down and sleepily scratches his butt—*eew*—then yawns and runs his fingers through his sculpted hair, which leaves them sticky and covered in glitter. He blinks a few times as he notices his sparkly palm and pink nails, and I have to pull Josh's sleeping bag up over my mouth to keep from giggling. "What the . . . ," he mutters, and then he notices the sash across his chest. He swings his feet onto the floor and twists it around so he can read it. "Lovelorn sap. Ha-ha, very funny," he says, and then he gets up and stumbles toward the bathroom, tearing down toilet paper streamers as he goes. "Groucho, Twizzler, I know this was you guys, you little snot factories," he calls, but he's obviously not looking very closely at the bunks, because he still doesn't notice we're not the boys. "I'm onto you, so you better—GAH!"

The familiar sound of a camera clicking punctuates Stuart's yelp, and then comes Roo's voice. "Good morning, sunshine!"

"What are *you* doing in here?" Stuart sounds so genuinely freaked out that none of us can keep it together anymore, and we all start giggling like crazy. Stuart runs back into the main room, and he lets out a melodramatic groan, which makes us laugh harder. "Ugh, I can't deal with all this *giggling* before coffee," he says, clutching his head. "How does Val stand it? Does she know where you are?"

"She'll probably figure it out when she wakes up surrounded by smelly boys," Petra says. "Don't you guys ever *clean* in here?"

"Says the girl who trashed our cabin." Stuart rips down a bunch of toilet paper tentacles and throws them in her face, and she laughs. "All right, she-monsters. Go crawl back in the hole you came from, and tell my boys I'll kick their scrawny butts if they're not here in ten minutes." He opens his drawer and pulls out a T-shirt, and we all start howling again as it sends a shower of glitter all over everything. Those industrial-size jugs hold a *lot*, and I dumped in every last bit.

Stuart's face darkens. "Oh my god, you guys are *the actual worst*," he shouts, and we grab our shoes and bolt before he totally snaps.

"Twinkle, twinkle, little Stu!" Petra shouts back at him.

As soon as we feel safe enough to slow to a walk, Lexi links her arm through mine, and we cross the dew-damp field together. "That was amazing," she says. "How did the pictures come out, Roo?"

"Epic," Roo says. "These are definitely going in the

slide show on Saturday. This was a really good idea." She smiles at me, and for the first time since before Color Wars, it seems totally genuine.

We're a few yards from our cabin when we hear Val's piercing shriek. "Oh my *god*! *Eew*, what *is* this?! Get these *off* me!" One of the boys starts laughing, and Val screams even louder. "What are you *doing*? Get out! *Get out!*"

The Wolverines fly out of the cabin, barefoot and bed-headed, all of them cackling and hooting. Josh's cheeks are pink with laughter, and he has pillow lines imprinted on his cheek. From *my pillow*. I have to try hard not to look at them as he runs up and high-fives me, afraid I'm going to start blushing.

"I take it everything went according to plan?" I ask. "She sounds *really* upset."

"We poured maple syrup in her hair," he says proudly. "And we covered her in our dirty socks and sprayed all her clothes with Stuart's body spray. Oh, and we left her a little surprise in the mess hall—you'll see it as soon as you walk in. How'd things go for you?"

"Stuart looks pretty snazzy with silver hair and a pink mustache," I say. "Your cabin's covered in glitter. Sorry about that."

"Totally worth it." Josh smiles, and I notice for the

first time that the way his bottom teeth overlap is kind of adorable. "We make a good team."

"Yeah, we do," I say.

Another incoherent scream comes from our cabin, and Josh shoots a look over his shoulder. "I think she found the turtle in her underwear drawer," he says.

"A turtle? Where did you get that?"

"The lake. Duh." He shrugs. "You guys should probably go straight to flag raising. I'm kind of afraid she might start breathing fire if you go in there."

"But we're in our pajamas," I say.

"Being in your pajamas is *way* better than being on fire."

I smile. "See you there."

"See you." And then, before I know what's happening, he takes my hand and squeezes it.

The pressure of his fingers lasts barely three seconds, and then he lets go and runs off with his friends. But it's more than enough to make my whole body feel like it's on fire after all.

I eat breakfast between Roo and Mei, and we spend the entire time giggling over Roo's pictures of Stuart's shocked, glittery face. Val doesn't show up until the very end of the meal—apparently it takes forever to wash maple syrup out of your hair. She's super grumpy and reeks of Axe body spray, but when she sees Stuart parading around with his Sharpie mustache and pink toenails, she lightens up a little. She even laughs when she notices that the Wolverines hung her lacy hot-pink bra from the antlers of the taxidermy moose head, especially when Stuart fishes it down with a broom handle and wears it over his shirt for the rest of breakfast. Before we head off to activities, Val and Stuart announce that the Willows and Wolverines have to clean each other's cabins during Cabin Group as punishment for sneaking out. It's not that bad, as punishments go, but it does seem kind of unfair, considering their cabin was way more disgusting to start.

It should be a perfect day. I win a race up the climbing wall with Josh, and I manage to get up on water skis for almost thirty seconds. Mei invites me to go on a trail ride with her during Free Time, and I get to ride my favorite horse, Roxanne. Even the cleaning is easy after we figure out that we can sweep the glitter into the gaps between the wide floorboards. I spend lunch and dinner surrounded by friends, when less than twenty-four hours ago I was a complete outcast.

But the weird thing is that after the euphoria of pulling

a successful prank wears off, I don't really feel any better, deep down. Taking revenge on Val and Stuart seems to have made the rest of the girls happy—nobody's giving Val the cold shoulder anymore. But when I look at my counselor across the table, I still feel that same gut-punch of betrayal I felt in the supply closet the last night of Color Wars. Pouring glitter all over everything can't fix the pain of thinking you have a special bond with someone and realizing, suddenly and horribly, that you don't. I'm not sure if *anything* can fix that kind of hurt.

I wish I at least had someone to talk to who would understand. The Willows are great, but it's not like I can tell any of them I'm upset because Val doesn't think I'm special enough. Josh would just look at me funny and say, "Girls are so weird." If Mackenzie were actually *speaking* to me, she might get what I'm feeling, because—

Oh no. Oh god. Mackenzie would understand *exactly* what I'm feeling, because I did the same thing to her that Val did to me.

Admitting that to myself feels like the time I got hit in the face with a basketball during PE and suddenly found myself flat on my back on the gym floor, dizzy and totally confused about how I'd gotten there. Everything in the mess hall sounds far away, like the rest of the camp is on another station I'm not picking up very well. I feel a hand on my back, and Mei's voice says, "Izzy? You okay?"

I realize I'm staring at my burger like it's grown a face. "Yeah," I say. "I'm . . . um . . . I'll be right back."

Somehow, my legs carry me off the bench, through the aisles of the mess hall, and out the back door. There's a narrow stretch of lawn that runs between the back of the building and the woods, and I pace along it, back and forth and back and forth and back and forth. I thought Mackenzie was being oversensitive about how I missed her birthday, even though I apologized again and again. I thought she was punishing me for not letting her be more involved in the prank war. But her anger was never about either of those things. It was about the fact that she spent nine years believing she could trust me, that we had a special bond, and then, out of nowhere, I made it seem like other people were way more important. I'm pretty sure she tried to tell me that, but I couldn't hear it because I was too wrapped up in my own drama.

The difference between this situation and the Val situation is that Mackenzie really *is* most important to me. But I've made that really hard to see lately.

I told Josh that apologies don't always work, that sometimes things are more complicated than that. But of course they don't work when you apologize for the wrong thing. A regular apology isn't nearly enough at this point, anyway. I need a seriously grand gesture to show Mackenzie how sorry I am.

And then I see the kitchen door, and I get an idea.

I walk over and knock, and after a few seconds, a bearded guy I've never seen before peers through the screen. His apron is streaked with red and he's carrying a pretty big knife, and for a second I lose my nerve. But when he says, "Can I help you?" his voice sounds pretty friendly.

"Um . . . is Danny here?" I ask.

"Yeah," the guy says, but he doesn't make any move to get him.

"Um, can I see him? I'm a . . . friend of his? And I need his help with something? Please?" I don't know why everything I say is coming out like a question. Probably it's the giant knife.

The guy turns away and shouts, "Danny! Some girl's here to see you."

"Who is it?"

"How should I know?"

"Redhead?" asks Danny. He sounds hopeful, and I realize he thinks I'm Val.

"No. Some kid."

A few seconds later Danny appears on the other side of the screen. "Hey, it's you again! Emmy, right?"

"It's Izzy, actually," I say.

"Oh, sorry. You here to extort me for more frozen treats? Is Val with you?"

"No, she's eating dinner," I say. "And I'm not here for Popsicles. But do you have any Marshmallow Fluff in there? And peanut butter? And chocolate syrup? And toaster waffles? And leftover bananas?"

"No waffles, but I think there might be a few jars of Fluff in the pantry," Danny says. "There's chocolate syrup and peanut butter for sure, and we've got a ton of bananas that are about to go bad. Why? Do you guys want to cook something during Cabin Group tomorrow?"

"No," I say. "This can't wait till tomorrow. Listen, I know this is a weird question, but . . . if I needed to make about a hundred chocolate-peanut-butter-banana-Fluff sandwiches after everyone goes to bed tonight, do you think you could help me make that happen?"

CHAPTER 27

For the second night in a row, I sneak out the back door of Willow Lodge after everyone's asleep. It's a lot scarier walking through the dark alone than it was with nine other girls—I jump at practically every sound— and I kind of wish I'd recruited a few of my friends to help me out tonight. Mei and Lexi and Josh all probably would've done it. But it wouldn't be fair of me to pawn any of this work off on someone else. This is a project I have to do alone.

Danny's in the kitchen when I arrive, and there's a welcoming golden rectangle of light splashing out of the screen door and onto the grass. He's got Spanish music playing through an iPod dock, and it makes me feel at home. "Hey," I say. "Is this Ximena Sariñana?"

"Yeah," he says, obviously surprised. "You know her?"

"My aunt's obsessed with her. She plays this album all the time."

"It's cool if you want to put on something else," Danny says. "I've got a bunch of stuff on my phone."

"No, leave it. I like it."

There's a huge pile of ingredients on the butcher block island in the center of the room: Fluff jars, Hershey's syrup bottles, an enormous, half-used vat of peanut butter, six loaves of bread, and a pile of bananas speckled with brown. Everything I need to craft the perfect apology. "This is great," I say. "Thank you so much for helping me. Are you going to get in huge trouble?"

"I hope not," he says. "It shouldn't be that big of a deal. Tomorrow's the last day of camp, and we can't donate left-over stuff to the food pantry if it's already been opened. So we'd have to throw out pretty much everything but the bread, anyway."

"Well, if you do get in trouble, tell them it was all my fault, okay? Tell them I held a knife to your throat and forced you."

Danny laughs. "I don't think that'll be necessary, but I appreciate the thought. I hope this friend of yours is worth it."

"She is," I say. "She *definitely* is."

"So, where do we start?"

Assembling the sandwiches would go a lot quicker with two people, but I feel like this gesture will mean more if I do everything myself. So I tell him all I need him to do is put each finished sandwich in a Zip-loc bag. He tries to argue with me at first, but he must sense how much this whole thing means to me, because he gives in pretty quickly.

The first couple of sandwiches take a while, but soon I fall into a rhythm. Peanut butter on one side, Fluff on the other, sliced banana and a liberal drizzling of chocolate in the middle, so the bread won't get soggy. I cut the sandwiches diagonally—the only acceptable way—and with each stroke of my knife, I think, *I'm so sorry, Mackenzie. Please forgive me.* My mom once told me about this book she read where a girl could taste the emotions of the people who prepared her food, and I hope that when Mackenzie eats one of these, she'll know exactly how I feel.

Danny's asleep on the butcher block island by the time I finish hours later. I poke him awake, and he helps me pack the sandwiches into boxes and carry them to the lawn outside Maple Lodge. I thank him again for helping me pull this off, but he's too tired to form sentences, so he just waves his hand like "don't mention it" and trudges off to get a few hours of sleep. Once I'm on my own, I pull out my flashlight and the reference drawing I made during Free Time, and I get to work.

Twenty minutes later, the lawn in front of Mackenzie's cabin is covered in one hundred and three ChocoNana-FlufferNutter Delights, spelling out I'M SORRY in gigantic letters. I don't know if it'll be enough to win Mackenzie back, but I finally feel like I've done my best for my best friend. I sit down next to the S, pull the hood of my sweatshirt up against the chill, and settle in to wait for morning.

I mean to stay awake all night as a punishment for being an awful friend, but I can't help it—I fall asleep almost immediately. The sun is all the way up when I jolt awake to the sound of Lauren's voice. "Mackenzie? Your . . . um . . . Izzy's out here." I hate the way she pauses. She was obviously going to say "your friend Izzy" and then thought better of it.

Mackenzie appears in the doorway in her seahorse pajamas, and I peel my face off the grass and scramble to my feet. Her eyes widen as she takes in my message on the lawn. I feel like I should have a boom box on my shoulder like in one of those cheesy old movies, or at least some sort of grand, eloquent speech prepared. But I fell asleep before I could come up with anything like that, so I guess the sandwiches will have to speak for themselves.

"I brought you something," I say, because I can't just stand here in silence like a weird creeper.

"Are those . . . sandwiches?" she asks.

"ChocoNanaFlufferNutter Delights. One hundred and three of them."

"Where did you get a hundred and three sandwiches?"

"I made them," I say, like that's a totally normal thing to do in the middle of the night. "Want one?"

Mackenzie starts to smile as she comes down off the steps, and I hand her the nearest sandwich. "Are you going to have one too?" she asks.

"Can I? They're yours."

"Of course. I can't eat a hundred and three sandwiches by myself."

"Okay." I take one, and we open our bags. I let Mackenzie take a bite first, and then I dig in.

"Not as good as Midnight Snack at Sweetwater," I say.

"Not bad, though." Mackenzie takes another bite. "It's kind of a good breakfast food, actually."

We chew in silence for a minute, and then I say, "Listen, I'm really sorry. About everything. In case that wasn't clear from the fact that these sandwiches literally spell out 'I'm sorry.' I should never have ditched you to hang out with Roo and Lexi and Ava. Having you as a friend is so much better than being in charge of a prank war. And I shouldn't have used your pranks without giving you credit, even if you said I could. I know I made you feel like you weren't important, but I think you're really, *really* important. Like, the *most* important. And I miss you so much, and I want everything to go back to how it was before. So can we just . . . make that happen? Please?"

Mackenzie's quiet for way too long, staring down at her half-eaten sandwich. "Thanks for saying all of that," she finally says. "But . . . I don't think so."

My stomach twists a little, but I guess I shouldn't have expected it to be that easy. "I'm not saying you have to forgive me right this second. You're probably still super-mad. I screwed up, and I get that. You can think about it as long as you need to. But you'll forgive me sometime, right? Sometime soonish!"

"It's just— Here's the thing," Mackenzie says. "I don't really *want* things to go back to how they were before."

"You don't? Not ever?"

She sighs and fiddles with the earpiece of her glasses. "No, it's not— I'm not saying I don't want to be friends with you. But things are kind of different now, after this

summer, you know? Like, when we first got here, I was . . .
I mean . . ."

She stops and shakes her head quickly, like she's trying
to erase her words. She always does that when she realizes
she's started a story in the wrong place and wants to try
again. We had a counselor at Camp Sweetwater who used
to call her the human Etch A Sketch, and I smile a little
at that memory.

Mackenzie takes a deep breath and starts over. "Okay.
So, you're, like, this amazing person, right? You're funny
and smart and brave, and you make friends in two seconds, and it's not even hard for you. You're not scared of
anything. And I've always just been, like, *there*. Hovering
in the background. Like I'm your sidekick or something."

I can't believe Mackenzie thinks I treat her like Roo
treats Lexi. "You're not in the background!" I say. "That's
ridiculous. You were never my sidekick. We do everything
together." I swallow hard. "I mean, we *did* everything
together."

"Do you know how people at home introduce me
when you're not around?" Mackenzie asks. "They say,
'This is Izzy's friend.'"

"Well . . . you *are* my friend."

"That's not the point, though. I don't want to be 'Izzy's

friend.' I want people to know who I am separate from you."

"Come on, people *do* know who you are," I say. "They just also know you're my friend. Is that really so awful?"

"No, but that's not *all* of who I am, and people seem to think it is. *You* seem to think it is, a lot of the time." Mackenzie twists the corner of her sandwich bag. "Fighting with you is horrible, and I don't want to do it anymore. But . . . maybe it wasn't the worst thing that we spent some time apart, you know? I'd never done *anything* on my own, because you were always there taking over, so I assumed I needed you for everything. But it turns out I can totally do stuff by myself, and I can make my own friends, and they know me as *me*, and that's . . ." She shrugs. "It's kind of great, honestly."

I once saw a movie where a bull charged straight into this bullfighter and stabbed him in the stomach with its horns. Mackenzie's comment makes me feel exactly like that bullfighter. I don't realize I'm crying until a tear drips off my chin and splashes onto my sandwich.

"Sorry," Mackenzie says, but it's not "sorry" like, *I didn't mean it*. It's "sorry" like, *I wish the truth didn't upset you.*

"I never tried to keep you from doing stuff," I say. "I was just trying to help you."

"I don't need help, though. I don't need you to protect me all the time, or talk for me, or tell me what I think about things. I know what I think. I'm not five."

"Well, I still need *you*."

"You don't, though. You had your own stuff going on, like, the second we got here. Stuff that had nothing to do with me. And it was awful when you started ditching me all the time, but I tried really hard to be okay with it and leave you alone. But then when *I* made some friends and started doing stuff on my own, you got so mad. It's like it was okay for you to have everything, but you only wanted me to have you."

I remember all the times I thought Mackenzie was holding me back. It's so weird to hear that she thought the same thing about me.

"It's okay with me if you have your own stuff," I say. "You can do whatever you want. But can we have *some* stuff together again? It doesn't have to be *all* the stuff."

She finally looks straight at me, and she must see in my eyes that I mean it, because she nods. "Some stuff would be good," she says. And then, slowly and tentatively, she holds out her pinkie. I'm so grateful that I grab on a little too hard, and she flinches, but she doesn't let go.

We're silent for a minute, and then she asks, "What are we going to do with all these sandwiches?"

"Huh," I say. "I didn't actually think about that. Give them out at flag raising?"

"If Doobie sees, won't you get in trouble for sneaking into the kitchen at night?"

I shrug. "What's she going to do, send me home? It's the last day of camp."

"I guess." Mackenzie takes another bite, and then she smiles. "Thanks for making them for me."

"I wish they'd had toaster waffles," I say. "These don't really taste right on bread, do they? And they'd be way better if the peanut butter were crunchy."

"Sure," Mackenzie says. "They're not perfect. But this is a good start."

CHAPTER 28

The second I get to Rock Climbing that morning, Doobie shows up to fetch me. She sits me down in her office and gives me a long, boring lecture about sneaking into the kitchen at night and how "all choices have consequences." I'm scared she's going to ban me from the camp forever, but it turns out all I have to do is come back during Free Time and spend an hour and a half sitting silently and "thinking about what I've done." I ask if Danny's going to be in trouble for helping me, but she won't tell me. I hope he uses the knife-to-the-throat excuse if she tries to fire him.

It's time for Water Skiing by the time she lets me go, but I'm basically a zombie—a wet lawn doesn't make a great bed—and I keep falling asleep in the back of the boat. It's clear I'm not going to make it through Ultimate

Frisbee, so Val says I can go back to the cabin right after lunch and take a nap. It's sad that I've basically missed my entire last day of activities, but the sandwiches were totally worth it. I barely manage to take my shoes off before I fall asleep facedown on top of my sleeping bag.

I wake up what feels like three seconds later to the banging of the screen door. "What time is it?" I ask Mei when I spot her near the foot of our bunk.

"Two thirty," she says. "Better get up, it's time for Cabin Group."

I'm a rumpled mess, my eyes feel sticky, and my mouth tastes like a moth flew into it and died. I fumble my way into the bathroom, brush my teeth, and redo my braid. When I come out, Val has arrived, and she calls for our attention. "The closing campfire always runs late, and we probably won't have time for Cabin Chat later," she says. "I thought we could go sit somewhere nice, like the amphitheater and do it now. What do you guys think?"

Everyone agrees, and we head outside. The amphitheater is beautiful at this time of day, all shady and cool and quiet. We sit in a circle in the center of the stage, the scene of our karaoke defeat, and the trees and tiers of stone steps surrounding us feel protective, like they're trying to hug us. I've only been here a few times, but a pang of sadness goes through me when I think about how I won't see it again until next summer. A few days ago I wouldn't have thought this was possible, but I'm really going to miss Camp Foxtail.

When we're all settled, I expect Val to ask a cheesy question like she did during our first Cabin Group, one that'll make Roo roll her eyes. Maybe it'll be something about accomplishing our goals or about our favorite thing that happened at camp. But instead she says, "I thought we'd do something different today. And I apologize in advance if it's too sentimental, but you guys know how I am."

Petra sighs. "Cheeseball McCheddar, right?"

"Correct," Val says. "Guys, this has been my very best summer at Camp Foxtail, and you ladies have been such a big part of that."

I bet Stuart has been a bigger part, says an annoying little part of my brain. I tell it to shut up.

"And so," Val continues, "I made you each something to express my appreciation." She reaches into her bag and pulls out what looks like a stack of paper plates, and I'm kind of intrigued even though I don't want to be.

"Lexi Silverman, please stand up," Val says, and Lexi gets to her feet. "I hereby present you with the Most

Likely to Be Taylor Swift's Best Friend Award. Taylor is a huge inspiration to young girls, and the way you conducted yourself with such poise, kindness, and selflessness during Color Wars showed us all that you have a lot of the same qualities. Plus, you both sing and dance so well. I'm sure you two would get along great."

Val turns the top plate around. It's decorated with swirly cursive handwriting, cutouts of Taylor Swift's face from magazines, and Lexi's name in silver glitter. I wonder where Val got more glitter. I thought I'd used it all up.

Lexi's eyes widen, and she takes the plate reverently. "OMG," she breathes. "That is the nicest thing anyone has ever said to me." She throws her arms around Val, who hugs her back, and she looks so happy that it's hard to feel jealous.

Val has made a paper plate award for each of us, which must've taken forever, and each one is perfectly suited to its winner. Mei gets Most Likely to Develop Superpowers, because she climbs so fast it's almost like she's levitating. Bailey gets Most Likely to Win the World Cup, and Hannah gets Most Likely to Win an Oscar for Special Effects Makeup. Summer gets Most Likely to Manage a Presidential Campaign, and Roo gets Most Likely to Take Over the World. Everyone laughs, but I can see how much it means to her. I wonder if she's freaking out about going home, where she won't be in charge anymore. Ordinarily, that's how I'd be feeling right now. But after this morning, I'm kind of excited to go home and spend some quality time with my best friend.

My award is last, and my heart starts beating faster when Val says, "Izzy Cervantes, please stand up." I get to my feet and force myself to look my counselor right in the eye, and she presents me with the Most Likely to Become a Criminal Mastermind Award. My paper plate is decorated with pictures of ninjas and spies and a cartoon bank robber, which makes me laugh. "Thank you for fearlessly leading us through the prank war, Iz," Val says. "You are much funnier and cleverer and more creative than I'll ever be, and I had so much fun watching you work your magic. Thanks for letting me be part of it."

The compliments soothe the sting of betrayal I've been feeling for days, and I'm suddenly afraid I might cry. Val holds out her arms for a hug, and half of me wants to run away, to fight against believing that she cares about me in case I get drawn in again. But the other half wants to hug her back and breathe in the smell of her shampoo and sunblock and moisturizer, so that's what I do. When it comes down to it, I'm pretty sure Val *does* care. It's possible to care about more than one person at a time. She made mistakes, and she hurt me, but I made much bigger mistakes this summer, and the people I hurt still managed to forgive me. So I say, "Thank you," and Val says, "Of course," and then we both pull away. It's not a lot, but it's enough.

"There's one more treat I want to give you guys," Val says. "The kitchen has agreed to let us have a few boxes of leftover Popsicles. Anyone want to come with me to get them?"

My heart leaps; if I volunteer, everything can be like it was before for a few short minutes. But that's just a reflex. Things *aren't* like they were before, and maybe that's okay.

"I'll go," Roo says. "Anyone else? Ava? Izzy?"

I smile and shake my head, and then I sit back down between Lexi and Mei. "No thanks," I say. "I think I'd rather stay here."

After the sun sinks below the horizon, we gather at the fire pit for our very last all-camp activity. The campfire's already blazing, shooting sparks up into the sky as the Willows take our places on an empty log in the second row. Mackenzie's perched on the very end of the next log over with the Maples, and I make all my cabinmates shift to the left so I can sit next to her. Lauren's on her other side, and for the first time ever she doesn't look annoyed to see me.

"Hi, Izzy," she says. "Thanks for the sandwich this morning. It was really good."

I'm still not Lauren's biggest fan, but I just say, "You're welcome," and Mackenzie smiles at me.

Someone taps my shoulder, and I turn around to find Josh sitting on the log behind us. "You better spend the next eleven months preparing some seriously epic pranks, because I'm not letting you off easy next year like I did this year."

I laugh. "Oh, please. You *know* you're no match for me. And anyway, you won't be part of the prank war next year, even if I end up in Willow again. Won't you be in Coyote?"

"Who cares about the official prank war? I'm talking about *us*. You round up a few girls, I'll round up a few guys, and may the best man win."

"The best woman, you mean."

"We'll see." Josh leans forward and tucks a slip of paper into my hand. "That's my e-mail. Let me know if you pull off anything really amazing during the school year, okay? Or just, you know, write to me about whatever."

"Okay," I say. "I will." I smile at him and tuck the paper

deep into the pocket of my shorts, where it'll be safe.

Doobie gets up on a log in the center of the circle and leads us in the Foxtail Anthem, and then she does a little good-bye speech. It's the normal clichéd stuff about how we're the best group of Foxes the camp has ever had and how she'll miss us, but it still makes a warm sense of belonging bloom inside me. The counselors have rigged up a screen on the far side of the fire pit, and when Doobie presses a button on her laptop, a battery-powered projector springs to life and starts showing Roo's famous slide show. Our entire summer flashes before my eyes, set to a medley of peppy songs about foxes. Mei was right when she told me being in Roo's cabin makes you a celebrity; there are way more pictures of us than of anyone else. There I am, posing with my arms around Lexi and Ava, wearing my dance costume over Val's FOXY shirt. There's Mei and me laughing in the mess hall after the spaghetti prank. There I am getting my hair braided by Val, leaping onto Stuart's back in my Sea Witch costume, holding up my medal after Color Wars. I feel really lucky that Roo was around to document everything. Although she *did* sneak in that one photo of me with hot sauce all over my face.

When the slide show ends, a bunch of the counselors

make their way into the center of the circle with giant drums. I look at Mackenzie like, *What's happening?* and she shrugs. It's nice to be able to communicate with her wordlessly again.

"Who is stronger than an ox?" all six counselors shout together.

"I am! I am! I'm a fox!" we shout back.

"Who here thinks outside the box?"

"I do! I do! I'm a fox!"

"Who's as steady as the rocks?"

"I am! I am! I'm a fox!"

"Who's more graceful than the hawks?"

"I am! I am! I'm a fox!"

I think about our first day of camp, when Mackenzie grumbled that this was the stupidest chant ever. Now my best friend and I have our hands up on our heads to represent fox ears, just like everyone else, and it doesn't seem stupid at all. It feels exactly right.

The counselors sit down around the fire, place their drums between their knees, and start to play. The rhythm is simple at first, and we all clap along, chanting, *"Foxtail, Foxtail, burning bright! You're my heart's one true delight!"* Then a couple of drummers start taking off in different directions and banging out more complicated patterns. It gets louder and louder until I can feel the rhythm thumping in the center of my chest, stronger than my own heartbeat.

I'm so caught up in watching them that it takes me a second to realize nearly all the campers are on their feet. Lexi holds out her hand to me and shouts, "Come on, Iz!"

I stand up and give her my left hand, then hold out my right to Mackenzie, who springs to her feet and takes it without a trace of her usual hesitation. She grabs on to Lauren on the other side, and everyone starts moving in circles around the fire together. For a second I wonder if this is one last choreographed Foxtail tradition I haven't learned, but everyone seems to be doing something different, swaying and hopping and shaking their hips to the beat. Lexi's whipping her hair around, and it reminds me of the way we danced with Val after the spaghetti prank. I shoot Mackenzie a smile over my shoulder, and she beams right back at me as she bops her head and stomps her purple-sneakered feet in time with the drums.

I raise my face to the star-splashed sky, grip my friends' hands tightly, and break into a dance that's entirely my own.

ACKNOWLEDGMENTS

It takes a summer camp to raise a book—wait, that's how that saying goes, right? Infinite thanks to the following people:

Camp director (and editor) Amy Cloud, who sees the big picture in ways I can't and makes my stories the best they can be.

Head counselor (and agent) Holly Root, who's always there to soothe me when I wake up in the middle of the night, homesick and scared.

Camp nurse (and copy editor) Adam Smith, who bandages my writing's scraped knees and medicates its poison-ivy-covered sentences.

All my camp chefs, the Aladdin staff, who work tirelessly behind the scenes to nourish my books and send them out into the world healthy and strong.

My cabinmates (and early readers): Caroline Carlson, Claire Legrand, Nicole Lisa, Jen Malone, Kayla Olson, Lindsay Ribar, Heidi Schulz, and Michelle Schusterman. Making lifelong friends is the best part of camp (and of being an author), and even on my darkest, most mosquito-bitten days, you ladies make it all worth it for me.

Camp groundskeepers—cover artist Angela Li and art director Jessica Handelman—who make my books look absolutely gorgeous.

Lifeguards Anna-Marie McLemore and Kim Baker, who blew their whistles when I swam out past the buoys. Thanks for answering all my questions about Izzy's heritage.

Camp historians Lauren Magaziner and Danny Rooney, whose stories gave me so many ideas for this book.

My old stomping ground, Camp Echo, where I learned to ride a horse, shoot a target, paddle a canoe, and convincingly pretend I knew the lyrics to pop songs.

And my mom and sister, Susan Cherry and Erica Kemmerling, who wrote me letters every single day I was away. Knowing you were waiting for me at home made leaving camp much easier.